A WEDDING QUILT FOR ELLA

JERRY S. EICHER

HARVEST HOUSE PUBLISHERS

EUGENE, OREGON

Cover by Garborg Design Works, Savage, Minnesota

All Scripture quotations are taken from the King James Version of the Bible.

A WEDDING QUILT FOR ELLA
Copyright © 2011 by Jerry S. Eicher
Published by Harvest House Publishers
Eugene, Oregon 97402
www.harvesthousepublishers.com

Library of Congress Cataloging-in-Publication Data

Eicher, Jerry S.
A wedding quilt for Ella / Jerry Eicher.
    p. cm.—(Little Valley series ; bk. 1)
ISBN 978-0-7369-2804-5 (pbk.)
1. Amish—Fiction. I. Title.
PS3605.I34W43 2011
813'.6—dc22
                                                    2010021563

Printed in the United States of America

11 12 13 14 15 16 17 18 / BP-NI / 10 9 8 7 6 5 4 3

One

The wedding was in June, and Ella Yoder smiled at the thought as she stood at the kitchen sink looking out over the long sweep of Little Valley's rolling hills. Low mountains lay to the west, and the scattered Amish farms of Cattaraugus County spread all around her. This was where she felt at home. Here on Seager Hill, her heart was secure, her love was found, and she had no plans to leave—ever. She and Aden would be so happy here.

Ella rinsed the last of the dishes, pausing to consider all the preparations for the wedding. In the months ahead, the house would bustle in an uproar of activity as the family pitched in to get ready for the big day. The extra work wasn't something the family needed right now. Still, they understood even if they didn't know Aden was quite the wonderful man that Ella knew him to be.

"It's the way of the Lord," her father had said, "when a man and a woman come together in marriage and pledge their lives together in His holy will."

He had stroked his long beard gravely, but Ella saw his eyes twinkling. She remembered the pleasure that came from his words and thought again of Aden. How good it was to have her dad's approval of her husband-to-be.

Her mother also seemed content with the choice of Aden, and so surely after the work of the wedding, life would quickly settle back to normal for everyone and continue on as it always had.

The clock on the kitchen wall showed a little past three as Ella put the last of the dried dishes away. Her sister Clara would be home from school at any moment. Her mom and other sister must be on their way back from town by now. In the fields behind the barn, her dad and brothers would soon be ready to call it a day. It would fall on Ella and Clara to prepare supper for the whole hungry family.

Ella glanced out the window toward the schoolhouse. A neighbor's buggy lumbered slowly up the long hill on its way home, the sun behind it casting wild shadows on the road as the horse shook its head. Farther back Ella could see Clara and some of her school friends walking briskly along, lunch buckets swinging in their hands. As they passed the houses on Seager Hill, they broke off from the group one by one. Clara was her best sister, the sweet one, but that was something best not said out loud.

Ella quickly returned to the kitchen table, grabbing the potatoes. She would peel them, and Clara could take over when she arrived. They needed to make the fire in the kitchen stove, bring the flour out for the gravy, and fry the hamburger patties.

"Hi," Ella hollered when the door slammed. "Did you have a good day in school?"

Clara looked through the kitchen doorway. "Not *gut*," she said.

Ella gave her a knowing smile. "Test blues perhaps? I used to have those."

Clara shook her head and marched quickly upstairs, muttering over her shoulder, "I'm going to change, and then I'll be down to help."

Ella drew in her breath. She would carry on with the conversation when Clara returned. A nice sisterly chat might be all the girl needed. She continued with the potatoes until moments later when Clara came into the kitchen, her face still dark.

"So, now," Ella said with older sister sympathy. "Sit yourself down here, and you can work on the potatoes while we talk. You can tell me about your day."

Clara plopped down in the chair and stared at the potatoes. "Why must everything come in one day?"

Ella waited. It might not be good to push too hard.

"Teacher asked us to draw a picture for social studies class," Clara went on. "Then we were to write a story about it."

"Yah," Ella said, nodding.

"Teacher Katie doesn't do that usually. At least it's the first time she has ever done it for us."

"This is Katie's first year, right?"

"Katie didn't do anything wrong. She's a good teacher," Clara said, meeting Ella's eyes.

"So it wasn't from too much work?"

"Nee," Clara said, sighing. "I can do the work."

"Then…what?"

"Well, I started to draw my picture. At first I didn't know what to draw, but then I saw Amanda's picture. She sits in the seat in front of me."

"You didn't cheat?" Ella asked firmly. "You know that's not right."

Clara shook her head. "Of course not. Amanda's picture didn't even give me an idea, really. Amanda's picture was of a clothesline. And besides, I finished before Amanda did."

"You shouldn't be proud about that," Ella said quickly, thankful this wasn't about copying someone else's work.

"I don't think I was proud. Anyway, that wasn't the problem. The trouble started when Amanda turned in her seat and saw my picture of the house. She gasped out loud. I was sure Katie would look up and see us, but she didn't."

"So it was a nice picture?" Ella said, thinking none of this sounded too serious yet.

"Yah, but I didn't know it was nice then. I thought Amanda didn't like it, and so I drew in some more things…so she would like it. Things like a horse and buggy, a fence, cows, and a bull like Dad just got. Then when I was done, I finished my story."

Ella motioned with her hand for Clara to wait as she lit the kindling in the woodstove. The little stream of smoke swirled out of the lid, and

Ella waved it back in with her hand. Slowly the flame grew, and the smoke circled up backwards in the stove. Ella added heavier wood and closed the lid. "Phew," she said, turning her attention back to Clara. "So you wrote a good story and made a nice drawing?"

"Yah, but I didn't know that yet. Amanda asked to look at my picture and story at recess. I gave it to her, and she took them both up to Katie. I could hear Amanda whisper that it wasn't fair I could draw and write so well and that she couldn't. Katie told her something I couldn't hear, but Amanda seemed happy about whatever Katie said to her."

"So what did Katie tell you? I hope she liked it."

"She said that I have to be careful about such things," Clara said, "that our people don't try to be good at drawing and writing stories, and that such things belong just to the *Englisha*." Clara paused. "Is that true, Ella?"

Ella opened the oven and placed another piece of wood inside. *What should I say to Clara? I certainly don't want to encourage Clara in disobedience to the faith. After all, Daett always says, "Destructive seeds are planted when the heart is still young." Is this a destructive seed?*

"Maybe...sometimes," was all Ella could muster up as an answer.

Clara looked distressed. "I wasn't *trying* to be good or even better than Amanda. It just happened."

"Then no one can blame you," Ella said, thinking that was surely safe advice.

"Katie didn't look happy," Clara said. "I could tell."

"I know what we can do," Ella said, turning quickly to face her sister. "Bring the drawing home with you from school so I can see it."

"But if it's wrong, why would you want to see it?"

Ella considered her answer. "Well, maybe we can make it right by what we do with it. Yah, that's what we can do. Your picture of a house may be what I've been looking for."

"For what?" Clara asked, raising her eyebrows.

"I can use the picture for my quilt. Bring it home. I expect it's going to be exactly what I need for my wedding quilt in the basement."

"Really?" Clara said, the faint hint of a smile crossing her face.

"It can be the centerpiece," Ella said. "I'm certain of it. I've been looking for a centerpiece for some time and found nothing that's just right. This might be exactly what I've been waiting for."

"I doubt if it will work," Clara said, her voice sinking.

"But it's nice, isn't it? Yah, you just said so."

Clara nodded. "But you haven't seen it yet."

"That's true," Ella said, pausing to slide a hamburger patty into the pan. "But you bring it home, and if I like it, we can pencil it in straight from your picture. What do think about that?"

Clara shrugged. "That might be nice, I guess."

"Aden will love it," Ella said, her voice soft. "We can use it on our bed—once we're married."

"But it still makes no sense," Clara said, unconvinced. "Katie said this was all wrong. How will using it in your quilt make it right?"

"Not everything in life makes sense," Ella said, "but I'm sure Katie wouldn't mind if we use your drawing for my quilt."

Clara met her eyes. "Then you think I can draw again…if it's for the right thing?"

Ella nodded, smiling.

"After this, I thought I never should try to draw anymore."

"Of course you may. You just can't do it when you might be…well, thought of as showing off. Prideful," Ella said, adding another piece of wood to the fire. When the flame looked satisfactory, she reached for a kettle, filled it with water from the water bucket, and gently set it on the stove to heat.

"There's something else I should be telling you," Clara said, her eyes focused on the floor.

Ella glanced at her. "Now what's wrong?"

"Paul…" Clara began and then hesitated. "He's in my class and sits right behind me."

"Has he been bothering you?" Ella asked, remembering her own days at school. That one boy—what was his name?—always used to kick his shoes against the underside of her desk even when she repeatedly told him not to.

"Not so much bothering," Clara said, "just looking. Whenever I turned around in my seat today, he was looking at me."

Ella waited.

Clara focused on her potatoes as she continued, "I never noticed before, but I did today. And, Ella...I *liked* that he was looking at me. Is that wrong? Wrong like my drawing?"

"Ach," Ella said, reaching an arm across to Clara's thin shoulders. "There's nothing wrong with that. It's a *gut* thing to feel, Clara. It's the life that our people get ready for—like what Aden and I are getting ready for with our wedding."

"Me...marry Paul?" Clara said, dropping her potato on the kitchen table.

Ella laughed. "Not now, you silly. You're still a girl. When you get older. There's plenty of time then to marry."

"Then why do I feel like this now?"

"It's just a feeling, that's all. You grow up and make choices about those feelings. Yah, I should know."

"That's what you and Aden feel?"

"That and a lot more," Ella said. "Love can start with a feeling... And then it grows until you become man and wife. That's how *Da Hah* made it to be."

"I saw Ezra look at me like that once. Except I didn't feel anything like I did today."

"Who's Ezra?" Ella asked.

"He's in the seventh grade and sits across the aisle from me. He was held back once. I think it was in the fifth grade."

"Ach, he's still probably a nice boy."

"Maybe," Clara said, shrugging, "but not as nice as Paul."

"Clara, slow people, like maybe Ezra, are not to be looked down on. You must always remember that. Yah, all you can see of Ezra is his schoolwork. What he does at home on the farm may be much better than what Paul does."

"Only Paul made me feel what I did," Clara said. "Ezra didn't."

"I'm not saying that's wrong," Ella said. "Some girl will like Ezra. There's someone for everyone."

"Like Aden is for you?"

A smile filled Ella's entire face. "Especially for me, Clara, there couldn't be anyone better."

Two

The sisters heard the sound of buggy wheels rattling up the driveway, quickly followed by the chattering of familiar voices.

"Mamm's here," Ella said. "They're finally back from town."

The front screen door slammed, and Dora appeared, her arms full of groceries. Their mother, Lizzie, and three younger sisters followed.

"Is supper done yet?" Lizzie asked as she bustled in, set the groceries down, and surveyed the kitchen.

"Just about," Ella said. "Did you have a good trip?"

The three youngest sisters nodded in unison with big smiles on their faces. They each carried a small bag of groceries into the house—except the youngest, Martha, who carried a single can of soup.

"It was a good trip," Mamm said. "The traffic was light for this time of the day. For that we can thank *Da Hah*. The way things are downtown sometimes is an outright fright. You'd think all the earth was on fire, the way people rush about."

Ella's laugh filled the kitchen.

Clara glanced up from digging through the bags of groceries. "Did you bring any corn candy, Mamm?" she asked after searching the first three bags and finding none.

"Now, why would I buy something like that?" Lizzie asked, keeping a straight face. "Your teeth are already in enough danger of rotting out. You have a dentist appointment as soon as school is out."

"Ach. Please?" Clara said, digging deeper into another bag, her eyes hungry.

"Why don't you help unpack those bags, Clara," Ella said. "Mamm might find what you want while you work."

"Now, that sounds like a good idea," Mamm said.

"You're just tricking me," Clara said but stopped emptying the contents of the grocery bags onto the kitchen table. Instead, she lifted a few items and set them in the cupboards. Mamm then acted like she would walk away but stepped back to the last bag, and with a flourish, she brought out what was left of the corn candy.

"There's not much here," Clara said, holding the half-empty bag aloft.

"You have more than I had," Dora said, her arms full of groceries and ready to go down the basement steps.

"They left enough for you," Mamm said. "You're not a child anymore."

"I'm not to be married like Ella," Clara said, "so I'm still very young."

Mamm laughed. "Now that's some logic. I have to raise all of you children right. Eating less candy is part of growing up—that and a lot of other things. Neither your daett or I want you to reach marrying age with us having to hang our heads in shame over the way we raised you."

"Clara helped me real well today," Ella said quickly. "She peeled the potatoes like a *gut* woman, I'd say. And Clara has her first time at chores tonight."

"Yah," Lizzie replied, nodding, "and it is high time too."

"So why did no one tell me?" Clara protested. "Tonight I have to milk cows?"

"I didn't decide this," Ella said. "Mamm and Daett decided last night after supper, and I just overheard. Don't worry, though. We'll start you in slow and give your hands a little time to get toughened up. But I can't say I don't feel sorry for you."

"Ach, then don't feel sorry," Mamm said. "Clara's a big girl now—almost out of the eighth grade. With the wedding coming up and you leaving us, Ella, we thought it was time Clara started evening choring. Dora had to learn even earlier. So, really, Clara's been having an easy time of it."

"That I did," Dora said, shutting the basement door behind her. "They needed me to help with chores right early. And they almost killed me."

"Now, now. No pity parties." Mamm laughed, but her voice was firm. "I'll take over supper from here. It's Dora's turn to be outside choring tonight. Daett and the boys will be in from the fields soon. Take Clara with you. Show her what she must learn."

Ella led the way upstairs to change into chore dresses. Clara and Dora followed close behind. When they were on their way out to the barn, Clara asked, "Do you think I can do this? Is it hard?"

"Of course, you can." Ella gave her a sideways hug for encouragement. "Just think of all the things you can do. You can draw. You can write. You've got Paul's eye now. After all that, why couldn't you be milking a cow?"

"What's that about Paul?" Dora asked, a few steps behind them.

"It's none of your beeswax," Clara said, marching forward.

Ella laughed heartily.

"She's kind of young for that sort of thing," Dora said dryly.

"Old enough or not, that's how these things go," Ella said.

"Ugh," Dora said, "I don't think Clara's going to like this at all."

"That's just because you're so black about things," Ella teased. "And say, how are you and…let's see—Norman, isn't it—getting along?"

"You don't have to make it sound worse than it is," Dora said, grinning. "He's not all bad."

"Can we talk about something else besides boys?" Clara asked.

"I suppose we could," Ella said.

"If I'd caught someone like that Aden of yours," Dora said, "I'd be cheerful too."

"Ach, the grass is always greener on the other side of the fence. And you're not getting my Aden," Ella said, trying to put a warning in her voice but failing. "*Da Hah*'s only made one of Aden, you know."

"You think he's a dream, that's what you do," Dora said. "But let me tell you, no boy's a dream. There's always trouble hidden in there somewhere. Aden probably snores all night, I'd guess, and you'll never be getting any sleep. That and the house will soon be full of babies."

"I really wish you two would be quiet," Clara said a little louder this time.

"Don't worry about Dora," Ella said, holding open the barn door. "Just remember what you felt when Paul was looking at you. That's the real thing."

"You'll be turning the poor girl's brain to mush yet," Dora said with a laugh.

Inside the barn, the low ceilings of the first floor surrounded them. Cobwebs hung on the rafters, and bits of hay fell from the mow. The cows—the first batch already in the stanchions—greedily scooped up the small portion of feed in front of them.

"Needs a good sweeping in here," Dora said and saw Ella nod in agreement as the girls took down their stainless steel milk buckets and three-legged stools.

"Evenin'," Eli, the oldest of the boys, hollered. "Late as usual, I see. Someday I'll be findin' me a girl who knows how to come to choring on time."

"We're not late," Dora said with a glare. She stood at the water bucket behind the cows and dipped the washrag in. "See, I'm ready to wash the cows."

As Eli turned to leave, Ella said, "Now, Clara, pay attention to what Dora is doing. That's the first thing to do. You have to wash the underside of the cow's udders because they're in the field mud—and even worse—all day."

Ella got her own washcloth, motioned Clara closer, and pressed her shoulder against the cow's side. "Sometimes you have to push the cow like this to get in. Then, once they're over like this, you scrub hard. Always watch out for the tail. It gives a person a nasty whack."

As if to demonstrate, the cow brought its tail around in a solid thump across Ella's back. "See," Ella said, "I think she must have heard me."

Clara bent over to look at the udder of the cow and noticed little droplets of water, leftover from the wash, clinging to it.

"You then do this," Ella said as she sat down on the three-legged stool. "You stroke the side of the cow a couple of times and wait a little bit for the milk to come down. If that doesn't work, then you have to try something else to relax her. Once the udder is full, you set your bucket on the floor, holding it tightly between your feet. That's just in case old Bossy tries to kick. They usually don't, but they do seem to know when someone new comes along. Now, with each hand squeeze and pull down. Don't just pull straight down. Do it with a roll. Start with the top fingers and move downward."

Ella squeezed, and a stream of white milk shot into the bucket with a loud metallic sound. Across from her, Dora started at the same time. As the spurts of milk made a fast tat-tat-tat sound, two cats dashed out of the shadows and paused in the aisle to stare at the girls.

"Good evening, kitty cats," Dora said, giving each a spray of milk. The liquid stream flew across the concrete floor and landed in the cat's mouth with practiced perfection.

"You're spoiling them again," Ella said, her voice a gentle chide. Then she turned and added her own stream to the mouths of the cats.

"Now who's spoiling whom?"

"I couldn't help myself," Ella said, "as cute as they are."

"Soon they'll be having kittens," Dora said dryly. "That's how these things go. We'll have to spray milk all night long."

"I don't know about that," Ella said, laughing, "but can't you just see the little fuzzy balls with milk running off their whiskers?"

"You'd be spoiling the whole world if left to yourself," Dora said, giving another shot of milk to the two cats before brushing them away with her foot.

Ella turned her attention back to Clara and handed her the three-legged stool. Clara reached for it, took a deep breath, and gingerly sat down.

"That's a big cow," she said, looking up at the hairy side that rose above her. "What if this thing falls on me?"

"Cows don't fall," Ella assured her. "Just take your hand and squeeze like I showed you."

Clara squeezed hard with both hands. "Oh no," she said as only a dribble of milk came out, "this will take a year."

"Harder," Ella said, encouraging her. "We all learn by doing. Squeeze. Pull. Squeeze."

Clara worked her hand as the cow, its tongue hanging out the side of its mouth, turned to look back at the young girl.

"She doesn't like me," Clara said in panic. "She's getting ready to kick."

"Oh, she likes you," Dora said from her stool. "Cows don't care who milks them as long as you don't pinch them."

"She's not pinching," Ella said. "Quit scaring her. She doesn't even have long fingernails."

Clara managed to get a longer squirt of milk out.

"I did it," she squealed.

"You've got a long ways to go there, little girl," Dora muttered as she got up to empty her bucket into one of the larger milk cans. Dora slowly poured the milk through the strainer and into the can, pausing momentarily when the strainer reached the overflow point. Moments later she emptied the last drops.

"Keep going, Clara," Ella said. "You're doing fine. I have to go milk my own cow now."

Clara worked slowly while Ella and Dora finished their cows and then two more apiece.

"My hands burn like fire," Clara said in despair, "but I think I'm finally done. No more milk comes out."

"That's all you need to do tonight," Ella said, walking over to her. "One cow's enough. Tomorrow night you can try again. It takes time for your muscles to grow stronger. Now, let me check how well you've done."

Clara stepped back from her cow, and Ella sat down. She quickly began with long even strokes and, to Clara's surprise, soon covered the bottom of her pail with milk.

"So I didn't finish the cow," Clara said, her face fallen.

"Don't be feeling bad," Ella said. "I had to check. It wouldn't be good for the cow if you left milk in it."

Three

With all of the others having already disappeared inside the house, Ella raced across the yard. Eli met her at the utility room door. "I thought I was always last," he said with a teasing tone. "So how come you're the tail tonight?"

"I was helping Clara," she said, then stopped, and waited outside while he washed at the washbasin. The evening had grown quiet. The noise of the cows in the barnyard was muffled. In the west the sun had set, and the deep shadows settled across the valley, replacing the light of day. Yet even the nighttime had its comfort and strength in the repose that came after a hard day's work.

She heard Eli splash around in the washroom. He would have the water dirty by now and wouldn't think to step outside to empty the contents. He was a fine enough young man, as was her younger brother, Monroe. They just needed to be taught some manners.

The noises in the washroom ceased, and Ella stepped inside and, as she expected, found the water dirty, Eli gone, and the soap bar skidded all the way to the back corner of the counter. With the water basin in her hand, she held the door open with her foot and threw the water into the yard.

"Supper, Ella," Mamm called from inside. "The boys are hungry."

Perhaps she ought to go on in, sit for the prayer, and then come back out to wash. But, no, they could wait. Eli could have dumped the water out if he had wanted to. That would have saved some time. She refilled the washbasin from the water bucket beside the cabinet and quickly washed her hands.

"We're hungry," one of her brother's roared from the kitchen as she splashed water on her face. There was a general murmur of voices and then silence.

Slowly she dried her hands and face on the towel. That would teach them. She smiled in the semidarkness and then opened the kitchen door with a great rush.

"She wouldn't be makin' Aden wait like that, now would she?" Monroe said. "Not when he's starvin' from a hard day's work in the fields like we are."

"My, my," their father said with a grin. "You boys will all make it—even as hungry as you are. And just remember this. If you get half as good a wife as Ella, you'll be doing real good. That's the kind of wife she'll make for Aden. Yah." He nodded his head sharply, his beard jerking with the motions of his chin.

"Ach. She's only so-so," Monroe said, waving his arms around. "Can't she hurry now? And Aden just wouldn't be a-knowin' any better, that's all."

Ella sat down, ignoring them.

"Are we ready to pray?" their father asked.

Both boys nodded vigorously and then followed the rest, bowing their heads in prayer.

Daett led out in German, "Our *grosser Gott im himmel,* You who never rest or grow weary, we now pause to give thanks and to bless Your great name. Your name is worthy of honor and glory and praise for as long as the earth stands and heavens shine. Even unto all eternity, You are and were and will forever be. Bless now our home and those who live here. Bless the food that is prepared. Be with those who hunger tonight in other lands and even in our own land. Give them grace, and when we meet them, give us compassion for their needs. In the name of the Father, the Son, and the Holy Spirit. Amen."

"Pass the mashed potatoes quick! I'm starving, and I won't last much longer," Eli blurted, motioning with both hands toward Dora who sat directly in front of the bowl of white, fluffy, mashed potatoes.

Unmoving, Dora stared at the bowl.

"Potatoes!" Monroe roared.

"Let's see now," Dora said slowly, "do I want one spoonful or… maybe I want…two. Or, then again, I think…I'm gaining too much weight. Do you think I should have any at all?" She pondered the question while staring at the bowl with great intensity.

"If you don't be passin' that bowl, I'll be throwin' a cow on your head," Eli bellowed, "like right now."

"Ach! Yah, he will," Dora said to the others in mock fear. "The great man has spoken, and shall I pass the potatoes, then?"

"I think you'd better," Daett said. "I could use some myself."

"Then I suppose I should," Dora said, taking a spoonful with a sigh. With a sweet smile on her face, she passed the bowl.

"We have to be warnin' the poor boy who gets her for a wife," Monroe whispered to Eli. "I wouldn't wish her on my worst enemy."

"You're a little late," Dora said with a smirk. "He's already smitten with my charms."

"Then he'll need *Da Hah* to help him!" Eli declared.

"Children, children," Daett said, "let's leave *Da Hah* out of this. He's helping all of us."

"Some more than others," Eli said with a smirk.

"I will pray for you when it comes time to find a girl," Dora said. "I'm sure you'll be needing lots of help."

"A good wife might help you boys," Ella said in defense of her sister. "She might show how you are to conduct yourself."

The boys shook their heads at each other.

"Somebody just drove in," Mamm said as she rose from her chair to look out the living room window. "It's Aden's daett. I wonder what he wants."

"He might be wantin' that Belgium for tomorrow," Daett said. "I told him he could have the horse for a day or two since I know he'll be careful with it."

"Maybe you'd best go see, Noah," Mamm said. "I hope your food won't be getting cold before you come back in."

"This can't take too long," Daett said. "The Belgium's in the barn already." He got up, grabbed his hat, and went out the front door.

There was silence around the table except for the sound of forks and spoons on ceramic plates.

The front door soon opened, and they clearly heard two pairs of footsteps on the floor.

Mamm raised her eyebrows and said, "They must want something from the house."

Noah appeared in the kitchen doorway and cleared his throat. His left hand gripped his beard tightly. He looked directly into Ella's eyes across the table.

"I thought he'd best tell you himself," he said and stepped aside to let Aden's father, Albert, through the doorway. He stood there, his head bowed, silent tears streaming down his face.

Ella rose from her chair, but Mamm motioned for her to sit back down.

"He has news for us," Daett said. "*Da Hah* has seen fit to move with His hand in ways we cannot understand. Yet we know that He is still God, and in this time of trouble, we must not question His ways. Yah, let us always remember that."

"Is it Lydian," Mamm asked as she scooted her chair away from the table, "or one of your girls, perhaps? Is there trouble with them?"

Aden's dad breathed deeply, his hands clasped together in front of him, and then he pulled his blue handkerchief out of his pocket and loudly blew his nose. His lips trembled as he spoke, the words a mere whisper. "Ella, our Aden passed away this afternoon. We only heard an hour ago ourselves."

"Aden?" Mamm rose to her feet. "But he was not ill."

Albert shook his head as sobs now racked his body. "I had to come…

to tell Ella at once. She is like family to us, like a daughter. Yah, but now this is all lost, and Aden has passed to his reward."

"What happened?" Mamm asked. All heads turned to Ella, who sat in stunned silence.

Albert didn't answer but walked slowly over to Ella. He placed his free hand on her shoulder and sobbed into his handkerchief. The moments were long before he found his voice again. "I have lost my son, the son whom I loved, but your pain will also be great. You have lost what you never really had."

"*Da Hah* will be with us," Daett said from across the table. "His grace is always enough—even in these times."

Ella tried to speak but found no words.

Albert gathered himself together, intending to finish his story. His voice caught, but he tried again. "Aden became ill some days ago. A real hard side ache, he said. We did the usual things for him. We thought he might have overworked himself. They'd been framin' a house with the work crew. Aden didn't want to go to the clinic. I guess I should have insisted, but he's a man now. He just stayed home from work a few days and seemed better after that. It looked as if he knew best… like he'd done the right thing. I didn't pay much attention anymore. Then he told us he ran a fever last evening. By this morning Laura told him something had to be done. He looked so bad. We took him down to the clinic right away. Doctor sent him right to Tri-County Hospital, and I guess they went to surgery. That's where he was when we came down. But he never woke out of it, and they told us the appendix had burst. It had burst a day or so ago. It was just too late."

Albert wiped his eyes. "It's just so unexpected. Yah, I never would have thought Aden—of all my boys—would go so soon. He was the best of them, and now *Da Hah* has taken him."

Mamm stood to her feet and walked over to stand behind Ella. Albert stepped aside. Ella knew her face must be white as she struggled again for words, but not a sound came out. It was useless to try.

"You want to come to the living room?" Mamm asked. "It might be easier there. Yah, come?"

Why was her blood so cold and the whole kitchen so out of place as if she had never seen it before? Ella tried to stand, to allow Mamm to lead her, but she didn't have the strength. *Surely this isn't true. Aden's dead? The words must be from a bad dream, but if they are, why can't I wake up?*

"Is Aden…really gone?" she asked, finally finding her voice.

Mamm nodded. "But you shouldn't talk about it here. Come into the living room."

What does the living room have to do with anything? I don't want to talk about this. I don't want to hear it. I would rather scream, run out the door, and go find Aden. I want to see that he is alive, feel his arms around me, hear him say everything is okay, and listen to his laugh. He would say someone had misunderstood. He would say that I'm still the most wonderful girl who ever lived and tell me not to be frightened.

"He's not dead," she whispered. "I would have known. He can't be dead. I just saw him Sunday."

Her mom helped her rise, placing her arms under Ella's. By the kitchen doorway, Ella heard Daett ask Albert, "When will the body be coming back?"

"Tomorrow," Albert said, his voice low. "We will have the viewin' in the evening."

"I will bring her tomorrow," Daett said. "We will stay with her till then."

Albert loudly blew his nose, and Daett held the front door open for him. Ella watched him go, unable to move.

Four

The kitchen had a hush of silence over it. Daett came back and took Ella by one arm, and Mamm took the other. They slowly moved to the living room and helped her sit.

"He's not dead," Ella said. "I know he's not, and I want to see him."

Mamm sat beside her, running her hand over her daughter's forehead. "This is not for you to think about. Just cry real good, now. It's what's for the best. This is the way of *Da Hah*. He decides who lives and who dies."

"Not Aden," she gasped. "No. I will not believe it until I see it. Not Aden. He was a good man, and I loved him. He cannot be gone. *No*."

"You'll be stayin' with her," Daett whispered to Mamm. He disappeared through the kitchen doorway and spoke in a low voice to the rest of the family amidst the intermittent soft rattle of metal utensils on dinner plates.

Mamm pulled Ella tight against her.

"It's not possible. I would have had some feeling about this. In here," Ella said as she lay her hand on her chest, "because I love him."

"I know," Mamm said, nodding. "We all did. He was a good boy. His family is heartbroken too. You're not the only one. They also have suffered a great loss along with you. You must think of them and not

23

just of yourself. Our people are like that. And others will stand with you."

Ella was quiet and then turned to Mamm. "It's true, then?"

Mamm nodded. "I'm sorry. *Da Hah* has taken him." Then she added, "You can hope to see him again."

"We were not married," Ella said, her eyes seeking her mom's face again.

"It's best you cry, Ella, and not think," Lizzie said, pulling Ella tight against herself again. "Let the pain come. That also is *Da Hah*'s way, and He can touch you, then, because He's the only one who understands when times like this come."

A few faces appeared in the kitchen opening but were withdrawn immediately.

"I think I'll be going up to my room," Ella said, making an effort to rise. "I want to be alone."

Mamm searched her daughter's face but said nothing. Together they moved upstairs, taking the steps slowly. Once inside her room, Ella sat on the bed while Mamm lit the kerosene lamp. The match caught on the wick, the flame flickered, but settled down when she replaced the glass chimney. Mamm sat down beside Ella.

"I'm okay, yah," Ella whispered.

"You'd best not be alone for the night. Perhaps I can be staying with you."

Ella shook her head. "I want to think about Aden—all night long—and where he has gone."

"Thinking's not good," her mom said with understanding. "It will not bring Aden back, and the will of *Da Hah* must not be questioned. We must believe that *Da Hah* knows what's best."

Ella lifted her face and said, "I must ask my questions, Mamm. I really must. They are in my heart, and I will ask them even if no one answers them. Does *Da Hah* ask that we love someone with all our heart and then forget without a struggle?" Ella stared at the blank wall, the wild shadows of light dancing on the blue color.

Mamm studied Ella's face for a long moment, before standing to her feet. "You can be alone, then. A little later I will look in on you, yah?"

Ella nodded, and Mamm, with one more careful look at her daughter's face, stepped into the hall and closed the door gently behind her.

Is Aden really gone?

Yet it had to be true. Aden's father had said so, and his sorrow was evidence enough.

She felt the need to walk, to pace the floor. But as soon as she stood, she sat down again. Her body was completely drained of strength. It was then that the sobs came, great waves shaking her frame. From the force of the fountain within, she tried again to stand.

She walked the floor, making no effort to keep the thoughts away, allowing the pain to rack her. Aden's face—so handsome, so young, and so beloved—came before her. That first time she saw him, even then, how much she had wanted him to ask if he could take her home. In the weeks after, how her heart trembled from the uncertainty of whether he ever would or not. His eyes held a smile on Sunday nights, not just for her but for other girls too.

Then there was that evening when she came close to him as he paused beside his buggy. How her hopes had risen and then crashed when the conversation had gone nowhere.

"Hi Ella," he had said. "It's a *gut* evening, isn't it? The stars are so bright tonight. One can see all the way into the heavens, it seems like."

She said something but couldn't remember the words. Her irritation at him astonished her—that he noticed the stars in the heavens but not the ones in her eyes. But then perhaps he did notice and was so used to seeing them in every girl's eyes that they meant nothing to him.

She agonized and walked slowly passed him, but he seemed more interested in getting his horse hitched to the buggy than with where she was headed.

It had been weeks—maybe months—later when he asked her if he could take her home. She had to struggle to stay calm, to not shout

"Yah!" Instead she just nodded her head and hoped the joy in her face didn't show too much.

She walked the floor, remembering the thrill of that first moment when she sat beside him in the buggy—so close to such strength, such powerful arms. She remembered how he held the horse's reins, how the stubble of a beard moved in the darkness, and how he talked and slapped the lines to hurry the horse out of the driveway.

"It was nice for you to be lettin' me take you home," he said. It was the first thing out of his mouth, as if she were the one who extended the favor and the one who gave all the pleasure.

He let his horse go that night, and she clung on to the side of the buggy because she didn't dare clutch his arm. She thought he was showing off but would learn in time that he really hung on to the lines, pulling his horse back from an even faster speed. He was like that—always had more than what he revealed. His body and soul contained strength above what one needed. After a time she learned this—after she understood his heart. She often marveled that God made such a man.

She fed him shoofly pie that night. He said halfway through, "I don't really like shoofly pie, but this is good. It must be because you made it."

"Aden," she had gasped and stood to take the plate from him.

"No, I'll eat it," he said, playfully pulling back from her outstretched hands.

"But you don't have to eat it. We still have a piece of cherry pie in the cupboard. It's better than making you eat something you don't like. I'm so embarrassed."

He laughed. "Don't be. This really does taste good."

She sat down on the couch again and watched him finish. The way he ate convinced her he really did like the pie. Either that or he was a really good actor.

"Can I come again?" he asked at the door when it was time to go.

She knew then she loved him. She loved him enough to be his wife long before he ever took her hands in his or kissed her. His hands were rugged, rough from his work in the outdoors. He laughed with a full sound as if the joy rolled up from inside of him and his life could never hold all of it.

Then there was that Sunday night. She was just nineteen. He had said the words, "You will marry me, yah?" Unable to speak, she had nodded.

He laughed. She had hoped it was for joy and not for her awkward silence at such a moment.

"If I could, I would marry you tomorrow, Ella. Do you know that? But we have to wait—until we're both twenty-one."

"It's so long," she said, clinging to his arm.

"I know. But you're worth the wait, worth every minute. To be married to you will be worth it all and then some."

She hung her head that night to hide the stars in her eyes from him. How badly she wanted to tell him she was unworthy, that his opinion was too high of her, but the words wouldn't come, just the rush of emotion as he kissed her again.

They talked for hours on the backless couch in her living room. The things they found to do, apparently other couples weren't that interested in doing. Together they took walks by the river at the bottom of Seager Hill. In the winter snow, they made snowmen on Sunday afternoons. They stood by his buggy and talked about the stars, argued about what they were called, and even visited the library in Randolph to find evidence for their arguments.

They visited his *grossmom* who lived in the *dawdy haus* behind his parents' place. They stopped the buggy once to listen to *Englisha* Christmas carolers singing outside a house.

"They are beautiful, those songs, even if they are *Englisha* songs," he said. "*Da Hah* in heaven might even listen to something so nice."

"Yah," she said in astonishment.

"The whole earth is beautiful, is it not?" he said. "Did not *Da Hah* make it all without the help of man? So who is to say He doesn't like beautiful things?"

She shivered. "You must not say such things. Preacher Stutzman might hear you. You should be careful with your words."

He laughed. "These are words for your ears only. You draw them out of my heart. We won't speak such things to Preacher Stutzman. And if you knew the truth, Preacher Stutzman is a nice man. You just have to get to know him."

He pulled her tight against him in the buggy so that she felt the warmth of his arm even through the blanket.

"Da Hah couldn't have made a more beautiful girl than you if He tried," he said. "I can't wait until you're my wife. I can't imagine how I deserve such a thing. I will build a house, Ella, just for you. It will be a great big house, one with plenty of rooms for love…and for all our children."

"Stop it," she told him. "Such nonsense you speak, and I am just a common, ordinary girl with plenty of faults like everyone else. If you don't quit your wild imaginations soon, you'll be in for a big disappointment."

He laughed beside her in the darkness, and she knew he wasn't persuaded. And she loved him even more for it.

Behind her Ella heard the bedroom door opened, and Mamm appeared. "Are you okay?" she asked.

"Yah," she said. "I loved him, Mamm. I loved him so very much."

"I know." Mamm wrapped her arms around her daughter for a long time. Then she released her hug and left quietly. Ella resumed her pacing and remembering and then the questions. *How could God do this to me? How could He place such a love in my heart and then allow it to be torn out with such brute force? How could such a God be trusted again?*

Yet she could not go on with such thoughts. It was forbidden. Surely it was her lack of understanding *Da Hah*'s ways. Was that not the real problem? Yet how could one understand with such pain throbbing in the heart, with such agony tearing at the soul, and with tears pouring out like water from a fountain?

Ella walked the floor and tore open the curtains, nearly bringing them down off the hooks on the wall. *I will ask my questions. I will ask why. Let the heavens say what they wish. Let faith lock the door, but I will walk through it anyway.*

Her eyes searched the heavens, studied the stars—those very stars she and Aden had shared. *Do they know the answer?* She waited but was greeted only with silence, with mockery, as if they laughed at her distress and promised her nothing with their stony silence. She was truly alone and forsaken in life.

Five

The next morning Daett softly called to the younger girls from the bottom of the stairs. Clara and Dora both stirred in their beds. Clara reluctantly swung her feet to the floor, and Dora lit the kerosene lamp, its shadows dancing wildly on the walls. Clara reached for her dress, which was beside the bed, and dressed quickly.

"We're one person short this morning," Dora whispered. "Ella will not be with us."

"I know," Clara grunted. "I thought of that last night." How would all the morning work be handled? Much of last evening had been spent in stunned silence in the living room. When bedtime came, the children had been bidden goodnight with strict instructions to be quiet and not bother Ella.

But as they crept past Ella's door, the children could all hear Ella's muffled sobs. How strange and confusing it all was. The world had simply turned upside down. Death had always been a distant thing, seen only when they walked past wooden boxes at funerals. Now it had arrived in their home and to their Ella, of all people, sweet self-sacrificing Ella.

Daett had led the family in a Scripture reading before they went to bed. His hands held the huge family Bible as he spoke the words in somber tones, "Yea, though I walk through the valley of the shadow of death, I will fear no evil: for thou art with me; thy rod and thy staff they comfort me. Thou preparest a table before me in the presence of mine enemies: thou anointest my head with oil; my cup runneth over. Surely goodness and mercy shall follow me all the days of my life: and I will dwell in the house of the Lord for ever."

He had read in English. That just made things all the stranger. The Scriptures were never read in English. Never. Clara had stared at her dad, but he simply closed the big Bible and said, "Everyone, off to bed. We all have a hard day ahead of us tomorrow." And they had tiptoed upstairs and climbed into their bedrooms.

The new day loomed before them all. Dora took the kerosene lamp and quietly stepped into the hall with Clara behind her. As they went by Ella's door, it opened suddenly, and there was Ella, still in her dress from last night, looking worn. Her face was red and puffy, and her eyes looked sad and lonely. The light from the kerosene lamp in Dora's hand splashed shadows on Ella's face.

"Is it time to chore?" Ella asked in a bare whisper.

"You're not supposed to get up," Dora said.

"I know," Ella said as she glanced down at her wrinkled dress, "but I can help, and I don't even have to get dressed. I must have slept in this."

"As you wish," Dora said, shaking her head, "but Mamm will have something to say about this."

The three made their way downstairs with Ella in the rear. They walked single file into the kitchen.

"Why is Ella up?" Mamm asked as if Ella wasn't there and Dora and Clara were to blame.

"She must have heard us." Dora said. "We didn't make any noise, and I told her not to come down."

"Then get right back upstairs," Mamm said, addressing Ella for the first time.

"I have to do something, Mamm. I can't just sit up in my room and think of him."

"Didn't you sleep at all?" Mamm asked.

"I don't know," Ella said. "I don't remember."

"Ach." Mamm said, relenting. "Well, perhaps that is for the best. Then stay with Clara inside while Dora and I do the barn chores."

Ella nodded, standing totally still while Dora and Mamm left. She turned to Clara and said, "You can set the table, Clara, as usual. I'll need help with the bacon after that."

Clara glanced at her sister. So Ella had plans for a full breakfast. Ella had her back turned, intent on the fire in the stove, the shadows of the kerosene lamps playing on her shoulders. Clara whispered the words, "I'm sorry about Aden, Ella."

Ella turned around, her face caught in the soft light. "He's gone, Clara. And I so loved him. I really did."

"Maybe *Da Hah* will send you someone else," Clara said without much thought, the words just coming out of her mouth.

Ella smiled gently. "No, Clara. It's not to be. There was just one Aden—my Aden—and I could never love like that again."

"I'm sorry," Clara said. It did feel like the right thing to say. "He was a *gut* man."

Ella paused at the words, the match in her hand. "He was more than *gut,* Clara. Aden was wonderful. He was the most wonderful boy I ever laid eyes on. He won my heart, and he loved me, Clara. I was to become his wife. I was to bear his children if *Da Hah* sent us any. We would have grown old together. Now he's dead and just gone. And it was *Da Hah* who took him."

"Daett read a real *gut* Scripture last night. It was about walking through the valley of the shadow of death. Mamm cried a lot."

"Yah," Ella said, her smile weak, "I have a very *gut* family, and here I am spilling all my tears on you. I'm the one who should be sorry about it. I'll be okay, Clara, really I will. Other people have gone through this before. Lots of them. It's just that it's me this time; me—little Ella Yoder—who has a broken heart."

Ella dropped the match on the stove, bent her head over the rusty black stove, and began to cry new tears. Clara felt the sting in her own eyes. She went into the living room where she remembered from last night a spare handkerchief lay folded. She came back and gently pushed the soft cloth into Ella's hand and then stood back to wait until Ella's emotion had spent itself. More than that, what was there to do?

"Ach," Ella finally said, "now I've gone and got the match wet too. It's wasted." Then the sobs came again.

Clara gently nudged Ella away from the stove. She found another match and lit the kindling. The flame flickered, sought fuel and oxygen, and burst into bright light. Carefully she added additional wood and shut the stove lid.

"You're *gut* at that, yah," Ella said, regaining her composure. "But if we don't get to work soon, we'll never have breakfast ready in time."

This was true, and Clara returned to the table, set the plates, and then went down to the basement for the bacon. By the time she returned, steam was rising from the heated pan Ella had placed on the stove. She cut the package open, pulled the bacon strips apart, and slid them into the pan. The crackle soon filled the kitchen.

They worked together in silence until the screen door slammed. The first people were back from choring. Mamm, her face still wet from a quick wash at the washbasin, came in through the washroom door first.

"Get the girls up," she said to Clara while looking for a long moment at Ella and then giving her a hug.

Clara wanted to join the two as they held each other tight but decided this was meant for Ella and her mother alone.

On her usual trips upstairs to wake her sisters, Clara thought to make as much racket as she could because this usually helped prepare her sisters for her arrival. With noise they might at least stir a little before she opened the door and lit the kerosene lamp. With a light in the room and a jerk on their covers, they would get up.

This morning, though, the usual methods didn't seem appropriate. Clara walked quietly up to the bedroom door and opened it. With a gentle shake of their shoulders and a whispered, "Time to get up," she roused her three younger sisters.

Ruth popped right up, as did Ada. Martha, the four-year-old, rolled over and pulled the quilt over her head.

"Go away," she said. "I'm still tired."

"You have to get up, yah," Clara said firmly.

Clara pulled on Martha's arms and stood her up beside the bed. She helped her slide on her dress. Ruth and Ada had already dressed themselves and were out the door by the time Clara followed with Martha's hand in hers.

Their footsteps sounded hollow in the morning silence. They didn't say a word when they arrived downstairs but slipped quietly onto the back bench of the kitchen table. They also must remember that something had gone terribly wrong last night.

Clara glanced around. The table was set, her mom was in the kitchen with Ella, and there was nothing more for her to do, and so she took her seat at the table.

The bowl of oatmeal steamed on the stove, and the bacon sizzled until the time came to serve it. Ella had the last batch of fried eggs in the pan. In the washroom the splash of water could be heard as the menfolk washed up. The murmur of their voices could be heard through the utility room wall.

Quietly they came in. Eli and Monroe sent guarded glances toward Ella as they took their seats. Their father sat at the head of the table as usual.

He cleared his throat. "This morning we will read a Scripture. We normally don't do this, but today is not normal."

Clara snuck a look at Ella's face. She was staring straight ahead at the wall. She then glanced over to Eli and Monroe. They were sitting in silence, and from the look on their faces, they were hungry. But this morning Ella's needs must come first.

Mamm got up and went into the living room, returned with the big Bible, and gave it to Daett. He leafed through the pages, found what he wanted, and began to read in German. The words, the holy language, were solemn.

"*Ich werde erheben.* I will lift up mine eyes unto the hills, from whence cometh my help. My help cometh from the Lord, which made heaven and earth. He will not suffer thy foot to be moved; he that keepeth thee will not slumber."

Then he spoke directly to Ella, "The Lord, He will have His mercy on you, Ella, even in your sorrow and loss. You have not sinned against Him, that He should be angry with you. We do not understand how this can be or why *Da Hah*'s hand has come down heavy on you. Yet we be trustin' His mercies are with you. He will give you and all of us strength for the way—for what lay ahead. He will give you His grace for this trial so that the darkness of this pain will not destroy you.

"We know your heart is broken, and though we don't feel the pain like you do, we do know what this pain is…to have our hearts broken. We also know that *Da Hah* does such things, and He alone understands what His hand does. He alone knows what the reasons are. In this trial you are asked to walk through, we know His mercies are still new every morning."

Ella said nothing, but fresh tears ran heavily down her face. Mamm cried too, and even Eli and Monroe sniffled a little.

"We will pray now," Daett said, continuing. "Then we must eat. Life will go on…even in this hour of trouble."

Six

After breakfast Clara helped with the dishes, packed her lunch, and left for school. The day had dawned into a magnificent morning without a cloud in the sky. Summer's heat was still a long time away and hard for Clara to imagine after the rough winter they had been through.

Clara stopped in the middle of the lawn to soak in the sun's warmth, and she felt almost guilty for enjoying the sensation. With Ella in such pain, wasn't it wrong to enjoy anything so much? She was nearly overcome but shoved the sad thoughts away, took a great deep breath, and let the air out slowly. She allowed her eyes to take in the view in front of her. It was the best spot in the whole valley. Like her older sister, she loved their house on Seager Hill. From here the swells of land rolled away across the valley for as far as the eye could see. Below them buggies drove along the strings of blacktop roads.

To the west, the low mountains stretched out, still white streaked with snow from the winter. Where the snow had melted, bare spots emerged with a blush of green. She laughed while she ran down the hill toward the schoolhouse, drawing in delicious breaths of air in great gulps.

From the other direction, a buggy came up the hill. Likely it was the Miller children, Ben and Susie. They sometimes walked but must have decided to drive this morning.

When the driver slapped his horse with the lines, the horse responded with a peculiar run. It really was Ben and his sister. Clara slowed to a walk and watched as Ben kept the horse moving at a good clip. Ben slapped the lines hard one last time and pulled left. With the speed he had, he almost made it but not quite. The old horse threw out its hooves in plenty of time, its legs spread, as if rebelling against the whole world. The driveway of the schoolyard was several yards away, but the horse was steadfast in its tracks as the buggy now blocked half the roadway.

What a nasty horse they had. Whatever entered the horse's brain at moments like this made it stop, and little could persuade it to continue until it decided of its own accord to move on.

Boys came out of the schoolhouse on the run, their hats held down on their heads with one hand. One got on each side of the horse's bridle and pulled. Two got on the back of the buggy and pushed. It was a futile effort. The horse, as usual, refused to budge.

Ben yelled from inside the buggy in exasperation, but this didn't do much good either. Susie climbed out, got her lunch bucket out of the back, and walked the rest of the way. The horse was Ben's problem, not hers.

Clara ran quickly to join Susie, having to go around the stalled buggy and exasperated boys. There was no sense in her offering to help. She didn't have any special knack to get a balking horse on the move again.

Down from the top of Seager Hill, one of the *Englisha's* cars came, having to slow down because of the obstruction in the road. There was no doubt the situation could fast become serious if the horse wasn't persuaded to move forward soon. In the schoolhouse, Katie would soon pull the bell rope with or without a stalled horse in the road.

With all the excitement on the outside, Clara was ready to go inside and tell Katie about the problem. Perhaps Katie wouldn't ring the bell until this was cleared up. She waited a moment longer while Paul, the boy who sat behind her in class, moved forward and took hold of the horse's bridle.

Clara watched, fascinated. Paul seemed to know just what to do. He pulled and petted the horse, talking to it and jerking firmly on the lines. Yet all was to no avail. The boys around the buggy waved their arms, pointed toward the road, and mouthed words Clara couldn't understand. Ben hopped down from the buggy, said something, and pointed. Two of the schoolboys left to walk down the road a ways in both directions. They held their hats in their hands and waved them like flags even though Clara could see no *Englisha* cars in the distance.

Clara was again ready to go inside and explain things to Katie when a movement on the hill caught her eye. She looked closer and recognized Ezra coming up the hill at a run.

Usually he and his sisters were late and often had to hurry, so seeing him running didn't seem unusual. He would want to offer his help. Ezra was holding his side by the time he arrived but marched right up to the front of the horse. He then said something to Paul, causing Paul to step back. Ezra, while talking quietly to the horse, took hold of the bridle, didn't pull or jerk on it, but reached out to stroke the horse's nose. Moments later the horse jerked its head in response and plunged forward as if to make up for lost time. Ezra hung on to the lines and soon brought the horse under control. Masterfully and quite astonishingly, the boy knew how to talk to horses.

When Ezra brought the buggy to a halt, the other boys swarmed around and quickly unhitched the horse. Ben led his now docile horse into the little stall they used for a horse barn during school days, and the others pushed his buggy back into place. They were just finishing when Katie pulled the bell rope.

Clara took her seat along with everyone else as Katie walked to the front of the classroom and cleared her throat.

"Boys and girls, as I think most of you know, our community has lost one of its members. Aden Wengerd has passed away. The funeral will be on Saturday. This is a tragedy for all of us, and our hearts go out to the family." She paused a moment as all the children considered the gravity of the loss of one who was only a few years older than the older students. Then Katie said, "Now we'll continue with our lessons. Will the first graders please come up for class?"

That was Katie's system. The eighth graders were called last on any subject. The first graders got to their feet and marched up the aisle to the front of the schoolhouse for class. Clara busied herself. It would be a while until Katie worked her way up to the eighth grade.

Far sooner than she expected, Clara heard Katie announce, "Eighth grade spelling." Clara got out of her seat and followed the others up to the benches in front. Katie waited for them to get comfortable and then gave them the spelling words orally. When the last word was given, the students handed in their completed work, and Katie dismissed the eighth graders by saying, "I'll check your papers this evening as usual and give them back to you in the morning. I hope everyone knew their words. Most of you are *gut* pupils, and I don't have to worry about you."

Clara smiled, still feeling as happy as she had on her way to school that morning. Even with the sad news of last night, life did go on. How strange that it should be so, Clara thought.

As she returned to her seat, Katie called the first grade math class forward. Clara slid into her seat, set up her math book, and started to work. The line of grades would move through the aisle throughout the rest of the morning, and the eighth graders would soon be called up again.

With her math book open in front of her, Clara struggled to concentrate, distracted by the figure of Ezra in the row across from her. He obviously struggled even harder than she did, not only with math but with almost all the subjects. Right now Ezra had his English book open.

How could it be that a boy who could talk a stubborn horse into moving forward couldn't complete English assignments with equal ease? It was a puzzling question. They all knew Ezra was slow, but obviously he wasn't slow in everything.

Returning to her own work, Clara focused on the math question in front of her. Whatever the answer was, it wasn't coming. If she could just solve her *pi* problem… No wonder the preachers said the *Englisha* didn't know what was important in the world. This something that looked like a curvy road on top of two posts that leaned sideways would never be studied at all if she had anything to say about it.

It then occurred to Clara to see if Paul, from his seat behind her, was staring at her again. She turned her head just slightly, searching with the edges of her vision. Yah, he was. Her heart jumped, and she wondered how it could be that his look could cause such feeling in her heart? But what about Ella and what happened to Aden? Wasn't this how such things started and could lead to such sorrow?

Carefully Clara kept her eyes straight ahead. *Think about the math problem, keep a clear head, and ignore him. Stay focused, and this will go away.* She pulled the drawing from yesterday out of her tablet and stared at it. *This is the drawing Ella said she would use in her wedding quilt. What now? Ella's lost her love. Is she going to complete her quilt? The work is almost done except for the edges. What would happen if Ella didn't finish it? Would someone else finish it and claim the quilt as their own after Ella has designed most of the pieces herself? Is this drawing now to be wasted? Surely no one else would want to use this in their quilt.*

Clara looked at the page more carefully. Against her better judgment, she had to admit it was beautiful and well done. It would look so wonderful on the quilt. Nee, Ella must complete the work. If not, perhaps Mamm could finish it, and they could keep the quilt in a closet until Ella healed. Perhaps she would eventually find another boy to marry. Yes, surely Ella would soon have someone else. After all, she had been snatched up quickly the first time.

Ella was too *gut* a girl to be without a wonderful man. Who would the boy be this time? All the older boys were already dating someone, but Ella would find someone, and then the quilt would be needed.

Clara placed the drawing of the house back in her tablet and returned her attention to the troublesome *pi* problem.

At recess time, she carefully transferred the picture to her lunch pail. She wouldn't let Ella see it just yet, but she wanted it at home where she could keep it safe and sound until it was needed.

Ella would not be home tonight. She would be over at Aden's house to sit with the body. Clara shivered. *Poor Ella.* What a dreadful thing to happen to so *gut* a sister.

After recess, Katie called the eighth-grade students forward for math. They all moved to the front of the classroom. Clara took her completed *pi* problems but kept the paper inside her tablet. *They are too scary to look at. What if my answers are all wrong?*

"So how's everyone doing with their *pi* problems?" Katie asked as if she suspected the truth.

Clara raised her hand. "I don't understand it, really. Do we have to learn things like this?"

"Yah," Katie said with a sympathetic smile. "Perhaps if I explained it again, it would help. And maybe we can do some practice on the chalkboard."

"I'd like that," Clara admitted, glancing at the others when no one else said anything. "Well, I do need the help even if no one else does."

"It's nothing to be ashamed of," Katie said. "How about the rest of you? Can I assume, then, that you all understood it perfectly?"

Paul grunted but didn't say anything as he and the rest of the class took their places at the chalkboard. The students worked under Katie's direction until their frowns turned into smiles of comprehension. On the way back to the bench, Clara glanced up and caught Paul's eye. He smiled a mischievous warm smile that sent thrills around her heart.

Thinking of Ella and Aden, she quickly caught herself. *Nee, I don't want this.* She slid into her seat and kept her head straight forward, but her mind couldn't forget that glance. Several long moments passed when nothing on her desk would stay in focus. *He is still looking.* She was sure of it. Finally she turned around slowly, letting her eyes meet his. They were simply too beautiful to stay away from.

Seven

Ella, dressed in black, left with Daett and Mamm in the surrey at around eleven. Thankfully no one was in the backseat with her. It was much better this way. Dora had wanted to come along, but Mamm wouldn't allow it. This way no one would speak extra words because they felt uncomfortable with her or, worse, pitied her.

"You're needed at home, Dora," Mamm had said. "Ella should be alone anyway. Let her grieve by herself. You, Eli, and Monroe can manage the chores. You can all come over afterward. Clara doesn't have to if she doesn't want to. Let her decide when she comes home from school."

Ella drew the vinyl doors closed on both sides of the surrey. The darkness inside deepened. It was cold outside, and she pulled the buggy blanket up higher. Mamm and Daett were vague, silent forms up front. She was alone and hidden inside. *Alone.* She considered the word. *Is that not what I am now—alone? I might as well get used to it.*

They drove down the hill and past the schoolhouse. Thankfully they passed no one on the road. Even at the usually busy intersection at the bottom of the hill with its multiple Amish homes and businesses, there was no one. Any Amish person who saw them would know where they were headed. Even their sympathy would be intrusive at the moment.

Later perhaps, after a little more time, the people could be faced. The funeral would be tomorrow with the house full of people. Was that not asking enough? For now each moment was a long event, a drawn-out effort to survive the pain. Each breath was a shameful event, one in which her heart went on beating and Aden's no longer did.

"It has been a beautiful morning," Daett said from the seat in front. "The Lord has given us grace again for this day."

Ella wanted to say there ought to be rain, great buckets of it, pouring out of the sky. But then her father's remark had not really been for her, though she couldn't help but hear it. He usually was more sensitive to her feelings than that.

"Yah, it is," her mother said, "but we best not speak of it today. It is the day of Ella's sorrow."

"I had not forgotten this," her father said. "I know my daughter's heart is broken, but we must still give thanks for what *Da Hah* gives us."

Ella gripped the edge of the buggy blanket. What was there to say? Words couldn't begin to describe how she felt. Even if she could say them, they wouldn't help this pain or cause it to ache any less.

Why had the God of her people done this? They taught He held all things in His hands and could do what He wished. *Why then has He chosen to take Aden? Why has He snatched Aden away before I could be his wife, spend time with him in a married state, and at least bear his child? To have his child now would ease the pain. To have a little piece of Aden, perhaps a son to carry on his name, his memory, and his looks would be a comfort. Now there would be nothing. It is as if Aden has been wiped off the face of the earth without any trace left behind. How could the earth be any darker—or crueler—than it is now?*

Not only had God let her down, her faith had let her down too. If it were not for tradition, she would already have been married.

"You have to be twenty-one, Ella." She could still hear the voices. "We all have to be. It's the way of our people. It's the blessing the forefathers left—where children learn to serve at home before they take on their own responsibilities."

Well, it had been no blessing to her. She had waited for more than two years and longed to share more with Aden than the infrequent embrace he gave her or the momentary kiss he allowed. She didn't want to breach the sacred privileges of married life. She had just wanted to marry him then, when they had first confessed their love. And they would have but for the rules. Now, it would never be possible. Soon they would bury his body and throw dirt on his brown wooden casket. The image was too awful to imagine, and she almost cried out.

No, I can't think that. Stop it. He's not dead at all.

Yet she was now going to where she would see for herself that Aden was dead. That dreaded moment lay ahead. It would be an awful moment of beholding his face frozen in death, his eyes forever closed, his lips hard, and his arms frigid and unable to ever move again. *Why did God so abruptly, with no attempt to warn me, take him away?* The question would not let her go.

"Why was I not allowed to marry Aden?" she whispered. The words came from tense lips that already knew the answer, yet the words must be said or something inside of her would surely break.

Her dad's head turned slightly, but he said nothing.

He heard me. "We had wanted to marry a long time ago," she said, loud enough for her parents to surely hear. "You knew that. Why couldn't we have been married then? I'd have his child with me now. Wouldn't that be better than this?"

"There is no answer to this," her dad said, turning his head to look at her.

Tears swam in his blue eyes. Ella's cries filled the buggy, rang in her ears. The pain was simply too much. Her people and her God had failed her—had left her alone.

Mamm reached back and gently gripped her shoulder. "We do what we know is best, and God decides from there. Even if you had been married to Aden, it still would have hurt this much—even more perhaps."

"I would then have had his child," Ella cried.

"Yah, this could be true," Daett said, "but we do not know. There are many, even among our people, who have no children. We can only know what is now, what happens this day, and what *Da Hah* has given. It is best you accept what His hand gives, even the sorrow."

"Yah," her mother said, "your daett knows what he speaks of."

"I only know how much I miss Aden," Ella said. "Why would God take him from me?"

"Are we not from the dust of the ground," her father answered, "frail and feeble and made by *Da Hah's* hands? Such questions, it is not our place to be askin'."

"Yah, but I ask them," she said, her voice resolute.

"Then *Da Hah* must answer them," he replied. "I cannot."

"It is a fearful thing," Mamm said, her voice tense, "to be questioning the Almighty."

"Yah," Daett said, "it is. Yet He has pity on the widows and the orphans. *Da Hah* knows your heart is broken. Ask of Him. Perhaps there will be an answer we know nothing of."

Ella settled back into the buggy seat. Yah, her father seemed to understand. Perhaps God wouldn't judge her harshly for her questions. She wiped her hand across her face, blowing into the handkerchief. Mamm took a deep breath in the front seat.

Daett pulled the buggy lines right at the next turn, and the gravel road rattled under the buggy wheels. They drove in silence across the open stretch of field and down the curves leading to the little creek.

The stream ran with clear water. Here and there, the spots sparkled where the sun's rays made their way through the tree branches and bounced off the ripples. Aden and she had stopped here many times on a Sunday afternoon, tied the horse to a tree, and walked along the banks.

Aden would take her hand as they talked about the future. Lately it had been the wedding, but Aden had once asked her, "Would it be too much for you if I were ever to be ordained a minister?"

"You…a minister?" She asked, knowing her face had registered the surprise. "You should not speak of such things. Is not the lot a sacred thing?"

He had laughed and answered, "Yes. And I do not desire it, nor am I looking for it. I just have this feeling sometimes. Like I hear my name called out by the bishop who says I've got the three votes. Then I walk up front to pick out the book. I must say that I wake up in a cold sweat—right scared stiff."

"It's just you're dreaming, then," she said, pulling his arm closer to her. "You would be making a good preacher, though."

He glanced at her. "Now, now," he said, "answer me. What would you be doing if that was to happen? Could you take being a preacher's wife? Would you be sorry you married me?"

"I'd never be sorry I married you," she said. "Never. I'd marry you right now. Yah, now, if I could!"

He had laughed that great sound that rolled off into the trees. It was as if the waters in the little steam joined in with their twinkling murmur.

"You are too *gut* for me—much too *gut,*" he said, looking her full in the face until she dropped her eyes. Then he swept her up into his arms and gently kissed her, setting her heart to pounding like a freight train on the valley tracks. Then ahead of them lay the long months of waiting for their wedding.

"You used to come here?" Mamm said, breaking into her thoughts.

Ella nodded, her eyes staring at the rushing water.

"It will be like this often," her mother said softly. "Each place, each day, each sound… Something will come to remind you of him. It will be like this until time can have its way and heal. So it is for all of us. *Da Hah* will bring healing for the hurt."

"Aden will be in heaven," Ella said, her voice firm. "He was too *gut* not to be."

"We must only hope he is," her mother said, turning around to look at her.

"You must let her talk, Lizzie. Yah," her dad said, "*Da Hah* will understand that. He knows she hurts."

"I know he's in heaven," Ella said. "I just *know* he is."

Her mother turned back around, her face grave. The buggy wheels rattled on the gravel as they passed Ben Raber's place with his *Hickory Rockers for Sale* sign out front. Ella saw Ben look out of the window of his shop and then pull back when he saw who was in the front seat. Ella leaned back as well. People would know who drove past, but they didn't need to see her.

That poor Ella. She could hear the voices now. *Almost married, she was. And so suddenly he's gone.*

The other schoolhouse, the one on the corner, came into view. Aden's parents' place was across from it. Ella took a deep breath. The body of what once was Aden was in there, and she would have to see it.

Eight

Noah Yoder drove the buggy onto the yard of the Wengerd's place and stopped by the sidewalk. One by one, buggies ahead of them parked in a long row beside the barn. Ella made no effort to get out until Mamm undid the vinyl door snaps and stood there waiting.

"You have to come. You can't stay here," she whispered.

Ella nodded. She pushed up on the seat with her hands and made her legs move under her. On the step down, she nearly slipped, and her mother caught her hand.

"Do be careful," Mamm said. "You don't want to be injuring yourself."

Mamm didn't release Ella's arm until they were at the walk. Behind them Daett drove forward to find a place to park and unhitch.

At the front door, Ella and Mamm were met by Aden's mother, Lydian, who motioned them inside. "He's still not here," she said.

Ella squeezed her eyes shut, stepping up into the house. She would have to find a way to bear the next few hours.

Mamm spoke first. "What a shock this was when Albert brought the news." She put her hand on Ella's shoulder, pulling her to a stop.

"I know," Lydian said, shutting the front door, stepping in front of

Ella, and embracing her. "This is so hard for all of us, and I know you loved him as much as we did."

Ella opened her eyes, taking in the darkness of the room, a single kerosene lamp burning on the counter. She returned the embrace. This was Aden's mamm, and she must also be hurting.

Around the living room, benches were set up. The bedroom door directly in front of them was open. That must be where the body would be taken. Daniel, Aden's younger brother, stood against the wall. His girlfriend, Arlene, sat in front of him. They came slowly toward her and then shook her hand. Other black-clad people stood, murmuring words she could hardly hear. When no one stood in front of her anymore, she wearily lowered herself down on a bench.

"The funeral will be tomorrow," Lydian whispered. "We have sent the word out, but I didn't know if it reached you yet."

"No, we didn't know," Mamm said, shaking her head, "but we figured on it."

"Lunch is ready. They brought in sandwiches. Some of the others have eaten already. There's no line at the moment," Lydian said, motioning toward the table. Behind them the door opened, and Ella's daett entered. He came to stand beside Mamm as she led Ella toward the table. Ella glanced over to where the sandwiches, soup, and crackers were set out. She shook her head and whispered, "I'm not hungry."

Mamm took her hand, insisting, and Ella gave in. What was the use?

"You'll be needing the strength," Mamm said, "even if it doesn't feel so now."

Ella took the round bowl her mom held out for her. She filled it with a little soup and several crackers. A sandwich was pushed into her other hand. They walked over to the benches and sat down. A few bites later, she still found it difficult to swallow. The rich soup felt like paste in her mouth, the sandwich dry. She was ready to stand and return the bowl to the table, eaten or not, when the long black *Englisha* hearse pulled into the yard.

Aden's body had arrived. She choked, placed the bowl on the table, the half-eaten sandwich beside it, and had no strength to even think of removing it. Several of the men in the room stood, picked up their hats, and went outside.

Through the window, Ella watched as the long wooden box was removed. With their black hats on their heads, the men gathered on either side of the coffin, bore the load, and stepped toward the front door. She stood, sobbing openly and hiding her eyes with her hands. Arms closed around her to help her move out of the way and over to the other side of the table while the procession slowly passed.

Ella closed her eyes, listening to the sounds in the house. How had she dared make such a fuss? She waited, her hands still on her face. They would just have to think what they wanted to. The sounds of bumping and scraping coming from the bedroom soon gave way to silence. The room where she stood also became quiet. The time had come to view Aden and acknowledge in their time-honored tradition what the hand of God had left.

Ella felt the hands of others helping her to sit. She opened her eyes. How much she wanted to rush out of the house but could not. Aden's parents stood beside the bedroom door, their arms around each other. She tried to breathe as they walked forward, heads bowed.

Their backs disappeared through the doorway. This was their son, and they would be together to see his departed face. The minutes passed as their muffled sobs rose and fell. No one would interfere or hasten the time they needed.

When they came out, their arms still around each other, their faces red from tears, Daniel made a motion with his hand toward Ella. As a sibling, he or one of the other children could have gone next. He was offering her a special place of honor. He knew and respected the deep love Aden and she had shared.

Ella rose, and her Mamm stood with her. This also was in order. It was *gut* that the mother should accompany her daughter to see the man who would have been her son-in-law. With Mamm's hand on her arm, the two approached the bedroom.

Through the open door, Ella saw the side of the wooden coffin, its plain wood sanded and varnished to a dull shine. She was about to see Aden, and yet, in reality, Aden was gone. What remained would only look like him. She dared her eyes to turn and see.

They had turned him so that his face looked away from the doorway and toward the window where the light streamed in. The wooden lid was ajar, laid back across a chair. She approached and sought his face, her breath a rough rasp in her throat.

The sunlight fell full across his face, illuminating his stubble of a beard and flushing his cheeks, just as she remembered him when he had been alive. She quietly gasped, reaching out with both hands to touch him, but Mamm pulled her back.

"He's gone, Ella," she whispered. "You mustn't touch him."

"I loved him, Mamm," she said, reaching again.

"Aden's in the hands of *Da Hah*, and you must be leaving him there. Yah, it is for the best."

"But I wanted him as my husband," she said, catching her breath. "Why must this be?"

"That is not for us to decide," her mom said, pulling Ella tight against herself. "Now we can only cry our tears."

Ella stood for a long time, the tender touch of her mamm on her arm. Long moments passed while those in the living room waited quietly. Time would never move again for her. This was the moment given to her to sorrow, to weep, and to know the pain…for after tomorrow, life must go on again.

After a time, Mamm gently tugged on her arm and tenderly pulled her away.

"Others will be needing to come," Mamm whispered, guiding her out of the room and back to the benches.

They waited in silence for the long hours of the afternoon while those in the room took their turns walking through the bedroom.

Eventually Ella whispered to her mom, "I'm okay if you and Daett want to go back home and help with the chores."

Mamm nodded and stood. She walked over to where Daett sat. Ella couldn't hear what they said, but soon her mother returned and shook her head. How blessed she was with such a mamm. Her parents had decided to stay with her even with the pressing duty of home and the farm.

When supper, which was brought by the neighbors, was served, Ella tried again to eat and managed to get some of the food down. After supper the official time of viewing started. Long lines of men and women formed outside and passed through the bedroom. Enough stayed to fill the benches inside, causing others to move on out to the yard.

Few words were spoken to Ella or to others from the family. The visitors shook their hands, embraced them, and extended comfort by the power of their presence and their willingness to be there. Dora, with Eli and Monroe, arrived just before dusk. They passed through the line, and Ella rose to join them.

She wanted to see Aden again when the sun was no longer on his face. Perhaps it would be different now. With Dora beside her, she didn't pause long, resolving to return later, to come back when there was enough time to be alone with him.

"It's such a sad thing," Dora said when they had taken their seats again. "I'm so sorry it has to be happening to you."

Ella nodded, squeezing Dora's arm. *It is* gut *to have a sister who cares.*

"It should be happening to me," Dora whispered. "I'm the real bad person. You and Aden were the *gut* people."

Ella shook her head. "It wasn't me. Aden was the *gut* one."

"I hope you'll be findin' someone as *gut* as he was," Dora whispered.

Ella shook her head. "There will never be another one. I loved him, Dora—really loved him."

"I know that," Dora said, nodding. They wrapped their arms around each other's shoulders.

Both of the mamms made their way over and sat beside them, one on each side. Neither woman said anything. They just sat in quiet support.

When the crowds thinned out an hour later, Ella leaned toward her mother and said, "Perhaps I should bring in my clothes from the buggy. I'm staying for the night."

"I expect so," Mamm said, nodding.

"I'm sorry 'bout the chores," Ella whispered. "I'll help after the funeral…something extra, perhaps. Yah?"

"You shouldn't even think about this," Lizzie said. "Dora and the boys…we can handle things. You don't have to worry."

It was *gut* for her mamm to say it, but the guilt and pain didn't go away. Slowly Ella got up. Eyes from all over the room turned to look at her as she went outside to get her night bag.

When Ella returned, Aden's mom met her at the front door and whispered, "Up the stairs. The spare bedroom is in the back."

Ella made her way slowly back through the benches, maneuvering around the gathered women and then upstairs. Likely she wouldn't spend the night up here, after all. Surely some visiting family would need the space, and she could just as easily sleep downstairs on the couch. Aden's body would be closer to her that way.

By eleven o'clock only the family—including Aden's older married siblings and their families—was left in the house, and the benches were moved back against the wall. Aden's daett gathered the family around for a Scripture reading before some of them would leave.

With a solemn air, he read from the last part of the first chapter of Job. "Then Job arose, and rent his mantle, and shaved his head, and fell down upon the ground, and worshipped, and said, 'Naked came I out of my mother's womb, and naked shall I return thither: the LORD gave, and the LORD hath taken away; blessed be the name of the LORD.' In all this, Job sinned not nor charged God foolishly."

In the silence that followed, Albert closed his Bible and wept with the great cries of a father who deeply loved his son.

Some of the married children left soon afterward. Others of them were led upstairs to spend the night. Ella gave up her room, insisting she would prefer the couch in the living room.

"You can sleep here. We might be up and down all night," Lydian said.

"That is perfectly all right," Ella said. "It really is. I want to be close to him."

Lydian nodded, wiping her eyes.

When the last person disappeared, Ella lay on the couch in the dress she had come in. Tomorrow morning she would change into her black dress for the funeral. Tired from grief, she soon dozed off.

With a start she awoke. The house was silent, and the moon had risen, hanging in the living room window in a small inverted slice. Slowly she sat up.

The time had come to see Aden again. With the desire to be close to him strong, Ella stood up on her unsteady legs. During the walk to the bedroom, fear clawed at her, but she pushed it aside. Lydian had left a kerosene lamp burning in the bedroom, its light turned low. This time there was no one to stop her when she saw his white face, his best shirt collar tight around his neck. Ella touched him, her hands on his. She kissed his cheek and wept softly until there were no tears left to cry.

"I'll be tellin' you goodbye now, here alone," she whispered. "Tomorrow there will be others. I loved you so much, Aden. I know that God must have you, whatever His reasons are, and so I find I can't hate Him. It would be as if I hated you."

She paused, her hands still holding his. "Goodbye, Aden. You were my dearest. I always loved you with all of my heart. Sleep your years in peace until I can join you again."

She turned and walked slowly back to the couch, drying her tears with her wet handkerchief. Then she lay quietly, watching the moon in the window until she fell asleep again.

Nine

Daniel awoke with the moonbeams from the east window on his face. What had awakened him? The moonbeams or the ache in his heart for his brother Aden? The events of last night and the day prior came back with great clarity. This all was such a shame and such a great loss, especially for Ella and Aden.

He hadn't cried much yet—only a few tears last night when Daett read the Scripture about Job. The words were very touching, especially the ones about still blessing the Lord whether He gave or took away. That seemed hard. How could one bless the Lord when a *gut* man like Aden had died so suddenly? Did the Holy Book always get things right? The preachers said so, but it sure didn't feel like it now.

He really must do something. That was much easier than speaking words. Aden had always been able to say things just right, but Daniel rarely could. Perhaps that was one of the reasons they had gotten along so well.

Why had Aden passed away? Daniel sat up in bed and struggled with the question. *Why would God just come down and take away my brother—a brother so close to marriage with Ella. The two were wonderful together. It seemed as if they were made for each other. Is God so wise that He can see what I cannot?*

It was not as if Daniel wanted to challenge God, but this tragedy seemed so very wrong. Sure, Aden carried some of the blame because he hadn't gone to the clinic when the pains started. Home remedies hadn't been enough this time.

The old people said one should crawl downstairs head first a couple of times to cure a stomach or side ache. It had always worked for him before, and Aden had seemed satisfied with the relief he received. He, at least, had rested well enough that one day to go back to work the next at the construction job near Randolph. They had driven down there together in the buggy instead of hiring an *Englisha* driver.

The weather had been good, Aden had looked okay, and they had worked hard all day. Aden hadn't eaten supper, though, and complained about having a fever. His mamm had checked his forehead.

"It's just the aftereffects of whatever you had," she said. "Perhaps if you sleep on it and get a good night's rest, you'll feel better in the morning."

Aden had his own room across the hall, and nothing unusual had happened that night. No groans or cries of agony as there should be from a man who would die the next day. It was strange. Maybe the preachers did know what they were talking about when they spoke of a God who chose to do what He wanted all without much warning.

Ella, the woman who was to have become like a sister, was downstairs, perhaps sleeping now. What could be done for her? Not much. She was obviously greatly distraught, more so than he was, perhaps. Aden had only been his brother. She was to be his wife. But maybe her pain would pass eventually. Maybe she could love again and marry. She was beautiful, that was for sure, even in her present agony.

Amish girls in similar situations married again unless they had some very good reason not to, and Ella obviously didn't. Her sorrow would be overcome with time. There had been young widows before in the community, and they all came to terms with their grief and married again.

Suddenly Daniel felt ashamed. *Where has such a thought come from anyway? It's terrible to think about Aden and Ella, Aden's body still lying downstairs. Another boy with Ella? No, the thought is best not considered. Yet it could happen. It is just a matter of time. No other boys have ever dated Ella that I know about. Aden had been the first and only one to ever take her home.*

He rolled over in bed. How much better it would be if Aden were still alive.

Since I can't help him with Ella, I'll have to figure out another way I can help. And then Daniel remembered that his brother's money needed to be dispersed in some fashion and that he was the other signature on the account in the bank at Randolph. The sum was considerable. By this time surely it was almost enough to build the house Aden wanted so badly to build for Ella.

Might this have been the reason Aden was hesitant to visit the clinic? Since Aden was over twenty-one—already twenty-four—and had no insurance, he would have had to pay the medical fees. If his reluctance to go the clinic was to save money, it was all really a big shame. What good was money without the life to go with it?

"I'm a ripe old age for an unmarried Amish man," Aden had said, "and I'm waiting for her, and she's worth it. Worth every day and minute it takes."

One morning at the job site, Aden had laughed about one of their preachers telling the story of Jacob from the Old Testament waiting seven years for Rachel. He then waited another seven when he was given Leah to marry first. Aden liked the point of the story—that others had walked this same road he was on and had found the prize to be worth the effort.

Daniel smiled as he remembered the look on Preacher Stutzman's face. He would snort in disgust if he knew of Aden's application of his sermon. Stutzman was just a young fellow, quite zealous about things, and certainly would have been repelled by the use of Scripture for such a mundane and carnal reason. In Preacher Stutzman's mind, all Scriptures were given by inspiration of God to support and defend the church *Ordnung.* Beyond that all uses of Scripture were less than godly.

Could Aden have been kept from a visit to the clinic by his desire to save money—the money he needed desperately to build the house for Ella and himself? Aden hadn't wanted to borrow money even though others in the community borrowed money under certain circumstances. Often farms were too large to be purchased totally with cash, or a person needed start-up money to begin a new business.

If Aden's obsession had affected his decision, Daniel decided he had better not mention the matter to anyone. He didn't know for sure, and, besides, what difference would it make now? Many of the Amish put off medical needs because of financial difficulties.

Daniel remembered, though, that Aden had based some other decisions on money. One had been the way they had conducted business. Aden and Daniel worked in the construction business, and often Aden contracted their work. According to the *Ordnung*, contracting was a great evil. It led many souls to the lust of money and from there to worse sins. A man would face temptations, the preachers said, beyond his ability to bear if he was allowed to state a price upfront and then perform the work afterward. He might be tempted to cut the quality of the work, work faster than the body was made to labor, and use materials that could fail later after the money had been collected and the check cashed. Only righteous work could be done when the labor was performed by the hour—at least according to the preachers and the *Ordnung*.

Aden had snorted through his nose at this idea, not in front of their daett but in private to Daniel. Aden also said he would take responsibility for breaking the *Ordnung* in this matter and would never allow Daniel's reputation to be compromised if they were ever caught. "It's all a bunch of baloney," he said. "A man is righteous because his heart is righteous. Out of the heart come the important things in life. That's in the Scriptures somewhere if Preacher Stutzman really cares to read it."

Aden had enough nerve to approach Bishop Mast one Sunday afternoon in Preacher Stutzman's hearing and start a conversation about contracting. The noon meal of peanut butter sandwiches, dill pickles, cheese, and coffee had just been eaten. Benches had been taken out to the lawn, and the men were relaxing in the shade, chewing on grass stems, and talking about whatever crossed their minds while the women folks cleaned up inside the house.

"It's not fair," Aden had said. "Why aren't the carpenters allowed to contract? All of you furniture makers set a price beforehand. The bakeries do it. The cabinet shops do too. Just about everyone else. Even milk has a set price."

Bishop Mast smiled. "S'pose that's just the way things are done, and they're not likely to change—at least while the church is my responsibility."

Stutzman, though, rose up in a glorious burst of righteous indignation and said, "I can't believe you bring this up today, Aden. I'm terribly disappointed to hear one of the young men of the church bringing up this question of contracting. This is all a great evil, and a greater one can hardly be imagined. It would be like a cancer in the soul of the church if contracting were allowed. The apostle James said, 'Ye ask amiss, that ye may consume it upon your lusts.'" He had quoted the verse in German, making the matter sound even more serious.

Stutzman continued to quote James, "Go to now, ye rich men, weep and howl for your miseries that shall come upon you. Your riches are corrupted, and your garments are moth eaten."

He then quoted the apostle Paul from Corinthians, "God hath chosen the foolish things of the world to confound the wise, and God hath chosen the weak things of the world to confound the things which are mighty."

Stutzman said the apostle also said, "My speech and my preaching was not with enticing words of man's wisdom, but in demonstration of the Spirit and of power."

Bishop Mast had cleared his throat loudly at that point and replied, "Yah, Stutzman, we know this is true. It's all well and good, but contracting won't be allowed in any case. It seems to me that's as good an answer as any. Besides, in all the other businesses Aden just mentioned, the customer can examine the product well before he makes the purchase. Is this not true? Yet it is not true for contracting. Besides that, contracting holds greater temptations because of the large sums of money involved."

That, of course, closed the matter but not in Aden's mind. He figured out a way he could contract, at least for a few years until he had enough money to pay for his house. He would simply do it, tell no one about it, and pay Daniel by the hour. No one need be the wiser for it.

If and when he built his house, he wouldn't need to lie about where the money came from. Everyone would just assume that it came from a loan. It would work out. Aden had smiled with great confidence. Ella deserved a new house, one that was paid off. "She's just that kind of girl," Aden had said.

So Aden had contracted the work. He paid Daniel and the rest of the crew their wages, and the rest of the money was now tucked away in the bank in Randolph. If he could, he would help his brother spend the money in the way it was supposed to be spent. Perhaps Aden had left some instructions somewhere.

Daniel, weary of his thoughts, got out of bed, stared out the window at the moon, but soon returned to bed. Hopefully he could sleep through the few remaining hours until morning and the dawn of a very sad day.

Ten

Ella woke up when the two neighbor ladies came to prepare breakfast for the family. The soft click of the front door brought her upright on the couch. Her head was pounding, her hands were shaking, and her stomach was ready for food—all of which seemed quite out of place. Her body shouldn't want to go on with life when her heart didn't.

"Good morning," the women greeted her.

"You must be Ella," the younger one said.

She nodded and stood a little shakily.

"The news about Aden was so sad," the younger one said, offering Ella a hug. "I'm Ida, and this is my mamm, Susan. We live just down the road a bit."

Susan gently shook Ella's hand. "I hope we didn't get the house up too early."

"No," Ella said, "I'm used to getting up at this time of the day, anyway."

"Then we'd best get busy," Susan said. "Food still has to be made, and I'm sure everyone is hungry. The body is the first to move on with life even if the heart no longer wants to live."

"Yah," Ella said, nodding, "it does seem so."

"Lost a child myself… It was years ago," Susan said. "He was just a small boy, my David, but I did sorrow for him. I imagine it would be worse if he had been full grown. I guess *Da Hah* always has mercy."

"It does hurt a lot," Ella said, unsure of how to reply. Then she added, "I think I'll just step outside for a little while."

"Yah, you do that, and we will get busy here," Ida said. "We'll have breakfast ready soon, and you can eat when you want."

Behind them the bedroom door opened, and Lydian stepped out, already dressed in her work clothes.

"Now, you get right back in there," Ida and Susan said at the same time. "We'll be takin' care of breakfast."

"But I should help," Lydian said.

"No, you rest," Ida said, her voice firm. "You get back in bed. We'll be callin' when breakfast's ready."

"You're much too kind," Lydian said, a catch in her voice.

"It's the least we can do," Susan said, stepping forward to give Lydian a hug. "I lost a son too. He just wasn't as old as yours."

"I remember that," Lydian said. "His name was David."

"Yah, David. Yet *Da Hah* has healed my wounds, as He will yours."

"This is true," Lydian agreed. "Even with this great a pain, *Da Hah* can be healin' it."

"Now, get a few more winks of sleep," Ida said. "We disturbed Ella enough already."

Ella smiled weakly. "I really want to go outside…to see the morning much more than I want to sleep."

"We will call you, then, when the food is ready," Susan said warmly.

Ella nodded and stepped outside as Lydian closed her bedroom door.

The predawn morning air held just enough chill to need a light coat. Ella paused. *Should I go back in? Nee, the cold feels good to my aching head.* It seemed to ease the throb.

Aden's parents' house lay in a hollow, surrounded by trees and the murmur of the little creek in the distance. Open farmland lay behind them, and the open swath ran up the hill a ways. From here none of the open sweeping vistas could be seen from Seager Hill.

To Ella this had always been Aden's place and still was today. Many times she had come here Sunday afternoons and for family occasions. To Ella this place had grown to seem much like her own home.

Few Amish ever moved from Cattaraugus County. It would have been the same for Aden and herself. Aden's parcel of land lay up on Chapman Road, and they would have brought their children down here and to Seager Hill, adding to both of their parents' list of grandchildren. She would have called this "Mommy and Dawdy's place" when speaking to her children. Now it was not to be.

It was yet another loss among the many she had experienced the last few days. The pain just seemed to continue like tearing away the layers of an onion one at a time. Surely the end would come soon; a time when the pain would be less.

Perhaps today after the funeral the lessening would start.

As if to add to her discomfort, the first rays of the morning sun broke over the ridge. Great streaks of light bathed the few low clouds, which hung on the horizon, in orange and red. Above them the half slice of moon still glowed, adding to the glory. Ella gasped at the beauty of it. Yet how could the dawning of Aden's funeral day bring such magnificence?

She wanted to shout into the stillness and tell God He must intervene. This was too cruel, too unfeeling to let alone. Her world had been stripped of beauty, love, and desire and left bruised, broken, and undone. What right did this day have to display such beauty?

The clouds ought to hang their heads in shame, weep in great thunderclouds of grief, and drive winds across the fields as a token of the destruction she felt. Aden, the man who should have lived, whose children she should have borne, was dead, and all the sky could do was show this beautiful sunrise. She lifted her face and wept at the injustice of it all and at a God who would decree it so.

As if in answer, the sky in front of her increased its brilliant display, adding green and yellow to the color scheme. Ella watched, her face still uplifted toward the heavens. The caw of crows came from the distance. She heard the faint beat of horse's hooves on the road, and a cow bellowed from the barn. Across the road a house door slammed.

After a few moments, Ella's thoughts turned to what would be expected of her after today. She would, of course, be expected to go on with her life. Tradition would be demanded of her. Amish girls didn't stay single, locked away from society, and lost in their own worlds. She was almost twenty-one. Soon she knew the questions would come. In a thousand ways, she would know she must show she was ready to live again. There would be little dropped hints and seemingly innocent questions raised, perhaps not immediately but soon enough.

"I wonder if the time's been long enough," they would say. "Has Ella healed from her sorrow yet?" Even her mamm and Dora would join in. "When are you going to move on, Ella? You know you mustn't waste your life. There's a man somewhere who needs you, who can love you, and whose children you can bear."

She held both hands out in front of her. No man's arms would ever be placed around her again. There would never be another to draw her into his embrace, to find her lips in love, or to feel the beat of her heart on his chest. In fact, she did not desire another man to love, and she would not allow herself to be drawn into another man's embrace. *I will stay true to Aden, to his memory, to his love, and to what we experienced together. Let people say what they want.* She raised her face to the sky. *Let the heavens dare to say nee.*

A soft whisper of a breeze flowed across her face, cooling her brow, soothing the throb of her headache. Ella took a deep breath and let it back out slowly. Her eyes were dry now, and her fingers were clenched in her hands. *Yah, I will live my days alone in my parents' house if necessary but not in another man's. Ella Yoder, you will not be untrue to Aden's memory, whatever the cost. My life will stretch out before me as long and lonely—*

"I saw you come out," the voice of a man called out behind her, the sound soft on the morning air.

Startled, she whirled around to find Daniel a few steps behind her, his eyes cast down.

"You surprised me," she said.

"I didn't mean to," he said, raising his gaze to hers. They were sad eyes, as hers must be. "He was a good brother, Aden was. Yah, as good a brother as one might ever have."

She nodded.

"I see the sun is putting on a right good display," he said.

She turned to look again at the colors in the sky. "It doesn't seem right," she said slowly. "This beauty…does it? Not today."

"Nee." He shook his head. "None of it makes much sense."

She glanced at this face, his eyes studying the bright colors above them.

"How can one understand such a loss as Aden?" he continued. "Aden was so alive, so full of life…only a few days ago. We worked on the job together the day before. It's so hard to believe that it could really have happened."

"Oh," she said, her interest rising, "you were with him?"

"Yah," Daniel said, nodding, "we worked hard all day. Aden, of course, always worked hard. With what we know now, that was the worst thing he could have done. It must have pumped the poisons all the way through his body, with his appendix ruptured like it was."

"Why didn't Aden visit the clinic? He could have seen a doctor."

"He could have," Daniel said, meeting her eyes. "He probably wanted to save money. I don't know. Aden didn't think it was serious enough, I guess, especially when the pain seemed to have gone away."

She nodded. Choosing to be frugal was a common trait in her people. Usually, though, the results weren't this tragic.

"By the evening I could tell he was tired," Daniel went on, "but I just thought he'd worked a little too hard too quickly. Mamm checked his temperature when we got home. She said he ran a fever and that he should eat supper and rest, which he did. I guess we all figured he'd be better by morning. I heard nothing from him all night. You would think I would have heard something, as sick as he was. I was just across the hall."

Ella nodded again.

"That's the kind of man he was. It took a lot to slow him down," Daniel said and then turned the topic to Ella. "I'm sorry for your sake, Ella. I know Aden loved you a whole lot. He told me so all the time. He thought you well worth the wait over all those years."

"I know. He told me that too."

"We all thought he'd just gotten the flu or something and that perhaps he needed antibiotics from the clinic at the worst. But we never thought of this." He shook his head. "Now my brother's gone, and I don't quite know what will be happening with the construction business. Aden pretty much ran the crew. I guess I can go on…if I can get the courage up. Maybe someone else will help."

"It's going away," Ella said, motioning toward the sky where the colors had faded. "Rain would be much more fitting on the day of his funeral."

"I know," he said with a long glance upward. "The moon woke me a while ago. I don't know exactly when. I spent some time thinking about Aden. I think he would like this morning, though, with the sky so full of colors."

Ella considered this. Perhaps the weather didn't suit her for the occasion, but Daniel was right. Aden would have loved the beauty of this morning.

Behind them the house door opened, and Ida called, "Breakfast is ready."

Eleven

Gathered around the table, they all bowed their heads in silent prayer and then ate breakfast with few words, the weight of the day's sorrow heavy on the house.

"You can go clean up and change your clothes in our bedroom," Lydian whispered to Ella as they finished their meal.

After she changed into her black dress, Ella glanced out the bedroom window to watch a few of the buggies pull in—mostly Aden's relatives. The clock on the dresser read a little after seven-thirty. In an hour the service would begin and the pain would start anew.

When Ella returned to the kitchen, the men had already started rearranging the benches in the living room. They soon had every corner full, quickly moving some into Lydian and Albert's bedroom. The body was brought out by the pallbearers and placed on short benches close to the front door.

Apparently an overflow crowd was expected because a wagon arrived bearing more benches. They were unloaded into the barn where, as customary, a separate service with separate preachers would be held.

By eight-thirty the house was full. The only sounds in the house were the soft cries of babies and the squeak of a bench when someone moved. Two men in charge of the seating made sure the immediate family sat in the proper front seats. Ella was placed with Lydian and Albert on the first bench. Behind them the brothers and sisters sat, followed by cousins and then more distant relatives.

Out of the corner of her eye, Ella saw her parents along with Dora and Clara ushered in and given seats in the house. Some of her aunts and uncles also made it inside, which was a nice gesture from the two ushers. They could have sent them out to the barn service, giving priority to the church people from Aden's district.

At a quarter of nine, one of the ushers gave a nod to Bishop Mast, who abruptly stood to his feet and began speaking. "We are gathered today to share in the sorrow of the Wengerd family. They have lost a son whom they loved, and their grief is great. We have been told by God to laugh with those who laugh and to mourn with those who mourn. Today we mourn with the Wengerd family.

"No man can comprehend the mind of *Da Hah* or understand why a tragedy like this happens. Even the wisest of mankind cannot begin to understand. Man's duty is to trust and to believe that *Da Hah* knows what is for the best. This hour may well be one of the darkest hours in the lives of the Wengerd family, and yet it could also be the one that bears the greatest fruit in eternal life."

Ella shifted on the hard bench, thinking that whatever the rewards were in eternity, she would still have preferred to have Aden here.

The bishop had a kind face, and his eyes were moist as he turned his look to the family seated in the front row.

"I have never lost a son," he said. "All of my children are still alive. Many might say that I can never understand what you feel, and that may be true. Yet in the Lord, we trust that we can share in your sorrow. Where we do not, *Da Hah* can fully understand. *Da Hah* lost His Son to death on a cruel cross, and He knows what those who have lost so much are feeling today.

"On Calvary the Son of God, the eternal One who had come to save the world, died. He was slain by evil men. That day of death was a terrible day, more terrible than anything men have ever experienced. The earth shook when Jesus died. His death was so awful that the sun hid its face in shame and darkness."

So she had been right this morning. *Death should be observed with awfulness and dark clouds. The rise of the sun had been an insult, after all. Does God, who cares so much about His own Son, not care about Albert and Lydian's son?* Ella glanced out the living room window at the open clear sky. *What does God think of my bold question being tossed into His face?* But what He thought really didn't matter. The pain was simply too much to ignore.

Why? Why doesn't God care about Aden? Certainly He can hear my question. He is God, after all. Will He strike me down for thinking such a thing? Will He take me as He has taken Aden? If so, at least then I'll be with Aden.

Ella's eyes were drawn to the wooden box between her and the bishop, who at that moment had stopped to pull a big blue handkerchief out of his trousers. He unfolded it with a shake and blew his nose with both hands.

"*Da Hah* will have mercy on all of us," he said and sat down.

The next speaker was a relative of Aden's, his older sister's husband. He stood with his hands clasped for a long time, his head bowed, before he started speaking.

"I know of many times," he said, "when Aden did many good things for others. In my mind the actions reflect on the kind of man Aden was. I myself was a recipient of Aden's kindness when he lent me money, a fairly large sum, a year ago when we had an emergency on our farm. Two of my best cows died in one week, and I needed funds to purchase replacements.

"I paid back the money I borrowed from Aden last week, and he didn't want interest on the money. He hadn't even once complained about the amount of time I took to repay. I almost thought Aden might have forgotten about the money if I hadn't brought the matter up.

"Then there was the time when Aden was still a young boy. I had been seeing Aden's sister, my wife now, and I forget exactly why, but Aden drove me home with his own horse and buggy. Once we set out, Aden's horse became lame from a stone it had picked up. We both got out, and Aden removed the stone from the hoof, but the horse still limped.

"Instead of riding the rest of the way back to his place where a new horse could be obtained, Aden insisted we walk the next two miles home. Aden led the horse by the bridle all the way. I told Aden this wasn't necessary and that the buggy wouldn't pull much harder with the two of us in it. But nothing could persuade Aden. The horse had to be favored. I know from experience that few young boys would have taken such kind actions."

He paused, produced his large handkerchief, and wiped his eyes before retaking his seat and allowing silence to settle over the room.

Ella had never heard either of these stories and had listened carefully, the desire to know more about Aden strong in her heart.

Preacher Stutzman slowly got to his feet. He let his eyes sweep the room for the longest time, his hands loosely at his side. Finally, he took a deep breath and then launched out with a great roar in his voice.

"Greatly beloved, I greet you in the name of the dear Lord, Jesus Christ. I fear that I do not have good tidings for you this morning but rather warnings from *Da Hah*. We must fear today…and fear it greatly. We must fear for our own souls and for our bodies. Dearly beloved, we must take great warning by this, the death of our brother. Much has been said about the good life he has lived, and this is all the truth as I can bear witness myself. Yah, it is so. Yet did not the Lord come for him in a sudden and dreadful way? We must then stand greatly warned. If this can happen to a good man, to one we can have good hope of a better life in eternity, can it not happen to any of us?

"Yah, it can." Stutzman answered his own question, his hands now held high, his pacing begun in front of the casket. "We must not be doubtful about this. This good man's death is a warning from *Da Hah* Himself. This is a wakeup call to all of us here that we repent of our sins and turn to *Da Hah* and to the church for help. There are those amongst us—perhaps some of our young people—who are playing with the temptations of the world. There are those who are living in secret lives of disobedience. There are those who are in transgression of the laws of *Da Hah* and of the voice of the church. To them this is, and let it forever be, a great and terrible warning of what is to come. Death can arrive in an instant. It could take us by the hand and usher us into eternity before we know what is happening. I ask you young people, have you been preparing yourselves? How about you older people, married and unmarried, have you been preparing?

"The Good Book says to seek your God while there is yet time. Seek your Creator in your youth because you know not when the evil day comes—as it has come for our brother. The day of calamity comes as it has come today."

Ella didn't even look at his face. *What in the world is he going to say about my earlier questions and how I threw angry words at God?* She held her hands tightly together. *Is he going to see me shaking? Does he already know what my thoughts are?* Only a few feet away, he strode past, his broad pants loose around his waist, his suspenders doubled up on the back on one button, his black dress shoes dull and unpolished. *Is God like him?* Ella wondered.

"The Word of God says," Preacher Stutzman said with his voice filling the room, "that the day of the Lord will come as a day of wrath, as a day of trouble and distress, as a day of waste and a day of desolation, as a day of darkness and gloominess, as a day of clouds and of much thick darkness."

His voice boomed out the German words, "*Zum Tag*...Today if ye will hear his voice, harden not your hearts."

For the next hour, Preacher Stutzman paced and lectured those assembled. Ella knew she heard Bishop Mast clear his throat once quite loudly. Perhaps he wanted to add to the tirade?

Then the sermon stopped as quickly as it began, and the long line of mourners began to file past the casket. Those from the service in the barn came in first, and then those in the house got to their feet. The family came last, and they stood together and walked forward. Ella stood with Albert and Lydian at the head of the wooden box. She forced herself to look, seeing him for one last time. But the man in the box no longer looked like Aden at all. Last night in the bedroom, with the kerosene lamp light on his face, she could imagine him as he used to be. Now he was stark, cold, and simply gone. She pulled her eyes away.

When Albert and Lydian moved on, she followed them. The crowd parted before them. Ella saw several people glance at her. Likely they wondered why she had no tears. They had been cried last night. She had said her goodbye then. Let them think what they wanted to. They had not lost their beloved.

They made their way to the yard, and then Ella rode to the cemetery with her own parents and three younger sisters. Somewhere behind them, Eli and Monroe had Clara and Dora with them. The long procession of buggies moved slowly toward the cemetery. At the state road, time was taken up in the crossing. Each buggy waited in turn until traffic was clear to cross over.

"Looks like quite a storm's building over the mountains," her daett said from the front seat.

Ella leaned out of the buggy door to see. It did look like a storm but why now? They almost had him buried. Why not earlier?

"It's just come up," her daett said. "I hope it gives us time for the burial before the rain starts."

When her dad parked, Ella got out of the buggy, helped her sisters down, and then took another look toward the western mountains. The storm did look ominous. Stiff winds off the lake drove the great stacks of black clouds.

Ella walked across the little graveyard, moving forward to stand beside Albert and Lydian by the graveside. The casket was set on small benches, and, again, the lines formed and viewed the body. Bishop Mast read a prayer, a great swelling of German words written to express the agony of the human heart that had suffered unspeakable grief yet still worships his God. Then slowly they lowered the coffin into the ground.

As Ella watched, they started throwing in the dirt. Gentle shovelfuls of dirt thudded against the wooden casket. The sound gradually became the soft sound of dirt thrown upon dirt. The mound grew slowly higher.

Ella glanced over her shoulder at the storm clouds, which were ready to break. The winds came first, great blasts that tore green leaves from the trees and drove them across the graveyard. Then the rain came, lashing them with an intense fury. Yet no one ran for shelter. They waited until the shovels ceased their work, little rivulets of water forming and running off of the now completed mound.

At last the mourners began slowly walking back to their buggies. Ella, however, stayed by the graveside, her head lifted toward heaven. The cold rain streaked down her face. *So this is what it feels like when God cares.*

Long moments later, Mamm pulled at her arm and whispered, "It's time to go."

Twelve

D aett pulled to a stop at the main highway and glanced each way before he crossed.

"Hard to see anything," he muttered. "S'pose the *Englisha* drive slower in this weather. You just never know, though."

"I'm glad it's raining," Ella said from the backseat. She so wanted to be on her way home, but instead they must go back one more time to the Wengerd's place.

"Why would you like the rain?" Ruth, who sat beside her older sister, asked. "I'm all wet from it."

"Because I think *Da Hah* must be sad," Ella said, "and I'm glad He's sad with us."

"I'm sad too," Ruth said. "Burying somebody in the ground is sad."

Ella pulled Ruth toward her in a tight hug. "We're all sad today."

"I'm sad too," five-year-old Ada spoke up. "Is Aden gone for always?"

Ella gave her a hug with her other arm and nodded.

"Do I have to die too?" Ada asked.

Mamm turned around in the front seat. The rain lashed against the vinyl sides of the buggy as Mamm said, "Everyone dies, Ada, sometime. It happens when *Da Hah* decides, but you'll not care then. You'll be in a much better place—up in heaven."

"Is that where Aden's gone to?" Ada asked.

"Yah," Mamm said, "and someday in heaven you'll see him again."

"I don't want to go there to see him," Ada said, finality in her voice. "Aden was a nice man. He should still be *here*."

Ella tightened her arm around her sister as she said, "You shouldn't think about this now. You need to grow up first."

"I don't want to grow up," Ada said, leaning against Ella. "Aden was all grown up. That's when he died."

"Most people stay big," Ruth said. "Look at Mamm and Daett. They're big, and they're not dead."

"You'll get big someday," Ella said. "You'll be marrying a boy then and have a whole house full of children."

"I just want to go to school," Ada said. "Is that big enough to be buried?"

Mamm and Ella traded smiles over Ada's sweet innocence. For Ella, the smile felt welcome. Was she healing already?

The buggy turned down Young's Road and then south to the Wengerd place. Ella and Mamm got out in the pouring rain and dashed inside with the younger girls while Daett went to tie the horse. Thankfully her dad didn't intend to unhitch, which meant he didn't plan to stay far into the afternoon after the noon meal. Oh, to be home now, safe in her own room, surrounded by all that was so familiar.

Inside, the line of people moved past the kitchen table. Soup, casserole, potato salad, and cake were being dished out. Ella and Mamm took their plates. Ruth and Ada held their own plates, but Mamm held on to one side of Martha's, the young girl's chubby fingers clutching the other side.

Behind each dish, a girl stood, measuring out the quantity of food by their own judgment or by whispered instructions.

"Just a little bit," Ella whispered to each girl. She really wanted nothing but knew she must try.

"I'm so sorry about Aden," several of the girls whispered their sympathies as they nodded at her instructions.

"Thanks," Ella whispered back. They were girls of her own age, all of them with boyfriends of their own. It was easy to read the compassion on their faces and feel their hearts reaching out to her.

They found a bench that was open or had been vacated for them in the crowded kitchen by someone who saw them coming. Martha got on her knees and used the bench as her table. They all ate slowly, surrounded by the mill of people.

Soon, with her plate empty, Ruth asked, "Can we go outside and play?"

Mamm shook her head. "It's still raining."

"We can run for the barn," Ruth persisted.

"Nee," Lizzie told her, "just be waiting inside."

Ruth let her disappointment show on her face and then moved across the room to where some of her cousins stood obviously commiserating over a similar answer to the same question. Soon, though, they were lost in animated conversation.

Across the room Ella saw her brothers and Clara get up and slowly work their way outside. Behind them her daett talked with Albert, his empty plate on his knees. Hopefully, he would be ready to leave soon.

Someone slid into the space on the bench beside her, and Ella turned to see Lydian. The older woman took Ella's arm and squeezed it gently.

"Ach, this has been such a sad day for you and for Albert and me," she said.

Ella nodded.

"We were all so looking forward to having you in the family," Lydian whispered. "You would have been a *gut* daughter to us, I know."

"I won't forget Aden—ever."

"No, of course you won't," Lydian said, "but your life must go on. Yah, you must not weep too long or too much."

Ella nodded and glanced away. Aden would always be the standard she held in front of her eyes. No other man would ever match him.

"Time goes on by, and the sorrows and troubles come and go," Lydian continued. "We all have our share of them in one way or the other. I'm just sorry yours had to come this early and so hard, at that."

Out of the corner of her eye, Ella saw her daett get up to leave. When Lydian said no more, Ella spoke. "Thanks for your kind words. I will do the best I can." She reached over to hug Lydian and said, "Daett is ready to go."

"Of course," Lydian said, releasing her hug. "We'll miss having you around."

"I'll miss you too," Ella said as she stood to follow Mamm.

It was true. She *would* miss them all—Aden's brothers and sisters and Lydian and Albert, who always seemed to be around in the background. In a way, this day was going to be the end of her participation in the Wengerd family.

As Ella and her mother moved toward the door, Mamm said, "I don't see Martha."

"I haven't seen her either," Ella said.

"Do you think she went outside after what I told her?" she asked. "Ella, see if Martha's in the bedroom."

Ella glanced outside. Already her dad had the horse untied. In the rain, the horse wouldn't want to wait long. Ella made her way as fast as she could through the crowded room. First she checked the bedroom where Aden's body had lain. With Martha not there, she moved on.

The main bedroom was also empty, and so Ella squeezed past two elderly ladies to open the door to the upstairs. She hurried up the steps and opened the first bedroom she came to. It was Aden's bedroom. Only on occasion had she been up here. Usually they spent their time downstairs or at her place. Now Aden's room seemed barren, forsaken. Ella could hear the voices of small children coming from somewhere close by.

She stood still, her hand on the doorknob. A pair of pants lay across the bed, a shirt was tossed beside pants, the covers on the bed remained unmade, and his Sunday shoes sat just outside the closet, the shoestrings tucked inside.

Aden always had his Sunday shoes on when she came up. Had he really tucked the strings in like that? How like Aden to be so neat and orderly. She crossed the room, bent down, and ran her fingers across their shiny surface. Aden always kept his shoes well blacked.

Ella picked them up in one hand and sat down, running her free fingers down the length of the pants lying on the bed. The air was full of Aden, yet he was gone. She let the memory of his face, the touch of his hand on hers, the presence he brought with him, and the man that had been Aden strike her full force. Would it always be like this—sudden and unexpected reminders of her loss?

Her fingers clutched his shoes and gripped his pant leg. *Let the pain come. Let it do its work. Then perhaps it will end sooner.* She breathed in and out, the sound heavy in the silence of the room.

Then she remembered that Daett and Mamm were waiting. She was supposed to find Martha. In great haste she replaced the shoes to the spot by the closet and smoothed out the bed where she had sat. Surely no one would notice, as rumpled as the covers were, but she did so just in case.

Outside in the hall, Ella followed the sound of the children's voices. Opening the next bedroom door, she found Martha surrounded by her cousins and other community girls.

"Come," she said. "Daett is waiting for us."

"I'm not done yet. We're playing."

"Daett's already outside. We have to go now."

"I don't want to. Mary is getting ready for a story."

"It can wait," Ella said, taking her sister's hand and leading her from the bedroom. At the bottom step, she opened the stair door and escorted Martha quietly through the crowd. It was a little thinner now but still took awhile to reach the front door.

"Where have you two been?" Mamm asked.

"I had to search upstairs," Ella whispered. "Then I found myself in Aden's room. I had to look. I just lost track of time. It was like he was just out for a while and would come back soon. His clothes, his shoes… they were there waiting."

Mamm understood that there was no answer she could make. "We have to go now. Daett's horse is hard to hold in this rain," she said gently.

They dashed across the yard with Ruth and Ada ahead of them.

Mamm took Martha's hand and helped her into the buggy. Ella entered last, after Martha was safely in the front. She carefully climbed up lest her foot slip on the slick step of the buggy. Already life was moving on, and she along with it.

Thirteen

"I'll help with choring," Ella said to Mamm when they arrived home. "I'll change and be ready in no time."

"It's been a hard enough day for you already," Mamm said. "We can manage. Dora can help with the milking, and Clara can work inside with me."

"No, I'm going to help," Ella insisted. "Everyone has told me that life has to go on, and so then let it go on."

"Yah," Mamm agreed with reluctance, "but it just doesn't have to be tonight."

Seeing Ella's face, Mamm relented. "Well, perhaps it's for the best. You always were wise for your age. Sitting around does no one any good. I'll still keep Clara inside, and you can work out in the barn. They do need you."

Behind them the stair door opened, and Dora came out in her chore clothes. "Any help in the barn tonight?" she asked.

"I'll be out as soon as I change," Ella said, moving toward the stair door.

"Are you sure?" Dora asked skeptically.

"Yes, I'm sure," Ella said. "Moping around won't be bringing Aden back. I'll see you out in the barn in a wee bit." And then she turned and opened the stair door, her footsteps landing softly on the steps and making the boards squeak in the usual places. The familiar sound was soothing, as if something in the world was still the way it ought to be.

Ella entered her room and sat on the bed. Her whole body felt exhausted. At the moment the bed looked mighty inviting, and the pillow appeared so soft. *Perhaps I will lie down for moment. Dora would understand if I fell asleep. But if I sleep now, I won't sleep later when it really matters. No, it would be better to work even though I'm exhausted. Then, for sure, I'll sleep better when the night hours come.*

She searched for her chore dress in the closet, and in the weak evening light, she finally found it and lifted it from the hanger. And then she froze. Her wedding dress. It still hung there, full of promise and mocking her.

She cried out, the sound filling the room, the chore dress sliding to the floor. *Get it away from me,* she thought even as her shaking hand reached out for the soft cloth of the bridal dress. She gently slipped it from the hanger. How beautiful it was, so lovely, so unworn, and now so dangerous. The dark blue material fairly shimmered. The color looked good on her. Aden had said so the day she wore another dark blue dress.

Ella turned the dress sideways and held it against her. Carefully she held her head away so the tears wouldn't fall on it. Aden would never see this dress. *When will this pain go away? Will it just go on and on?*

Gently she replaced the dress on the closet rod and gathered herself together. She heard the sound of footsteps coming up the stairs behind her, and then the door burst open. "Is there something wrong?" Mamm gasped, her hand on her heart. "I heard you cry out."

Ella pointed to the dress. "I forgot that I left it out last week. Did *Da Hah* plan this to torment me?"

"He never planned anything to torment you," Mamm said, wrapping her arms around her. "Come here. Shouldn't you just stay in tonight and rest perhaps?"

Ella shook her head. "No, I'll be okay now."

"If you're sure…" Mamm said, backing out of the room and shutting the door.

Quickly Ella picked up the chore dress from the floor, slipped it on, and hurried downstairs.

"I'm off," she called into the kitchen and hurried outside. The weather had partially cleared, the sun was low on the horizon, and the evening dusk already sat heavily in the sky. Ella walked across the yard with only a quick glance around. There was a light on in the barn, and the cows would already be in the stanchions.

She opened the barn door, finding Dora and both of her brothers already seated beside a cow. The steady sound of milk jets squirting into foamy buckets filled the low ceiling barn.

"Washed all the cows on this side," Dora said. She didn't look up but kept her back bent and her hands busy with the steady rhythm of milking.

"Thanks," Ella said.

"No problem, and you still don't have to be out here."

"I know, but I want to," Ella said, her voice catching. "I saw my wedding dress when I was changing. I wasn't ready for that." Ella got her milk bucket and stool and headed toward one of the stanchions.

"I wouldn't be either," Dora said. "I guess the world just gets dark all at once. It had to go and pour down rain at the graveyard."

"That was the most touching time of the day," Ella said, setting her stool down beside the cow.

Dora glanced up. "You thought the storm was touching? I thought *I* was the dark one."

"It made me feel like *Da Hah* cared about us. That's what the bishop said, didn't he?"

"I suppose you could take it that way," Dora grunted. "It's just that I got my shawl soaked the whole way through. We got to the buggy as soon as we could, but didn't you stay out for a while longer?"

"Yah, it felt so good," Ella said. "I think *Da Hah* remembered us. I was beginning to think He never would."

"If the sadness keeps on, I suppose we could get you some of those *Englisha* pills from the doctor at the clinic," Dora said, standing up to empty her pail into the milk can. "They say it helps keep the head turned on right."

"I don't need my head turned on right," Ella said. "I just need the hurt to stop."

"It won't stop for an awful long time. That's what the deacon's wife was telling Emma Troyer when her husband died last year. Emma's in her thirties and has six children." Dora sat down again, her stool scraping on the concrete floor.

"I'll not be taking any pills," Ella said. "You're too dark."

"The world is dark, Ella," Dora said without looking up, "really, really dark like it was today, and it's getting darker the older you get."

"You still have your boyfriend, Dora. Just be thankful for that."

"Yah, I suppose so," Dora said, her voice weary.

Ella got up, emptied her milk pail, and released several of the cows. She slapped their backs as they moved out to the barnyard. With Dora almost done, she waited before she allowed more cows in. Dora hurried with the cow she was milking and then set the milk bucket on the concrete while she stepped up to release the cow. Ella saw the accident before it happened. She opened her mouth to shout a warning, but it was too late.

The released cow backed up, straight for the bucket of milk. A belated yell from Dora only made matters worse. The cow jerked sideways and caught its leg on the bucket. The milk spilled out in a white flood, its contents rapidly spreading thin as it crept into the straw, debris, and cow dung on the concrete floor.

"A whole bucket!" Dora wailed. "What a waste, and it was all my fault. A perfectly horrible, dark, and dreary day this is. You naughty, naughty cow."

"It's just a cow, yah," Ella said. "Now get out," she told the animal, which had set its gaze on the running milk as if wondering why these humans went to so much trouble if they can't be more careful.

"Why do you girls spill the milk?" Monroe asked, stepping across the gutter. "Don't you know how to milk a cow by now?"

"You could have a little bit of sympathy," Dora said. "I just set the pail down to let the cow loose."

"Never, never do that," Monroe said. "Never, never just set the pail down."

"Quit bothering her," Eli said, speaking up for the first time. "We've all had a long day."

"Long day or not, it still needs sayin'," Monroe said, his voice firm.

"I heard you, and I already knew," Dora said. "Now don't be rubbin' it in."

Monroe looked like he wanted to say something but held his tongue when the next batch of cows swarmed around them, anxious to get at the feed in the stanchions.

Fourteen

They bowed their heads together for prayer. It was so *gut* to be home with everyone gathered together around the table again, just as it should be.

"Dora spilled milk all over the barn," Monroe said, waving his arms around like Preacher Stutzman. "Ella knows what she's doing, but Dora and Clara are another matter. Dora still sets buckets of milk on the floor. Daett taught Eli and me that lesson the first time we were in the barn."

At the head of the table, Noah cleared his throat, and silence fell.

"Yah, it's not *gut* to waste milk," Noah said slowly, "and we do need to be careful. But milk can be replaced. The cows will make more of it. What happened with Aden is the real sorrow. It's Aden who can never be replaced. We thank *Da Hah* we can have a good hope for him and that we will see him again in heaven if we are living lives of obedience ourselves. We can be comforted, but it's still hard, especially for Ella. I want all of you to do what you can for her in the comin' days. Give her time to grieve if she wants to. It's nothing to be ashamed of. She has had a great loss, as have all of us."

Ella resisted the temptation to wipe her eyes.

"She even helped chore tonight," Dora said with admiration.

"I noticed that," Noah said. "I suppose she knows what is best in this. Work can often bring healin' to the heart."

"If that's true, then I'll work all the time," Ella said, "both day and night."

"It might be best if you depended on *Da Hah* to help you," Noah said gently. "He's the one who made the heart, and He's the one who can fix the heart."

Ella nodded, thankful for her dad's words.

They ate quickly. When the rest were done, Ella still had food on her plate. She pushed it back, saying, "I can't finish. I'm sorry."

Mamm nodded. "We understand. Why don't you go upstairs now? The girls and I will clean up the kitchen."

"But I should be helping."

"No," Mamm said, her voice firm. "You need the rest, and a long night's sleep is for the best."

"There'll be no church tomorrow," Ella said, her mind racing ahead.

"Then you can sleep in, yah."

Ella managed a weak smile. "I'll be up with the sun."

Mamm shrugged. "Then you'd best get to bed."

Ella nodded, pushed back from the table, and made her way up to her room. Outside, darkness had fallen. She walked over and looked out the window. The night sky was thick with stars now that the clouds had cleared. Her eyes searched the grand sweep of brilliance, her heart throbbing with pain. The night was here, and how was she to face it?

She undressed and slipped into bed, the mattress soft beneath her. Waves of tiredness swept over her. She didn't know how anyone could find any pleasure in such a sorrowful world, and yet at that moment she did. Sleep felt wonderful.

Ella awoke with the sky still dark and the stars bright in the window. For a long moment, she lay still. *What time is it?* Her eyes searched the top of her dresser where the alarm clock should have been but found nothing. With an effort, she swung her feet to the floor, the surface cool to the touch, and sat up. *I must wake up.*

A step toward the dresser revealed where the alarm clock was hidden behind two books that had been left on the dresser top. The clock hands showed a little after two o'clock. Weary, she lay back down, but sleep wouldn't come. Her mind went slowly over the events of the last few days—over each moment and each hour—until an urge came to write it all down.

Ella pushed back the covers and got up again. She struck a match on the underside of the dresser drawer and quickly transferred the little flame to the kerosene wick. By the flickering light, she crept downstairs, taking each groan of the steps with bated breath. She found a tablet and pen in the living room desk and slowly made her way back upstairs.

With the lamp on the dresser, the tablet lying on her lap, and her eyes wide awake, she began.

Dear journal or whatever you are,

I haven't done this since my school years, but something terrible happened on Thursday. My beloved Aden died from a ruptured appendix, and my world has come to a screeching halt. I don't know how to describe the pain I feel because I've never felt it before. It is terrible. The pain is now a dull ache. I suppose that's because it's nighttime, and even it must sleep. Tomorrow it will be back again like a fire in my stomach that eats all that lives.

It has eaten my hopes, my dreams, my love, and my Aden—stolen it all away like the preachers say a thief in the night does. I still can't believe it happened, but I know it's true because I was there and saw Aden in the casket at his parents' house. After they brought us the news, I had wild thoughts that perhaps it wasn't true. Maybe it had been someone else who they mistook for Aden, but it wasn't.

It's now Sunday morning after two o'clock, and I know all too well it's true. The funeral was yesterday, and I was there. Now I can't sleep. My thoughts are about him, about his face, his laugh, his smile, his hands, and just about everything, I guess. I was in his room this afternoon, and it almost seemed he was there. The whole room smelled of him. The memories are still fresh, pretty raw, and very painful.

Today, because we don't have church and his district doesn't either, he had planned to bring me the plans for our new house—the one he was to build on his land on Chapman Road. I sit here now, and I can almost hear his buggy wheels in the driveway if I listen carefully enough.

I wonder what kind of house Aden planned to build. I only know the house from what he described. Aden said it was large and had plenty of room. He never said the house was for our children because he didn't need to. I already knew. I know I would have been a good mom, and he would have been a very good dad.

Right now the time in front of me stretches out like the Englisha's road—on and on as far as I can see, without much meaning or end to it. Now I wonder if it was wrong to love another person so much. I don't think I can ever love another man. I guess I'll be an old maid.

They say Da Hah knows what He's doing. I suppose that's true, even if I was angry with Him. Who wouldn't be mad after your heart is so painfully torn apart? The preachers say we are being made into something good for eternity, something about God needing pain to accomplish His work. They say all of God's people have always suffered and that we really don't suffer that much.

I'm ashamed to say that with how much I hurt inside, I doubt them.

Choring tonight helped with the pain—for a few moments at least. Dora even made me laugh. I have a wonderful family and plan to continue to help around the house as much as I can. When I'm twenty-one in May, I don't know what I'll do. I suppose Daett will let me stay home and go on helping around here in exchange for my room and board.

If only Aden were alive...

Ella closed the tablet. She couldn't finish the sentence. She placed the tablet in the top dresser drawer and crawled back into bed. Sleep came quickly, and she awoke with a start to the sound of footsteps in the hallway. Outside, the rain lashed the window pane. Apparently the Sunday weather would match her mood.

She got out of bed, lit the kerosene lamp again, and dressed. The tablet in the dresser caught her attention, but she pushed it toward the back. No secrets were written on it, and so what did it matter if someone saw the pages.

Downstairs, her mom had the stove fire started, the lid still off. Ella waited as Mamm watched the flames slowly lick the dry wood and seek a path upward. She added two pieces of wood and replaced the round lid with the fire handle.

"I'll be takin' care of breakfast," Ella said.

Her mother nodded, got her coat, and went outside. The wind blew the door shut behind her as Ella began to work quickly. The routine was familiar. Her mom had left no instructions, but that would be no problem. She would simply stick to their regular Sunday morning routine of oatmeal, bacon, eggs, and toast.

She still had the toast to do when the washroom door slammed, and water splashed in the basin.

"Nasty weather out there," Dora said as she peeked quickly into the kitchen. "Wind's all over the place."

"Fits my mood," Ella said.

"Mine too," Dora said, disappearing. Ella heard the splash of water outside the house. Dora, at least, had enough manners to empty her basin when she was done.

Mamm came in a few minutes later, followed by Noah, Eli, and Monroe. They washed quickly and with few words gathered at the table. Ella had just finished holding the last piece of bread over the open flames, toasting it to a light golden brown. She laid the plate of toast on the table and took a seat.

Noah bowed his head and prayed, "We thank You, o holy Father, for this day, for the gifts and grace You have given us, for the breath in our bodies, for the food on this table, and for Your holy Son, Jesus, who walked among us. Grant us now grace for this day and forgive us our sins as we forgive those who sin against us. Amen."

Ella watched them eat. Her body was hungry, yah, but her emotions were still unwilling. She carefully slid an egg onto her plate, hesitated, and then picked up two pieces of bacon. With a piece of toast in her hand, she buttered the surface and then slowly took a bite.

Fifteen

Daniel awoke troubled, his mind disturbed by the emptiness of his brother's room across the hall. Even in his sleep, he had sensed the grief like a heavy weight pressing down on his body. He threw the covers off with great energy as if to cast the burden away from him.

He dressed and went downstairs. His mother was up and busy preparing breakfast at the stove.

"Good morning," he said, his voice hoarse.

She nodded, her face red from tears.

It occurred to Daniel that, ironically, Aden would know what to say at a time like this.

With his coat in his hand, he went to his mom, who was bent over the kettle of oatmeal. Clumsily he pulled her tight against himself with one arm. It was the best he could muster.

"He won't be comin' back," she said, sobbing.

"I know," he said, his arm around her, his grip firm.

"He was just a *bobli* not that long ago."

"I have to be doin' the chores," he said, starting to pull away.

"I still have you, at least," she said, attempting a smile.

"You have the others too—all the rest of the family."

"Yah, I know. I want to be thankful for them—and you're all precious to me—but I still will miss Aden."

"We all will," Daniel said as he slipped his coat on and left.

The lantern glowed in the barn window. His dad must already be out, but Daniel lit another lantern anyway. Neither of them had a lot of chores, but they were in different parts of the barn. As he crossed the yard, he protected the gas lantern from the rain by holding it at his side and under his coat, causing the hiss to grow louder. A brisk wind blew steady as, overhead, the sunrise slowly cast its pale light on the grey clouds.

Yesterday morning Ella had been out here by herself to watch the sunrise. How like Aden she was in that way, much more attune to such things then he himself was. Aden had always been the one to wander the fields early in the morning and saw the first daffodils sprout along the fencerow in spring.

Aden and Ella did things on Sundays he and Arlene never did. They stopped and walked the creek on Stoddard Road, bringing home bouquets of flowers they had found along the water's edge for his mom. Two weeks ago Ella and Aden had brought back purple and yellow flowers. Daniel had no names for them, but Aden and Ella knew, as did his mom.

Aden even kept a book of poems upstairs from some *Englisha* author named Emily Dickinson. Occasionally Aden would read selections to Ella while they sat on the couch in the living room. Although Daniel never paid much attention to them, sometimes he would walk through the house and see them laughing about the lines. His parents were open minded about most things, especially with Aden, but this book from the *Englisha* author came close to pushing the line, especially with his dad. Such *Englisha* things were best left alone in his opinion. Daniel smiled at the sky. What would Ivan Stutzman have said if he had found out? Even Aden's charm couldn't have gotten him out of that one.

It was Aden who got to Stutzman, especially when Aden talked about the Amish people using tobacco products. Although Daniel didn't think Stutzman used tobacco, the preacher had said that all plants that God allowed to grow out of the ground were for the proper use of mankind and for his benefit. He even had a Scripture to prove his point and quoted it one Sunday afternoon when the men had gathered on the benches.

"For every creature of *Da Hah* is good, and nothing to be refused, if it be received with thanksgiving," Stutzman quoted. "We don't need any self-righteous, religious do-gooders, even if they be Amish people, speakin' out against what *Da Hah* has made. Tobacco was good enough for our forefathers, and it's good enough for me, even if I use none."

"I thought you might be lookin' for an *Ordnung* change," Bishop Mast had said, teasing.

Stutzman apparently didn't think the remark funny, even when everyone else laughed. "I see no reason to be changin'," he said. "One change is as bad as the next one."

Daniel opened the barn door and saw his dad at the back of the barn, his lantern hung on a nail in the ceiling. His own chores were at the other end of the barn where the horses were kept when they weren't outdoors. Aden's horse, as well as his own, needed to be looked after.

What would they do with the horse? Although they didn't need to make the decision this morning, it was just one of the many decisions—some of which were not yet apparent—that needed to be made in the days ahead. Great voids were left by his brother's death, voids that would have to be filled by someone.

Aden's horse would be easy to sell if that's what they decided to do. It was still fairly young, a fast buggy horse, and yet safe—sort of like Aden. He was steady, quick, sure, and dependable. Many of the young boys would jump at the chance to make the purchase.

If he could afford it, he wouldn't mind buying the horse himself. He certainly couldn't just take the animal—even if Aden was his brother—without payment to Aden's account at the bank in Randolph. That was the problem. He didn't have an abundance of money, and marriage to Arlene was somewhere in the future. They had dated for two years already, but he just hadn't gotten around to bringing the subject up. Their relationship was comfortable like that, no pressure. As far as he could see, Arlene belonged to him, and she seemed to feel the same.

His attention was distracted by an open stall door. *How did that happen?* The stall doors were always kept securely fastened, double-checked if necessary, yet the door was open and bent completely back on its hinges. A horse stood inside, and Daniel moved closer for a look.

The horse was Aden's. It stood on all four legs but in a sprawled out fashion as if to get its stomach into a lower position. When Daniel stepped closer, the horse stayed where it was but turned its head repeatedly toward its flank. Daniel stroked its neck, and the next time the head came forward, he grasped the halter. The horse curled its upper lip and pawed the ground.

His own horse, one stall down, stuck its head over the divider and neighed.

"What's the problem with you?" he asked.

Obviously the horse was in distress. With the stall door open behind him, his mind quickly jumped to a conclusion. *The horse must have gotten into the bag of oats stored on the barn floor just outside its stall.*

"Daett," he called toward the other end of the barn, "you'd best come over here."

Daniel stroked the horse's neck again and backed it to the rear of the stall.

"We'll take care of you, young fellow," he said softly.

"What's wrong?" his dad asked. He had come up to look through the stall slats. "Heard you talk worried back here."

"Horse got into the oats, I'm afraid," Daniel said, walking over to the bin where the oat bags were kept and glancing in. One bag was torn open roughly, and much of the contents were gone.

"How did the stall door get left open?" his dad asked. "I thought I checked them all last night."

"I was out here myself yesterday afternoon," Daniel said, searching his mind. "Who knows with so many people around all day."

"The horse is definitely foundering and bad too," Albert said. "You'd best be callin' the vet right away."

"On a Sunday mornin'?"

"Yah, we can't take any chances, not in the condition it's in."

"Should I walk it a bit first?"

"I'll be doin' that while you run and call. Stop in at the house and tell your mamm we'll be late for breakfast—maybe by a half an hour or so. That will give me time to take the horse around the barnyard for a few walks. We might have time to eat after that while we wait on the vet."

"Yah, I will call, then," Daniel said, leaving.

He stopped at the house to tell his mamm the news.

"It's bad, then?" she asked.

"I think so. I'm going for the vet now."

"Seems we've had enough tragedy," she said, moving the pan of eggs toward the back of the stove. "Maybe the horse'll get over it soon. I'll keep breakfast warm for you."

Daniel grabbed some coins out of the drawer where they kept change for such emergencies and walked down to the pay phone shack. It was a good half mile away and tucked off the road among some driveway trees. A sign on top read *Pay Phone* so it was accessible to anyone who wished to use it—not just the Amish. This was an important distinction to Preacher Stutzman. He believed no Amish person should solely own any portion of a phone, even if the phone was kept in a shack.

Daniel flipped through the pages and found the vet's number in Randolph. There was one in Little Valley, but he charged higher fees. On a Sunday morning like this, there would likely be an even greater difference.

A woman's sleepy voice answered, "Hello, veterinary services."

"I'm Daniel Wengerd," he said. "We have a horse that foundered. Would it be possible for the doctor to come out?"

"Certainly. I will let him know," the woman said. "Just leave me directions."

Daniel spoke slowly, mapping the roads from Randolph in his mind as he talked.

"I will have him come right away," the woman said, the faint scratch of a pencil on paper coming over the phone line.

"Thank you," he said and hung up. The last of the coins in his pocket had been used, but would help arrive in time? Aden's horse seemed to be in bad shape. How strange that a horse might die the day after its master was buried—an accident, perhaps, a curious coincidence and no more. Still, it was an awful thing.

Sixteen

D aniel jumped onto the front porch and opened the front door.
"The horse doesn't look good at all," Albert said from his seat
on the old rocker.

Daniel stopped in his tracks, "Can't we do anything more? I can't
let that horse die. Not after Aden's passing."

"You two, come in and eat your breakfast," Lydian said from the
kitchen doorway.

Albert nodded and got up. "I don't think there's much we can do.
That horse has eaten a lot of grain, and it looks to me as if it got to the
water trough earlier. Sometimes you can save 'em in time if you can
keep 'em away from water."

"Shouldn't we stay with the horse?" Daniel asked.

"I think walkin' it right now seems to make it worse," his dad said.
"This is a matter for the vet, I'm fearin'."

"There's nothing you can do," his mom said firmly this time. "No
sense in starvin' yourself about it either."

"I'm so sorry about this," Daniel said, sitting down heavily at the
kitchen table. "I should have been paying more attention last night.
What with all the people around, I should have known this could happen. Any one of the little boys could have left the latch open."

"They should all know better," his dad said, "but there are small ones who don't. Now let us pray for the food."

In silence they bowed their heads and then ate slowly. How empty and heavy the still house was without Aden.

"When do we decide what needs to be done with Aden's things?" Daniel finally asked. "My signature's on the checkbook. The bank told him it would be a good idea, and so he had me sign up for it."

"Is there a lot of money involved in this?" his dad asked.

"I haven't looked, but I think so."

"We shouldn't talk about this so soon," Lydian said quietly. "It's not right. It isn't. This was too sudden—all of this is. If there had been time, we could have talked with Aden. I don't think any of us should go into his things for a while. Just leave the money alone, wherever it is. I'll even be leavin' his room as it is for a few months, other than pick up his dirty clothes. We'll know when the time is right to do otherwise."

"Your mamm is wise," Albert said, nodding. "Aden never told me what he would want done. How could he have? He had no thoughts of dying. Daniel, did he ever tell you anything?"

Daniel shook his head.

"Then we'll have your mamm look through his desk upstairs—just to be sure. Sometimes people know and leave notes. Perhaps *Da Hah* lets them feel somethin' ahead of time. If that was the case, Aden wouldn't have wanted to say anything, but he could have left something, a little scribble perhaps. I once heard tell of a man who went grocery shoppin' the night before his heart attack. His wife said he never shopped for her before. Yet that evenin' he brought home bags of groceries and placed them all carefully in the cupboards before they went to bed. When she asked him what he was doin', he only smiled and said he wanted to take care of her."

"I will check today, then," Lydian said reluctantly, "but if I don't find anything, we will leave his things be for a while."

"I'll take the business on," Daniel said. "I think I can do that. Maybe if I hire someone else on, we can manage. There should be plenty of boys available who would be willing to help."

"You can do this without Aden's checkin' account?" his dad asked.

Daniel nodded.

"Then we can decide a fair price later, when the rest of the matter is decided. Your mamm will know when the proper time comes."

Outside a truck pulled into the driveway. Both Daniel and his father set their forks down and moved toward the door. They walked outside together to greet the vet who was just climbing out of his truck.

"Glad you could come out so soon," Albert said, "especially since it's a Sunday morning."

"Sounded serious," the vet said, glancing toward the barn. "The horse still up and walking?"

"Yah, at least it was thirty minutes ago."

"Got to some grain, then, you reckon?"

"From the looks of the bag, yes."

"Water? Did it have time and access?"

"All last night, I'm afraid. We didn't find the horse till this morning."

"Then let's take a look," the vet said, grabbing his bag. Albert led him to the barn.

Daniel swung the stall door open. Inside, Aden's horse pawed the ground.

"Not good. Not good at all," the vet said and brushed past in haste. He dropped his bag within reach, ran his hand down the horse's side, and then went to the head to open the eyelids. A soft groan was the only reaction he got from the horse.

"Afraid we have a rupture already," the vet said. "Sorry about that. Even if you'd called earlier, we might not have been able to save it. Tough when things like this happen. You want me to put it down? It might save it some suffering."

Watching the horse slowly lower itself to the ground, Albert said, "I don't rightly know. It's my son's horse."

"That one?" the vet asked, motioning with his head toward Daniel.

Albert shook his head.

"You had a funeral out this way yesterday, I heard. Wouldn't have been your son?"

"Yah," Albert said. "He passed away right suddenly."

"I'm sorry to hear that. I've never lost a child myself. It must be an awful thing."

"You have children?" Albert asked him.

"Three—two boys and a girl. Just young, all three of them."

"Only the Lord knows when their time will come," Albert said. "Doesn't make it any easier, but my son's in His hands now. We had good hope for him."

The vet crossed himself reverently and glanced skyward. "The Father, the Son, and the Holy Spirit. May he rest with God."

"The Lord's will be done," Albert said, his voice hesitant at this display of piety.

"I'm Catholic," the vet said. "Sorry again for your loss. I'm afraid it looks like his horse is gone too."

The vet knelt to lift the horse's eyelid again. He felt for a heartbeat with his hand and shook his head.

"It's only a horse this mornin'," Albert said. "My son was the great loss."

"You want me to call the truck…to pick it up?"

Albert glanced at Daniel and then nodded. "That would be best. We really have no way of disposing of the body."

"Will someone be around all day?"

"Yah, it's our Sunday off."

"That's what I thought since I didn't pass any buggies on the road coming in. I'll have the truck come out, then, and send the bill in the mail. Is that okay?"

Both Daniel and Albert nodded.

The vet picked his bag up, waved, and left.

"You can pay the bill out of Aden's checkin' account," Albert said when the vet's truck had pulled out of the driveway. "Aden would want it so because it was his horse."

"I will do that," Daniel agreed. "The checks are in his desk upstairs."

"I wouldn't know, but you can be handling it next week. People ought to be arriving here soon."

"I think I'll be going over to Arlene's place," Daniel said as they walked in to the house together.

"Give us a few hours here—with your mamm and me," his dad said with a weak smile, "and the rest of the family when they come. Arlene will still be there for you."

Daniel grinned and agreed with a nod. A few hours spent in the living room in conversation with his married siblings and their partners was not that unpleasant. Conversation with Arlene would have been better, but that would come later.

Not long after, David and his wife, Saloma, arrived, and Daniel went outside to help unhitch. They had all six children in the surrey, and Saloma was expecting another child any week now. Daniel helped unfasten the tugs as Saloma climbed down, hanging on with both hands. She managed well despite her size.

I wonder how it feels to have six children and another on the way? David seemed to enjoy them all, and Daniel imagined he would too. *Arlene will make a* gut *mamm, the way she carries a peaceful attitude around with her. Whatever children God sees fit to grace our home with, we will manage.*

The time would come soon when he would have to ask Arlene the question. She had been patient enough these last years, never acting like she was in a hurry, but with his twenty-first birthday coming in a few months, Arlene would start to wonder. She was only a few months younger than he was, and so there really was no reason their wedding date couldn't be set.

"What's the vet doing out this way on a Sunday morning?" David asked. "Surely he didn't have any business here, did he?"

"Afraid so," Daniel said, shaking his head. "We lost Aden's horse. It foundered last night and ruptured this morning. It ate all night, I suppose. Someone must have left the stall unlatched yesterday. I feel bad about it. I guess I should have paid more attention yesterday."

"Hard day, yesterday was," David said as he led his own horse forward. Daniel held the shafts up and then set them on the ground.

The sound of buggy wheels rattling behind them announced the arrival of Myron Raber and Daniel's sister, Susan. As they drove in the driveway, Daniel went to help unhitch, and David took his horse into the barn.

"Good mornin'," Daniel greeted them. "Nice day even with the rain comin'."

"Yah," Myron said as he got out of the buggy. He was a short-legged fellow with a beard that came down at least four buttons on his shirt. He was a nephew of Ivan Stutzman, a fact Daniel supposed couldn't be held against him.

The couple had three children now, all of them reflecting Susan's good looks. Of all Daniel's nieces and nephews, these were his favorites.

"Are you okay?" he asked Susan as she came out of the buggy. Her hand reached back up to help her youngest down the step.

"As good as I can be," she said with a catch in her voice, "when we just buried our brother yesterday."

"*Da Hah* gives grace to His people," Myron said, pronouncing the words in almost an exact imitation of Preacher Stutzman.

Daniel wondered why *Da Hah* made certain people and then thought, *Perhaps without them, there wouldn't be as great a need for grace.* "Yah, He does give grace," he said, smiling to Susan. "David and Saloma are here already."

"I thought that was their buggy," Susan said.

Daniel held the shafts for Myron as he pulled his horse forward. He followed Myron out to the barn because there were no signs of any other buggies at the moment. David was already over at the stall, and Myron joined him when he had his horse tied. Daniel felt obliged to fill Myron in on the details about Aden's horse.

"*Da Hah's villa,*" Myron said, all sober sounding. "No man can understand His ways."

That's true, but why do the words need to be said? Daniel thought. *It's sort of like salt rubbed in a wound.* Thankfully another buggy was arriving. Daniel turned to go, leaving Myron and David leaning against the stall rail as they talked.

Outside his oldest brother Levi and his wife, Sarah, had arrived. Levi was already out of the buggy, and Sarah was halfway to the house. Daniel helped unhitch—the little that was left to do—and after that, another buggy came. More arrived until the brothers and sisters had all arrived and gathered in the living room.

They were all married now except Daniel. With Aden gone Daniel felt it all the more—that comfortable, safe, cozy feeling of belonging; of fitting into a place you know is yours.

Seventeen

Daniel let his gaze rest on the family gathered in the living room. Moments earlier he had run upstairs to bring down more chairs for the children. Some of the older ones had become tired of the outdoors and sat around listening to the adults' conversation.

He placed himself toward the back, listening to the ebb and flow of the quiet chatter flow through the room. The younger children moved in and out. The girls played upstairs, and the boys carried on in the barn. When a storm threatened around eleven o'clock, Daniel checked for any open doors. In its brief downpour, all movement between the house and barn stopped until the rain moved on.

Daniel watched an occasional tear slide down the face of his sisters or mom. His own face reflected the other menfolks' stoic faces. Tears might come when he was alone but not in public. Daniel hadn't seen his dad cry much since the afternoon when the news of Aden's death arrived. He had wept then, but the storm seemed to have passed. He knew that in the years ahead, his father would bear his loss with a quiet dignity as befitting his age and the way of his people.

Eventually, conversation stopped as Lydian stepped from the kitchen and into the living room and announced, "Lunch is ready." Daniel glanced at the clock. It was already twelve o'clock. How quickly the time had passed.

"Let us pray first," Albert said. With all the voices hushed, he led out in prayer.

Afterward, the family adjourned to the kitchen where Lydian served food from the counter. Each family member took a plate, got in line, and filled it before being seated again. Children sat on the floor, their plates between their feet. Daniel went through last, ate, and then excused himself.

"Goin' to see someone special?" David teased.

Daniel just grinned and walked out the door. The rain had stopped, but a layer of fog drifted in piles along the river's edge. There was no way the truck could have come yet for Aden's horse, or he would have heard it. But Daniel knew his dad and brothers could handle the unpleasant chore without him.

As he went to get his own horse, he averted his eyes from the stall where Aden's horse had been. He tried to call his own horse from the back barn door, but when the horse didn't come, he decided to try to lure it in rather than traipse through the muddy barnyard in pursuit. The horse was good on the road but just didn't like to get started.

With a few oats spread in the bottom of a bucket, Daniel rattled the contents at the barn door and got immediate results. He heard the high whinny of delight and soon saw a horse that couldn't wait to get in the barn. He held the oats out of reach and led the horse inside. The horse then ate lustily while Daniel threw the harness on.

When he came out of the barn, two of his nephews held up the shafts of the buggy for him. They then held on to the bridle—one on each side—as he climbed in.

"Thanks," he said as they stepped back. He let out the lines, took off, and waved.

Once on the road, Daniel pulled the vinyl blanket out from under the seat and placed it across his lap. The air was chillier than he had thought. Winter was past already, but there was still an occasional nip in the air. Soon he would have to change to a wool blanket. If he didn't,

Arlene would surely suggest it in her calm manner. Not that she wasn't nice about such subjects, but he just wanted to use the vinyl blanket longer than she did. He supposed differences like that were what marriage was about—two people with different tastes learning from each other.

Did Aden and Ella ever have disagreements over winter and summer blankets? It's hard to imagine them having such a conversation. They probably quoted that Emily poet to each other under whatever blanket they used.

Why did God break up such a couple and leave Arlene and me, just an average couple, alone? It was a deep question, and Daniel squirmed on the buggy seat. It might be best to leave that one alone.

"Dangerous, such thoughts are," Preacher Stutzman would say. "And so is the man who thinks he can understand the mind of God. He is foolish and very unwise."

Daniel turned left at the next road and glanced at the river as he went by. Fog still hung in the valley, little curls of cloud swimming by his buggy wheels. It was a strange Sunday in ways he couldn't put his finger on.

A mile later he pulled into Arlene's parents' place on John Darling Road. He laughed. It was good to find some source of amusement today. The name had that effect on him. On the first night he had brought Arlene home, he had wondered whether he qualified as Arlene's John Darling but hadn't dared ask her. That was a question Aden would have asked Ella with a mischievous chuckle in his voice. It was a question that Ella would have answered with a smile. The two couples were just different, and that was simply the way it was.

He tied up by the barn because no one seemed to be around. The horse could wait here as well as be tied up inside the barn. There was a singing tonight in the neighboring district, and even with Aden's death this week, he wanted to attend. A good youth song service might cheer up his spirits.

As he finished securing the buggy, he heard the front door burst open behind him. Daniel turned, half expecting to see Arlene rush down the walks toward him. Not that she usually made such sudden appearances, but this had been a strange Sunday.

Instead, Arlene's two younger brothers approached at a run. Norman, the oldest, was in the lead, and the younger one, Mervin, was only a few steps behind.

"Whoa," Daniel said with a laugh as their youthful rush came to a halt in front of him, "what's the big hurry?"

"We saw somethin'!" Norman said with great soberness. "*Three* of them. We saw them all by ourselves."

"Yah," Mervin said, and Norman nodded vigorously.

"And what was that?" Daniel asked, thinking they had likely seen some boy thing, like a bull frog or praying mantis.

"Angels!" Norman said. "We saw three of them in the sky, and then one flew away."

"One went zoom!" Mervin said, making a quick gesture with his hand toward the sky.

"My, my!" Daniel said, smiling. "That must have been something. Where were these—you said angels?"

"Up in the sky. Up in front of the great big black clouds, the ones that brung all the rain," Norman said. "Mervin and I—we seen them."

"Well, shall we go inside and see if anyone else saw these angels?"

"They didn't," Norman said. "Just Mervin and me."

Daniel started up the walk, expecting the boys to follow him. When they didn't, he looked behind him.

"We're going to play in the barn," Mervin said, already following Norman in that direction.

"Okay," Daniel said, watching as the boys rushed through the barn door. It was a strange Sunday, a very strange one, indeed.

Arlene met him at the door, holding it open with her hand, a smile on her face. *She is such a sweet girl, so tender and kind. Now, if I could just find the words to express my feelings. Aden wouldn't have had any problems doing that.*

"How's the day been?" she asked as they moved into the living room.

"We thought of comin' over but figured the house was full with family. Aden's death was such a terrible shock to all of us."

He nodded. "Daett took it pretty hard, and Mamm did too, of course. Poor Ella, she took it hardest of all, I think."

"I imagine so. And you? Aden and you were close, yah? Are you okay?"

"Still hurts some," he said, "deep down inside of me."

She reached for his arm and squeezed it. "I would think it would. I don't have an older brother, but it must be awful hard. At least you have good hope for Aden. He wasn't wild or anything like that."

"Nah," he said, smiling crookedly, "I suppose even Stutzman would think there was good hope."

"Preacher Stutzman?"

"Yah," he answered with a laugh.

"I wouldn't worry about what he thinks," she said. "Half the church has no hope according to him."

"You think he has hope for himself?" Daniel asked, the thought just presenting itself.

"One would think so. I would certainly imagine so with the way he talks and all."

The front door opened suddenly, and Norman burst in with Mervin close behind.

"Daniel believes what we've seen in the sky," he said to his sister, great joy in his voice.

"I thought you were going to play in the barn," Daniel said.

"We had to come and tell Arlene. Nobody else believes us," Mervin said.

"So why did you two tell Daniel, then?" Arlene asked, tousling the younger one's hair. "Those were just clouds in the sky, moving along with the storm."

"I saw real angels, and Mervin saw them too," Norman said, his voice firm. "They were really angels, flying across the sky."

"Maybe they were," Daniel said, tilting his head. This strange Sunday made about anything seem possible.

"See?" Norman said, pouncing on the words. "He believes us. I knew someone would."

"Then thank him and go play," Arlene said not unkindly, but her voice was skeptical.

"Yah, he believes us," Norman said as he turned and went back out through the door and headed in the direction of the barn, Mervin in tow.

"We've been hearin' about those angels since before lunch," Arlene said when they were gone. "I hope they don't tell it around school. Norman's liable to, though, if I know him."

"They're boys," Daniel said. "I think people will understand that they think they saw something that looked like angels."

"I suppose so," she said. "You want to stay in the living room? Mamm and Daett are taking naps."

He nodded. Aden would have had something clever to say at just this moment. Something nice, no doubt, but he couldn't think of anything, and so he just followed her and took a seat on the couch.

There were steps from the upstairs, and Daniel turned when the door opened.

"Greetings," he said as Arlene's married sister, Naomi, appeared with her baby in her arms.

"Expected it was you," she said, taking a seat on the other couch and setting the baby on the floor on his stomach. He promptly began to crawl toward the kitchen.

"Is Duane around?" he asked.

"He was here for lunch, but he takes his Sunday nap better at home," Naomi said. "He'll be back later."

Arlene gasped as a chair clattered over in the kitchen, followed by the cries of the baby. Naomi jumped up and rushed out, lifting the baby up to examine him carefully.

"Is he hurt?" Arlene asked.

"Nah," Naomi said, righting the chair. "He's just started that lately, pullin' on things till they tip over. I just didn't think he'd try it out on chairs yet."

"Rowdy already," Arlene said, laughing.

"He's just being a Hostetler," Naomi said, her voice indignant. "I'm hoping he will start taking a little bit after our side of the family—just a little, little bit. You know we are the *nice* side."

"So what do you think of the boys' story about these angels?" Daniel asked Naomi.

"Oh, I guess there could be somethin' to it," she said. "Norman seems so sure of himself."

"What do you mean, 'somethin' to it'?" Arlene asked, her skepticism obvious.

"If they really saw angels," Naomi shrugged, "it could be a sign of things to come."

"Yah, you've always been into the old wives' tales, Naomi," Arlene scoffed.

"There's somethin' to such tales," Naomi said. "I've always had that feelin' about them."

"So what would this mean?" Daniel asked. "A sign of what?"

Naomi had no hesitation in her voice. "Three angels probably means three deaths. These things often come in threes anyway."

"I wouldn't be placin' much stock in that foolishness," Arlene said.

Daniel let the matter drop, and the conversation turned to other subjects as the afternoon passed quickly. He left the house with Arlene at five-thirty. She snuggled up close to him in the buggy, pulling the vinyl buggy blanket tight up to her chin.

"We'll be needin' the summer blanket soon," she said.

"I know," he said and laughed, remembering how he had somehow known she'd be asking for the wool blanket soon.

As they pulled in the driveway, the youth were still milling around the yard. Obviously they had arrived at the singing in plenty of time for supper. Daniel dropped Arlene off at the end of the sidewalks and headed for the barn.

Two boys came over to help him unhitch. Apparently rumors had already started. "Daniel, do you think Aden's death is a start of the string of three things?" the oldest asked him. There was fear in the air already.

"I don't know," he said, "but it might be best not to speak of such things."

They held the shafts for him as he led the horse forward. He found a good place to tie the horse not far from the sliding doors.

When he entered the house, Daniel caught sight of Arlene across the room deep in conversation. Hopefully she wasn't talking about Norman's angels. There was no sense in adding fuel to this fire.

Eighteen

Clara slid into her school desk on Monday morning, the echoes of the bell still in her ears. Teacher Katie walked briskly to the front of the classroom and called the first-grade English class forward. The little guys jumped into the aisle and hurried forward. Two of them almost ran, but Katie gave the offenders a stern "no-running" look, and they slowed to a walk.

"Are your assignments done?" Katie asked over the sound of tablets opening. Heads nodded vigorously as they passed their papers forward.

Clara watched the first graders a few more minutes and then turned back to her own classwork. Seated in front of her, Amanda had her English book open and her tablet set beside it. Amanda diligently wrote the words of a story to fulfill the class assignment.

Clara looked down at her own tablet. The picture of the house she had drawn was in it. Would Ella still want the drawing now that there would surely be no wedding quilt? She hadn't dared ask yet, but because Ella had wanted the drawing, she kept it.

Ella had refused to go along to the singing on Sunday night even though both of her brothers and Dora went. Dora had even made a special effort to persuade Ella but to no avail.

This morning it had been Dora's turn to prepare breakfast, and Clara had helped. Their conversation hadn't gone well, though.

"Some of the young folks think this might not be the end of things," Dora had whispered to her in the flickering light of the kerosene lamps. "Aden's death could be the start of more to come. Some think it could be the dreaded series of three. I sure hope they're wrong, but my own feelings say it might be so. I can see that these kinds of things never stop with just one. So who will it be next? That's the question. It could be someone young or old. Clara, it could be anyone *Da Hah* comes calling for."

Dora's eyes had looked large, dark, and gloomy in the dim light of the kitchen, as if she thought Clara might even be next in line to have dirt shoveled on her.

When they were all seated at the table, her dad led out in prayer. His voice was deep and full of comfort, and she listened to the words, feeling a little better. Still, she had wanted to ask her mom if she thought Dora's idea of more deaths was true, but it was too hard to get up the courage.

Usually, for such hard questions, she'd ask Ella but not this time. *I miss the Ella from a few days ago. The happy Ella—the Ella who was so glad to be alive—surely wouldn't think three people needed to die because* Da Hah *wanted to take them.*

Clara jerked herself out of her thoughts before Katie scolded her for staring into space. A quick emotion urged her to pull the drawing out of her tablet, quietly crumple the paper in her hand, and at recess drop the offensive paper in the wastebasket. She shifted on the seat, hesitating. *The drawing of the house, including the red barn and farm animals, is so beautiful and peaceful.* Slowly she reached for the paper, pulled it out, and held it in front of her. She ran her eyes over the drawing again. *It is lovely. The picture is as well drawn as I remembered. So this is evil? Katie apparently thinks so or at least she thinks it is wrong in some way. Preacher Stutzman is sure to agree with her.* His voice had thundered at the funeral, and she now drew her breath in sharply at the memory.

Do I dare have an opinion of my own about this drawing? The question seemed to pull her to the edge of a mighty cliff above a vast canyon with no way to see to the other side. Something deep in her mind warned of danger and calamity if she tried to cross. Yet the other side called her.

Clara looked at the picture again and then around the schoolhouse. *No one seems to be paying any attention. No one will know if I did or did not destroy the drawing. If I do not destroy it, am I, Clara Yoder, committing a great sin?* From what she could see, the answer was yes. With a deep breath, Clara took the leap because there seemed no other right choice. *I will not destroy this drawing. I like it, and if that is evil, then it will just have to be.* Her breath came fast as she waited, wondering at the sinfulness of her decision. *Is the page going to disappear in front of my eyes, taken away by a God who would save me from myself?* Anything seemed possible, yet the page stayed where it was, and soon her hands ceased to tremble.

A little rush of joy rose in her heart, but Clara stopped it. *Why should I be happy for my disobedience? At the moment it's enough that the drawing is mine to keep. Tonight I will take the drawing home again and see if Mamm thinks it should be used on the quilt. If she objects or thinks Ella doesn't want it now that such sorrow has come, then the paper will take its place in my dresser for safekeeping.*

That decided, her thoughts returned to the present assignment. The class had an assignment to write a short composition about frogs or any other small pond dweller the pupils wished to write a story about. Since Friday, the encyclopedia volume on frogs had not been available from the library bookshelf. She had seen Paul and then Ezra use the book, and now Amanda had the book beside her on her seat. Apparently quite a few of the eighth graders planned to use frogs as their composition subject.

She would simply choose another subject. The paper needed to be done before noon, which left her just enough time.

All at once it finally occurred to her what she should do. *I'll take special care to not write well. Then Katie won't think I've made a display of my natural talents. That solves things for the present assignment and perhaps for the future. If another drawing comes up, I'll do the same or take the good one home and do a lesser one for schoolwork.* To Clara, this seemed a sensible decision.

With a glance around, she saw the coast was clear to retrieve an encyclopedia from the library bookshelf. No one else was on the floor. Katie's rule said that students didn't have to ask permission to use the library during school hours, but they could only be on the floor one at a time.

Ready to stand, she caught Paul watching her from his seat behind her. She stopped, frozen for a moment. He had been watching her for some time already. Likely he even saw her look at her picture and put it back into the tablet. *Does he know what went through my mind? Is he going to tell on me?*

Clara searched his eyes, and he slowly smiled. The warmth was really *gut* to feel. His eyes spoke approval of her, of her person, even beyond her actions. She flushed a deep red.

She glanced away and stood to her feet. Katie had just dismissed a class, which she hadn't noticed in the confusion of her emotions. The pupils moved down the aisle on the other side of her, but the rule would still be violated if she made her way to the library now. Clara caught herself in time and waited by her desk until everyone was seated.

Katie looked at Clara and nodded her thanks. It felt good to have Katie's approval. *Perhaps I'm not an evil person after all, even if I like what is forbidden.*

With the last of the class settled in their seats, she continued to wait. Katie would want to call the next class, and with her on the floor, this would complicate the situation. Again her judgment was correct. Katie smiled and nodded as she called for the third-grade English class. They weren't quite as quick on their feet, but the class got up and moved forward.

Across the aisle, she caught sight of Ezra, who was seated in the seventh-grade row. The intensity of his eyes drew her. They were sad, solemn, and filled with longing as if he wanted something badly but was certain he would never obtain his goal. Clara looked away quickly. *What could Ezra possibly want so much?*

He had trouble with grades. *Perhaps he wants better grades like Paul and I earn. Maybe he saw my drawing and wants to draw, or perhaps his family is having money problems. They do seem to be quite poor.*

Clara glanced at him as she moved into the aisle, but he had his gaze on the top of his desk. Up in front, Katie gave instructions to the third-grade class. Ezra suddenly looked up at Clara, and she read the answer to her question in his eyes. The floor grew fuzzy in front of her, and she reached out to grab a desk to steady herself. "Sorry," she whispered to the girl seated in it and then moved on.

Paul admired her, but Ezra's eyes reflected need—stark soul need. Clara moved down the aisle and stopped in front of the row of library books. They swam unsteadily before her eyes. *Surely, I don't need to be afraid of Ezra. I've known him for years! He is kind to a fault, quiet, and never draws much attention to himself.*

Her mind searched for answers, as her eyes searched for the *P* encyclopedia. She would simply look up *pond* quickly and see what creatures inhabited its waters. In normal conditions, she could come up with some choice on her own right quickly, but now was not normal. Her fingers flipped through the pages and found the right one. A picture of a great blue heron stood right there, its legs stuck deep in the pond water. That was her answer—plain, easy, and simple. She replaced the book, pulled out the *H* encyclopedia, and took it with her.

Passing Ezra, he met her eyes again.

How strange the world is. It might be best to stay completely away from all boys. She walked back to her desk, sat down, and with a focus on her assignment, she began to work.

Nineteen

Clara walked slowly up the long hill from the schoolhouse, her lunch pail swinging at her side. The beat of horse's hooves on the road made her turn around and step toward the ditch to let the buggy pass. She waved, recognizing Karen Byler, who lived at the bottom of the hill, and her oldest daughter, Betty.

When they had passed, Clara stepped back out of the ditch. *Where did Karen and Betty go?* Their house was within sight on the other side of the hill, clear at the bottom of the valley, but the church district line passed between them. *Perhaps they went to visit relatives for the day.*

She skipped a few steps. The day had been a *gut* one at school, especially the English composition assignment. Katie had given her paper a ninety-five and another smile to go with it. Amanda had also gotten a ninety-five, as did Paul. Clara felt as though she accomplished what she set out to do by not writing as well as she knew she could.

All she'd had to do was stay with the facts from the encyclopedia, place quotation marks around the direct copy, and add a few of her own thoughts. No embellishments or ventures into story form, and Katie had liked the paper.

Still, how easily she could have made so much more out of the assignment. Clara slowed down, looking over the valley. *With a little more effort,*

I could have written a much better paper. I can easily see a great blue heron flying across the pond in search of its next meal. He is hungry, and his name is Moses. With his long legs sticking out behind him like the rod the preachers said Moses always carried around, he flaps along.

A night of hunger has Moses's stomach in knots. In the last pond, all the fish fled and hid under the logs. Still Moses is very hungry. The desperation increases at the next pond and still no fish. Moses is ready to do almost anything to find food, even fly off in search of a new pond if he has to. Clara envisioned it all. *Moses lands on the new pond and meets Henry, the bullfrog. Henry feels sorry for Moses and helps him find fish.*

It would have made a great story if Katie had let me write it and even draw pictures to illustrate it. But, of course, that's not to be.

In sight of the house, Clara quickened her step. Her imaginary story had given her courage to face what she needed to do. Because she had decided not to crumple and throw her drawing of the house in the wastebasket, she wanted—even more than before—the drawing used in some way.

She entered the front door and found her mom seated on the couch, a mending basket at her feet and the finished clothes stacked beside her. Neither Ella nor Dora were around.

"Did you have a good day at school?" her mom asked.

"Got a ninety-five on English," she said, "and most of the rest of the day was *gut.*"

"So like our life. Yah, part *gut,* part bad." Her mom picked up a shirt and examined the tear at the shoulder.

Clara slowly pulled the drawing from her tablet. "Can you look at this?"

"What?" her mom asked, her eyes meeting Clara's.

"It's a drawing from school I did."

Mamm reached for it, looked it over carefully, and then set the drawing on the couch. "You do draw well."

Clara cringed, but when nothing else came, she said, "Ella said it would make a good centerpiece for her wedding quilt. That was last week. You know…before—"

Her mom nodded.

"I haven't asked her since then whether she still wants to use it. Do you think we could…when you finish the quilt, perhaps?"

Her mom raised her eyebrows, "This may not be the best time to be talking about the quilt. Not yet."

"But it still has to be finished and go somewhere—even if not for Ella."

"I thought we might just roll it up and put it in the attic as it is."

"Unfinished? But it has to be finished."

"Sometimes *Da Hah* has other plans, Clara. Ella's life with Aden was ended unfinished. That happens sometimes. Even with wedding quilts."

Her face fallen, Clara stood motionless and then stepped forward to pick up her drawing.

"You're welcome to ask Ella yourself," Mamm said with sympathy, "but I don't know what she would say."

Clara thought for a moment. "Would that be okay, then?"

Mamm shrugged, "It might do her good. She does need something to do. Right now she just stays in her room when we don't have work to do. She's up there now."

Clara nodded, made her way upstairs, and tapped on Ella's door. A muffled voice answered, "Come on in."

The dark blue drape in the window was drawn even though it was four o'clock in the afternoon. Clara quietly stepped inside and shut the door. It was obvious that Ella was still not over Aden's passing. She sat on the bed, her head held aloft as if the weight was too much to bear.

"I'd like to ask you something," Clara whispered, "if it's all right."

"It's all right. Sit down here," Ella said, motioning toward the bed. "I'm still…not quite myself, as you can see. Don't let it bother you. We have to do chores before too long, and I'll get straightened up by then. I think it's your turn outside tonight, yah?"

Clara nodded and then pulled herself up on the bed. The mattress bent even further under her weight.

"What is it you want to ask me?" Ella asked, pulling Clara close to her. "You know it's nice to have a little sister like you."

"Well," Clara began, smiling weakly. Carefully she unfolded the drawing. "This is the picture of the house. The one we talked about last week, remember? Well, I was wondering if it would be okay with you if Mamm finishes your quilt…and uses my drawing just like we planned."

Ella took the drawing and studied it intently, silent for a long moment.

Clara began wondering if perhaps Ella had forgotten the question. *Should I ask it again?*

"You'd like that, wouldn't you?" Ella suddenly asked.

Clara nodded.

"Then why don't we draw it in? It would still look beautiful."

"Really? You would do that?"

"Let's go down and get the quilt before chores and start!" Ella replied.

"Okay," Clara said with relief. *This is wonderful! It might mean I'm not as evil as I had imagined. If the drawing takes its place on the quilt, the wrong would surely be cleaned out of it and also out of me.*

"Then let's be goin'," Ella said, standing up. Clara clutched the drawing as they walked into the hall.

"What are you two up to?" Dora asked when they came downstairs. She sounded breathless.

"Clara wants to draw in the missing piece of my quilt."

"Your quilt? Your *wedding* quilt?" Dora asked, standing ramrod straight.

At the tone of Dora's voice, Clara suddenly turned to Ella and said, "You don't have to be doin' this. Really, you don't. Not just for me, you don't."

"Maybe we'll do it for Aden, then," Ella said softly. "I think he'd like us to finish the quilt. He'd like the house you drew too. I'm sure of it. You did such a good job."

Dora shook her head. "Well, I guess it's better than sittin' in your room cryin' your eyes out."

"And that's likely what I'd be doin'," Ella said, "but we're on the way down to look at the quilt now. Chore time will be here soon if we don't hurry."

They left Dora standing there and went downstairs to where the quilt was. As they stood in front of the frame, Ella drew her breath in sharply.

"Are you okay?" Clara asked.

"I'll be okay in just a minute," Ella said quietly. "It's the first time I've seen the quilt since it happened."

"We don't have to, really," Clara whispered. *Why did I ever start this? I was thinking only of myself.*

Ella ignored her sister's remarks and said, "Let's see the drawing." She took the paper and held it over the centerpiece of the quilt. Other than a better color match, the effect couldn't have been better. Clara held her breath and waited for Ella's opinion.

A few moments later, Ella finally said, "It's so lovely, Clara. It really is."

"I'm so glad you like it."

"Aden would have loved the house," Ella said, tearing up.

Ella wiped her eyes, smiled weakly, and then stepped back for another look. "It couldn't be any better," she said. "You'll have to draw it in as soon as possible. I can work on the stitching as I have time."

"Mamm will help," Clara said, wishing she could help too by producing as fine a stitch necessary for the drawing.

"I expect it's time we'd better go chore," Ella said a few minutes later.

Clara nodded. "Thanks for bein' so nice, Ella, about this. I feel much better now."

Twenty

Ella felt numb and confused as she walked out to the barn. *Why did I ever consider giving the drawing so much as a glance? Sure, I wanted to please Clara, but there was more to the decision than that. Was I moved by the thought that Aden would have wanted me to finish the quilt?* That thought had deeply touched her.

Life did move on, and work did seem to soothe the haunting ache inside. Clara's drawing, though, had moved her where she hadn't expected to go. In a way the decision opened up the pain again, yet also it strangely seemed to bring relief.

Her thoughts were interrupted by a loud and fierce bawl from the barnyard. She jumped even as she realized the source of the ruckus. The new bull had still not settled into its new home, or maybe it had settled in too well, staking its claim on the cows and the whole barnyard. The bull bawled again, trumpeting its displeasure about something. Its head was down as it stomped about, kicking up the dust.

Ella shivered at the fury. Surely the bull had no hope of access to the outside world. Her dad and brothers made sure the barnyard fences stayed strong and in good repair. With a new bull, and one so foultempered, extra care would have been taken.

As she watched the bull, its anger brought back the unpleasant whispers from last night when Dora and her brothers had returned from the singing. She didn't have the heart to go, and thankfully they hadn't stayed home for her sake.

When the buggy had rattled in—home from the singing—she had gone downstairs and opened the stair door to hear Dora's hushed whispers in the kitchen. "They think it might be *three* before it's over."

Ella didn't need to be told details to understand what that meant. Surely, there wouldn't be more deaths. *Does God really want others to go through what I endured?* This seemed impossible, but then so had Aden's death. The bull, its nostrils raised in a great snort of anger, seemed to drive home the point that anything was possible.

"Ella," Clara, dressed in her chore clothes, called from the door of the house, "did you see the sunset?"

Ella stopped and glanced up at the sky. "No," she said loud enough for Clara to hear.

"Then step around the barn. It's well worth it," Clara said.

That might be a welcome distraction. Ella walked around the edge of the barn, the spectacle in the sky taking her breath away. Streaks of dark blue hung above great folds of red and orange where the sun had just set. There were splashes of red and gold in the sky, the whole area lit up in colors.

"It's beautiful," Ella said, realizing by the sound of Clara's steps that her sister had stopped beside her.

"At least it means a nice day tomorrow."

"That's what it usually means," Ella said, wishing there was a sign in the sky that her heart would be okay tomorrow.

"There will come a good day for you too," Clara said as if reading her thoughts. "There will be plenty of young men who'll be wantin' to marry you."

"Nah," Ella said, shaking her head, "I don't want anyone else. I can't ever be findin' another Aden."

She and Clara walked toward the barn. Inside, the familiar sounds and smells of cows, hay, and fresh dropped feed greeted them.

"Where are the boys?" Clara asked at the sight of the cows in their stanchions. The closest one calmly munched its feed and raised its head to look at them.

"They'll be in soon. You'll be milkin' two cows tonight to toughen up your hands as fast as you can."

"I ache already, I do declare," Clara said, groaning.

"You were born to be a farmer's daughter," Ella said, teasing her, "and then a farmer's wife."

Clara joined in with Ella's soft laugh.

"Remember, wipe down first," Ella said, pointing toward the bucket of water by the milk house door, "and watch for the tail."

"I remember that much," Clara said, groaning again. "They sure can hurt with those things."

Ella handed Clara the rag and watched while she wiped down the cow's udder.

"You have the hang of it, yah," she said, taking the rag.

While she worked on her own cow, the hesitant pings of milk started from Clara's direction. By the time Ella had finished, Clara's pings were already stronger.

"This is hard work," Clara muttered, her head tight against the cow's side.

"You'll be doin' four in no time."

Clara groaned, her voice drowned out by the loud bellow of the bull from the barnyard.

Ella stopped, and Clara brought her head up sharply.

"That awful thing," she said.

"I know. It was mad when I came out of the house."

The bull bellowed again. The sound of a loud crash of broken wood followed.

"What was that?" Clara asked, turning from her cow and standing up.

"You'd best go on milkin'," Ella told Clara. "Bulls are that way—at least most of the ones Daett buys."

Clara had just sat down again and reached under the udder when the bellow came again. This time it was followed by the sound of a desperate cry—a male voice.

"That was Eli," Clara said, standing again.

"I think so too," Ella said, not moving. "We better check on it."

"We should," Clara said, setting her milk bucket in the aisle.

Their daett's voice came from the barnyard, loud, urgent, and clear with its instructions. "Stay up there, Eli. Don't be comin' down now."

Ella set her bucket of milk aside and ran toward the barnyard. Clara followed tight behind her. They stopped at the split barn door, its top open, the lower level still securely fastened.

"No!" Clara screamed.

Eli was as high up on the wooden barnyard fence as he could get. The bull stood below, its nose in the air. Lowering its head to the ground and stomping in the dirt in a rage, it rammed its head repeatedly against the wood fence.

"I can't stay up here long," Eli said, his voice weak. Noah had approached the bull from inside the barnyard and stood only a few feet away.

Ella watched as the bull turned toward Noah, lifted its head, and then headed in his direction. The race across the dirt lot was swift and decisive. Ella had never seen her dad run so rapidly. His legs were a blur and his beard blew to the side as he crossed the barnyard. Both hands caught the middle of the board fence. In one smooth motion, Noah leaped upward as the bull came to an abrupt stop with a great bellow of rage at its missed prey.

"Oh, Ella!" Clara gasped from beside her.

Ella found her voice and yelled to Eli, "Climb down now! You can make it before it comes back to you."

The bull bellowed and started in their direction.

Clara screamed, pulled Ella sideways, and slammed the upper door shut.

"You can't do that," Ella said. "We have to see, and we have to help somehow."

"We can't help. It's comin' here," Clara said, her eyes wide.

Ella pulled the door open a crack and peeked out. "The bull has gone back," she whispered and then swung the upper door open all the way.

Noah had already climbed down the side of the fence and approached Eli's perch from the back.

"Climb down!" she yelled in Eli's direction.

He shook his head. Clutching at his chest, he said, "I'm hurt bad."

The bull approached again, bellowed, and rammed the post with its head. The board held, but Ella saw Eli lose his grip. His feet slipped, and he slid downward. He hung on to the top board for a moment by his fingertips and then dropped to the ground.

The bull bellowed and slammed its head into Eli's back. Ella screamed, "No!" as her hand found the latch to the lower door. It swung open with the force of her body's forward propulsion.

She raced across the barnyard. Her dad's voice reached her faintly through the pounding in her head. "Don't, Ella! You be stayin' back! Listen to me!"

The bull raised its head at her approach and then leaped back, its legs scraping across Eli's body. Ella never stopped or slowed down till she knelt down beside Eli. Her hand brushed his brow with never a glance back at the bull.

The bellow of the bull filled the barnyard as it lowered its head. Ella finally looked up but didn't move away from Eli. She stood instead and yelled at the top of her voice. "You rotten, mean thing! Get away from here!"

The bull seemed momentarily stunned, shook its head, and then stomped the ground. Little chunks of dirt flew into the air. Then it bellowed again and seemed to gather its rage.

Ella held her ground over Eli, trembling. She raised her arms and yelled again, "Get away from here, you ugly, wicked thing!"

The bull stood its ground, shaking its head. It would soon smash its head right into her chest, and she would surely be joining Aden, who had already crossed over to the other side. Her time had come.

For a moment, Ella felt the joy of the coming reunion with her beloved. She would leap into his arms and never let him go. She would kiss him until she had no strength left. Death was a friend. Ella could laugh in the bull's face as it rolled its eyes. At least she could save Eli by diverting the bull away from him. Ella stepped toward the bull, moving further down the fence line.

The bull shook its head again as Ella walked straight at it. To her astonishment it leaped aside. The bull remained too close to Eli, and so she repeated the walk, and again the bull backed down.

She stared at the bull, and it seemed to do the same. Wasn't it going to run at her? It jerked its black head around and looked to the side. She paused, also hearing the sound, and then turned to look. Her dad came at a run, his face taut, his eyes wild. He carried a short gate with him.

Without a word, he rushed up and placed the gate between Ella and the bull. His whole body shook as he pulled in great gulps of air. "Get out of here," he shouted. "Run, Ella!"

"I'm not going," she said through clenched teeth.

The bull seemed to ponder the situation and must have decided it had been bested. The bull bellowed softly and walked off. Noah followed, his gate in front of him, until the bull had been driven from the barnyard into the stall at the other end. With a click of the latch Noah fastened the gate.

When he came back, Ella had already returned to kneel beside Eli. There was blood on his chest and hands, and blood came out of his ears.

"Does he breathe?" Noah asked, kneeling beside her.

"Yah," she said.

"*Da Hah sie lob*," he said. "Let's be gettin' him to the house."

Twenty-one

"I don't think he should be moved," Ella said, her mind racing. "The *Englisha* always say not to move them. It could injure him even more."

"We can't leave him here, lying in the dirt," Noah said. "He has to be taken to the house. Then someone can go for the doctor."

"Is Eli dead?" Clara's voice asked from somewhere inside the barn.

Ella looked up, shook her head, and turned her attention back to her brother.

Noah looked around. Arriving at a decision, he said, "We will lift him onto the gate with Monroe's help. Monroe! We need your help."

"He wasn't in for milk'n yet," Ella said. "It was just Clara and me."

"Then he's up in the silo." Noah turned, ran in that direction, and hollered loudly up the outside chute, "Monroe! We need you now!"

A muffled cry answered him, and Noah motioned up the chute with his hand. Monroe's legs soon appeared, followed by a hurried descent.

"What's wrong?" Monroe asked.

"The bull got to Eli," Noah said, "and we need your help carrying him to the house."

"What was Eli doin' around the bull?" Monroe asked as they ran back. "He knows better than that."

"I don't know," Noah said. "It doesn't matter now. Let's just get him into the house."

Ella stepped away from Eli when they brought the gate over. Eli's breath now came in ragged gasps. With Noah at his shoulders and Monroe at his feet, they lifted. Ella went on her knees in the dirt and lifted from the side. His body settled on the metal rails, and Eli groaned deeply.

Noah and Monroe lifted together, one on each end, while Ella ran ahead to open the barnyard gate. The strange litter crossed the front yard to the house. Clara had come out of the barn to clutch Ella's arm as she shut the gate and followed behind.

At the house, Mamm came down the front steps two at a time. Dora slowly came out behind her but stopped at the top of the steps as if frozen. Behind her all three younger girls looked on with wide eyes.

Wordlessly Mamm knelt beside the gate as Noah and Monroe lowered it to the ground.

"The bull got to him," Noah said, his voice hoarse.

Mamm cradled Eli's head in her hands. "You must take him to the clinic, to Dr. Mast's. He will know what to do," she said, looking up at Noah's face.

He nodded. "We will hitch up the flatbed wagon."

"Please," Lizzie pled, "can you call the ambulance, yah? He may die before you drive him down."

"I will not have that *Englisha* machine with its lights and noise on our place," Noah said. "It does not befit our people even in this hour of trouble."

"He's your son," Mamm said, and Ella saw the pain on her mom's face.

Her dad seemed to ponder this, his hands by his side, his face suddenly much older than it had been this morning.

"I just thought of something. Alex Adams will drive him. He has a pickup," Noah said, his face showing his relief.

"Ask him quickly, then," Mamm said, looking down at Eli's still form. "He still breathes but not by much."

Noah answered by sprinting across the yard but slowing to a walk at the road. When he arrived on the porch of their only non-Amish neighbors, he knocked rapidly on the door. Mr. Adams appeared, and after a brief exchange, the two men moved rapidly to the garage. The sound of a truck motor quickly turned into the crunch of gravel as Mr. Adams drove across the road and backed up carefully to the metal gate.

"Blankets!" Mr. Adams said loudly before he was even out of the pickup door. "Lots of them, ladies! Quick about it!"

Dora and Ella made a dash for the house. Mamm stayed where she was, her hands cradled under Eli's head.

"What shall we use?" Dora asked. "Blankets from the cedar chest, perhaps?"

"Yah," Ella said as an idea rushed into her mind. "Get those, but I'll be gettin' something heavier."

As Dora went for the bedroom and the cedar chest, Ella took the basement stairs. Once down, she removed the quilt from the frame without any hesitation. Dora was already outside and had handed the blankets into the outstretched hands of Noah and Mr. Adams when Ella arrived back in the yard.

She stood ready to offer her quilt, but Dora still held one in her hands. Noah jumped down from the pickup bed, motioning for Monroe to help with the lift. With Mr. Adam's aid, the three picked Eli off the gate and set him onto the pickup bed. Dora held out her last blanket, and Noah covered Eli with it.

"Your quilt," her mom said. "He'll be needin' more warmth."

Ella held out the quilt, and her mom's eyes widened as she unfolded it.

"It's your wedding quilt."

"Use it," Ella whispered.

Her mom hesitated and then nodded. She tucked the quilt snugly around the blankets and under Eli and stepped back. Noah jumped in the back of the pickup truck.

"Monroe can ride in front," he said. "He'd best go along with me. We might need help to get Eli out of the truck at the clinic."

The pickup lurched onto the blacktop and accelerated down the road. Noah clutched the metal side of the truck with one hand, and his beard whipped backwards straight off his shoulders. He held on to his hat with the other hand.

Ella stepped over to her mom's side. Dora came up and placed her arms around both of them. The two sisters helped Mamm walk to the porch, and Clara followed close behind. When they reached the top step, Mamm sat down and sobbed into her hands with great gasps.

"Maybe he'll be okay," Ella said. But her mom hadn't seen the worst—the bull standing over Eli, Eli's blood mixed with the barnyard mud, and the hopelessness in Eli's eyes before he passed out.

"*Da Hah* has seen fit to visit us with much sorrow," her mom said. "I don't think I can lose my son yet."

Ella didn't know what to say, and Dora remained silent too. *It's just as well,* Ella thought, *because Dora might foolishly mention the tale about three deaths in a row.*

"Dr. Mast from the clinic is good. He'll be knowing what to do," Ella said. Beside her Dora cleared her throat, but Ella silenced her with a quick glance.

"Tell me what happened," Mamm said, her sobs subsiding.

"Clara and I were milkin'," Ella said. "We heard this hollering and the bull bellowing in the barnyard. When we went to look, Eli had already climbed the fence but couldn't get down. The bull must have run into him once already."

"Did you see that?" Mamm asked.

"No," Ella said.

"Go on," her mom said.

"Daett tried to get Eli away from the bull but was chased himself. I thought that bull was going to catch Daett, but he got over the fence just in time. Then the bull went back to Eli. It hit the fence and knocked Eli off. When he fell to the ground…the bull gored him."

Ella was silent again.

"How did you get the bull off Eli?" her mom finally asked.

"Daett got a gate and chased it back to its pen," Ella said, leaving her own part in the rescue out.

"Ella helped too," Clara said, but added nothing more when Ella shook her head at her.

"I've always been tellin' Noah to watch those new bulls," Mamm said. "He tries to be careful—I know he does, but…"

"Maybe Eli forgot we had a new bull," Ella said. "I didn't hear anyone say why he was in the barnyard with it. Maybe he took a shortcut across it. He was late to help us with choring."

"It could have been anything," Mamm said. "These things happen all the time. I had hoped they wouldn't happen to us."

"The milkin'!" Dora said, remembering. "It's not done."

"Oh, my." Mamm stood up. "Yah, those poor cows. The milking has to be done now…and the little girls." She glanced up at the three girls on the porch. "They saw all of this, and they are much too small. They should have been taken inside."

"They'll be okay, and you're not goin' out to the barn," Ella said, her voice firm. "We'll take care of the chores."

"I don't think I could if I wanted to," her mom said with a sigh and sat down on the porch steps again.

"Don't worry 'bout supper either," Ella told her. "No one's hungry anyway."

Clara and Dora nodded in agreement.

"We'll see 'bout that," Mamm said, "but the milkin' has to be done right away."

Ella squeezed her mom's shoulder, leaving her on the porch steps, and led the way back to the barn. Inside, the cows greeted her with what sounded like both irate and discouraged moos.

Immediately Ella and Dora got busy by grabbing their stools and locating their buckets.

Ella turned and said to Clara, "You'll have to help until we're done. These cows are in pain."

"Like we aren't," Dora said. "Eli. He's dead. As sure as anything, he is. It's comin' like everyone knew it was comin'. They talked 'bout it last night at the singing. These things always come in threes and don't stop until they're done. Just who would have thought it would be us? We already had one tragedy. Doesn't *Da Hah* know better than that? Loadin' people down with more than they can bear? This will give Mamm more than she can bear. And you too, Ella. You already lost your beloved, and now your oldest brother will be gone. I don't understand any of this, I do declare. It makes no sense at all."

"Maybe he'll be makin' it," Ella said, daring to hope. "We don't know how badly Eli is injured."

Dora set her stool down on the concrete barn floor and turned back to face Ella. "You saw him, Ella. There was blood all over him. He even had blood coming out of his ears. That's a sure sign he won't make it. But I guess it doesn't matter what you and I think. Things are out of our hands and even out of Dr. Mast's hands—out of everyone's hands in fact. You can't change what is to be. Don't you see that, Ella?"

A picture of her wedding quilt on top of Eli's broken body rose in Ella's mind. She stopped, unable to move for a long minute. *Did that perhaps doom Eli? Did it send him to the same fate as Aden? Did I condemn my own brother when I only meant to help him?*

"It's a foregone conclusion," Dora said. "We'll be burying him in a few days. I just know this. I now know we have lost our brother."

"I don't want to lose my brother," Clara said, protesting from beside her cow.

"Aden's family wasn't given much choice," Dora said. "Why do you think we should be given one?"

"He doesn't even have a girlfriend," Clara said. "He won't have anyone but us to mourn him."

"Then we'll have to do more than our share," Dora said. "Mamm will do more than her part, and Daett too. I know I'll be mournin' my share."

Ella rallied herself from under the cloud of despair tearing at her own heart. "Perhaps *Da Hah* will spare us," she said, surprised at her own words.

"I wouldn't depend on it," Dora said, standing to dump her first bucket of milk into the strainer.

"My hands ache," Clara said.

"They're going to be burnin' by the time you're done tonight," Dora said. "Just take a break once in a while. It's all you can do, and we do need your help."

Silence settled on the barn, broken only by the moo of uncomfortable cows and the steady spit of milk streaming into the bottom of the buckets.

Twenty-two

Mr. Adams' pickup truck pulled into the yard, bouncing to a stop by the front door. Mamm was already at the door when Monroe climbed out. She told the three smaller girls to stay inside as she rushed onto the porch and down the steps. Mr. Adams climbed out of the truck when he saw her approach.

"Your son has been taken to Tri-County by ambulance," he said when she stopped in front of him.

"He's alive, then?"

"He was when he left the clinic. Dr. Mast accompanied the ambulance, and he's in good hands, ma'am."

"With Dr. Mast, yah, he is. Where was he hurt?"

Mr. Adams shook his head. "It was all kind of a rush around there, and I didn't hear anything."

Mamm glanced at Monroe, and he shook his head.

The barn door opened, and Ella looked out. She thought she had heard a vehicle pull in.

"Monroe's back," she announced, turning to her sisters.

Dora stood up quickly and emptied her bucket into the strainer. "Be back in a moment, miss cow," she muttered. "Got to see whether my brother is alive."

Clara had just started to work on a fresh bucket, so she had little milk to dump into the strainer. When she stood up, the cow brought her tail around with a solid thump and caught her across the face. She stumbled into the aisle and lost her hold on the milk bucket. It clattered to the ground, and the milk flew against the wall. Clara shrieked and wanted to cry, but Ella took her hand and said, "Come. There's more important things than spilled milk right now. We'll clean it up later."

"The milk," Clara said, "it spilled!"

"It doesn't matter," Ella whispered, hurrying out.

Halfway across the yard, Dora had waited for them. Together they walked quickly toward the house.

"Good evening," Mr. Adams said, smiling as they approached. "Your brother has been taken to the hospital."

"So he's not dead?" Clara asked.

"No," Mr. Adams said. "We'll hope for the best. He's quite injured, I'm sure. You don't get mauled by a bull without injuries. But Dr. Mast is doing what he can."

"We thank you very much for your help," Mamm said. "It means so much to us."

"I'm more than glad I could help," he said, "and if you need transportation to the hospital tomorrow, I think I can offer my wife's services. I myself won't be home during the daytime."

"That would be too much," Mamm said, her voice catching. "We don't want to impose even more on you and your wife."

Mr. Adams smiled. "Until your son is well, consider us available to transport you to the hospital."

"You're too kind," Mamm said.

"Not at all, Mrs. Yoder. We will pray God brings a swift healing for your son."

"If it is His will," Mamm said.

"Then we will pray that it *be* His will," Mr. Adams said firmly.

"Thank you," Mamm whispered.

By the look on her mom's face, Ella knew her mother hoped this man's great boldness in asking the Almighty to make up His mind would not end up as an offense.

"Let us know," Mr. Adams said, getting back into his pickup.

They watched him drive out the driveway.

"Oh, the poor cows," Ella said, remembering their duties again. "We're still not done."

"I'll help," Monroe offered. "I'll finish my silage afterwards."

"I think I'll be makin' supper," Mamm said. "I feel like I can breathe again."

"The worst may still not be over," Dora said. "There could still be bad news to come. We should keep our hope in check."

"You had to say that," Ella said, giving Dora a sharp look.

"I'm sorry," Dora said at once. "I guess I can't help myself."

"Perhaps the news will continue to be good," Mamm replied hopefully. "There has been one good sign already. Mr. Adams was home tonight, and so he was able to drive Eli to the clinic. Yah, perhaps *Da Hah* will continue to help us out."

Ella remembered her quilt and wondered if it had helped or made things worse. *Surely it isn't a sign that makes Eli's chances even worse. I shouldn't think about such things. Surely a quilt doesn't make a difference one way or the other.*

"Let's go finish the chores," Monroe said. "It's late enough already."

"Clara can stay with me," Mamm said. "I need help with supper, and you're almost done, aren't you?"

"Three cows, I think," Ella said. "We can handle those. Her hands hurt by now, anyway."

Clara nodded, and they left for the barn. When Ella got done with two cows, she checked the ones Clara had done. One still needed finishing. When she finished that cow, she stepped back as Dora released the long line of cows. They moved out to the barnyard, pushing and shoving as usual against those who paused.

With the last one outside, Ella went to check on Monroe. Normally she wouldn't have concerned herself because Monroe was well able to take care of himself, but the earlier events had inspired fear.

"Are you okay?" she asked, hollering up the silage chute.

A fork load of silage thundered down, and she had to step out of the way.

She hollered up again. This time Monroe stuck his head out of the opening, halfway up.

"Something wrong?" he asked.

"Just checkin' on you. Are you okay?"

"I'll be right in," he said. "Just got a little more to pitch down, and then I'll have to spread it out."

"Want me to help you?"

He grinned. "Guess it would be nice—it's kind of late. The fork's over there in the corner."

She knew what to do and went to look for the fork. The pile of silage Monroe threw down would need to be distributed along the wooden feed bins where the cows would have access later.

With her fork in hand, she got to work and had several loads drug to the other end by the time Monroe came down. He helped, and the job was finished quickly. Monroe went to open the gate for the cows and let the now subdued bull out of its pen. A few cows came in immediately, which alerted the others. By the time they left the barn, the whole herd was in line and scooping up the silage in great gulps.

The table was set and ready when they arrived inside. Monroe let Ella wash at the basin first while he waited. By the time Monroe was done, the others had seated themselves. Without Noah present, they bowed their heads in silence.

Ella didn't feel hungry and noticed her mom didn't have much on her plate either. Monroe and Clara seemed to have their full appetite, though. They took seconds of most everything. Since it was the family custom, she waited at the table until everyone was done and then stood to help clear the dishes.

"I'm going down to call at the phone shack," Mamm said. "Maybe the hospital will have news."

"I'll drive you," Monroe said as he stood, his plate finished and scraped clean.

"You don't have to," Mamm said. "It might do me good to walk down."

"It's too far," Monroe said, his voice firm, "especially after dark."

"I guess you're right," Lizzie said, giving in. "I hope I can find out something from Noah."

"He'll have good news," Ella said, uncertain where her hopefulness came from.

A few minutes later, Mamm and Monroe left, the noise of the buggy wheels rattling in the driveway. Dora, who still sat at the table, sighed and got up to help.

Clara, sitting at her place at the table, asked, "What do you want me to do?"

"Dry dishes," Ella said. "Ruth can help. Ada and Martha, you two stay in the living room and out of the way. I'll start to wash, and Dora can clear the table."

Dora nodded and diligently began to scrape the dishes into the scrap bucket before handing them to Ella to wash.

When the last dish was finally scraped, Dora took the pail outside to dump. She took no light along. They all knew the way by heart, and with the faint glow from the kitchen door, the path was easy to follow.

A few minutes after Dora had let the screen door slam, a loud shriek pierced the night air. Ella caught her breath and raced for the kitchen door. *What now? Did some awful creature assault Dora? Is there a robber man in the yard? Did he come to assault them when none of the men are home?*

"Oh, no!" Clara said, following close behind her.

The two looked at each other, pale faces in the light of the kerosene lamp, and then they crept slowly toward the screen door. Ruth stood stock-still, frozen by the sink.

Dora's voice reached them as the two made their way cautiously to the door. "Don't come out here!" Dora yelled, her voice sounding muffled. Loud sniffles and coughs followed.

"Why not?" Ella asked from the doorway.

Dora yelled again. Her voice sounded more angry now rather than anything else. "Of all the stupid, hideous, awful things to do! And on a night like this! Stupid! Stupid! Stupid!"

A wave of putrid smell rolled up the porch, and Ella gagged.

"A skunk," Clara said with a howl. "Where did she find a skunk?"

"I threw the slop on it!" Dora sputtered as loud as she could.

"Now I've heard everything," Ella said. "Did it get you?"

"How would I know?" Dora hollered with fury. "You want to come out and see?"

"I don't think so," Clara said. "I'm stayin' inside."

"Someone has to help her," Ella said, unable to keep the laughter out of her voice.

"It's *not* funny!" Dora said, fairly bellowing.

"So what do you need?" Ella asked.

"How 'bout a tub of hot water? That would be a start."

"Out there? How are we supposed to get it outside? It stinks all over in here."

"How do you think it smells out here?"

"I can't imagine," Clara said. "Don't want to find out either."

"Get some water heated," Ella said. "She'll need a wash."

"That'll take a while," Clara said, hesitating.

"Well, she can't clean up in cold water."

Clara went to add wood to the fire while Ella ventured outside. Dora stood on the edge of the garden where the kitchen light reached. Farther into the garden, the darkness was deep and the smell was awful.

"So did it get you?" Ella asked, struggling to breathe.

"Get a flashlight so we have some light. Maybe I can tell then."

"Clara's heating water for you. We'll bring it to the tub in the basement."

"I can't go in there with this much smell on me."

"Maybe the skunk didn't hit you fully. If it didn't, you could leave your dress outside."

"Get the flashlight, then, and another dress and a blanket. I have to be takin' this dress off as quick as I can."

Ella left, got the items Dora wanted, and returned. The flashlight revealed no wetness on Dora's dress.

"Let's move away from this spot," Ella said, and when they did the smell decreased.

"I guess it did miss me," Dora said, her voice low and disgusted.

Ella couldn't keep from laughing.

"So what do we do now?" Dora asked, coughing loudly.

"Come to the basement steps and take your dress off there. You can go inside then. The smell won't stay in the house without the dress."

"That's what you think. What about on me?"

"We'll worry about that later. There's got to be some way of gettin' it off."

At the concrete steps, Dora got ready to remove her dress. "Turn out the light," she said.

"The neighbors have seen girls in their underclothes before." Ella laughed in spite of the evening.

"They haven't seen *me*," Dora retorted.

Ella handed Dora the flashlight, and she shined the light ahead of herself.

"Go on, now," Ella said. "I'll bring you a dress and a blanket."

"Bring a complete change," Dora said. "I smell all the way through."

Dora carefully found her way down the steps, her flashlight winked on only at intervals. Ella got a stick to pick up the dress. She carried it over to the wash line, its wire just visible from the kitchen light. Gingerly she held the stick up and draped the dress over the line. Tomorrow her mom could decide how to salvage the smelly thing.

Twenty-three

Ella let the screen door slam on her way in, the sound snapping in the night stillness. *What time is it? There is a late feel to the air.* A quick glance at the kitchen clock proved it was a little past nine-thirty.

"Is the water warm?" she asked Clara, who stood beside the large kettle used to heat bath water.

"A little," Clara said. "I put in plenty of water, but doesn't she smell? It will take more than soap to get her right again. Isn't that just the most awful thing to have happen to you?" Clara then dissolved into giggles. "She'll have the whole house stunk up by the end of the night."

"The skunk didn't get a good hit from the looks of things."

"Smells like it," Clara laughed. "Wouldn't this have to happen to Dora, of all people? Do you think the skunk saw her comin'?"

"It was probably as scared as she was."

"I wouldn't like a bucket of slop thrown on me either." Clara giggled again. Ruth, her face still pale, went into the living room to join her two younger sisters.

"Read them a story," Ella hollered after Ruth.

Just then they heard the rattle of buggy wheels in the driveway. Mamm must be home with whatever unpleasant news she carried.

"Okay," Ella said, "the water's warm enough. I'll dip some of the water out, and you take the bucket downstairs. After Dora starts washing, come back up for another bucketful. She'll be needin' all the clean water she can get."

"You thinking water and soap will take that smell off?" Clara asked, unconvinced.

"Let's see," Ella said, her mind whirling. "Vinegar. I think that works better than soap."

She dropped the dipper beside the kettle and reached under the counter for the bottle of vinegar. A quick twist of her hand, and a generous splash found its way into the bucket.

"Poor Dora," Clara said.

"She needs it, and she'll thank us later. Now light another kerosene lamp, and take it with you. Dora's only got the flashlight with her."

"There's one downstairs," Clara said.

"Good. Dora can shine the flashlight for you while you go down, and you won't have to carry the lamp."

Ella held the door open for her, and Clara hollered from the first step, "I want light, please."

Dora made some strange sort of noise in the basement, and the feeble beam of the flashlight bounced on the top steps.

Clara contorted her face to suppress a giggle, and Ella shut the basement door with a smile. Behind her the front door opened, and Ella rushed over to meet Mamm.

"*Da Hah sie lob,*" her mom said with emotion. "He will live, they think. I got to speak with your daett. Eli's still in surgery, but earlier one of the doctors gave a *gut* report."

"That is good news," Ella said as Mamm seated herself on the couch.

"What a night this has been. But we are to be spared, it seems. I don't know if my heart could've taken more sorrow. And you...with Aden just passed away. It would have torn all of us apart."

"Ah, Mamm," Ella began, reluctant to go on.

Lizzie glanced at her face and then stopped, startled. "Is there something wrong? Something I don't know about?"

"Dora got sprayed by a skunk. She's in the basement cleaning up."

"A skunk! I thought I smelled one coming in from the barn. It got worse when I walked past the garden, but I figured we just had one wandering about. Why would Dora go after the thing?"

"Dora threw the slop bucket on it."

"On purpose? The slop bucket?" Mamm asked. "Why would she do that?"

"No, not on purpose," Ella said. "She just walked out, as usual, and dumped it off into the night."

Mamm sat still for a long moment, and then she started to laugh. "Now I've heard everything."

"She smells pretty bad," Ella said, relieved to see the change in her mother's mood.

"I imagine so! A skunk would do that, but on a night like this… *Da Hah* must be trying to cheer us up!" Mamm laughed and then cried till the tears ran down her face.

"Are you okay?" Ella asked.

"Ach, I guess I'm not," Mamm said. "My nerves are 'bout shot, I suppose. So where is Dora? In the basement, you said? Have you given her somethin' to clean up with?"

"Warm water and vinegar."

Mamm thought for a moment. "That's a good start. Have her rinse in water with baking soda and hydrogen peroxide."

"That stuff?"

"It will help, yah," Mamm assured her. "I'll fix it. Bring the peroxide in from the medicine cabinet, and I'll fill the bucket in the kitchen."

"Clara should be up with the empty bucket any minute." Ella said as she turned to get the peroxide. Clara was back in the kitchen when she returned.

"I'm so glad Eli'll make it," Clara said. "I was afraid he would die, and then Dora went and got herself sprayed. How can you laugh and cry all in the same evening?"

"It just works that way sometimes," Mamm said. "Now the perox-ide." She reached for the bottle in Ella's hand and dumped a generous splash in the water, already white from the baking soda. Mamm stirred the contents briskly with her hand.

"Poor Dora," Clara said again. "She wasn't happy with the vinegar water. What will she say about this? It's like she's being made ready for the oven."

Mamm had little sympathy. "She shouldn't throw slop on skunks. Maybe this will help her remember in the days ahead."

"I'm sure she won't again," Ella said. "This is not a lesson to be learned twice."

"She already smells better," Clara said. "But her clothes stink pretty badly."

"Then take them outside," Lizzie said quickly. "Surely you didn't let her wear her dress into the house."

"Nee, I didn't," Ella said. "She took it off at the basement door. It's on the wash line now, and I'll be takin' the rest of her things out there too."

"Good," Mamm said with relief. "We can save the clothes for tomorrow. I think vinegar will probably work for them and do a *gut* job on the smell. If not, we can soak them until it does."

Ella turned to Clara. "Here, take the bucket down, and I'll bring Dora her clean clothes."

Clara walked to the basement door, the bucket firmly in her hand. It looked like she would spill the contents on the kitchen floor when her dress caught on a kitchen chair, but Clara unhooked her dress in time. Ella followed her down the stairs with the clean clothes.

In the basement, Clara found the still sputtering Dora busy washing herself behind the plastic divider they used for baths.

"Am I to be tortured all night?" she complained.

"That's the last treatment," Ella said, laughing. "Clara can get you a clean bucket of water now."

"Without all this junk in it, I'm hoping. I smell like a cake ready for the fire."

"Just water, now," Ella said, "to rinse with."

She gathered up Dora's underclothes and carried them outside, holding them at a distance as she hung them on the wire beside the dress. On the walk back, she paused to look at the night sky. Here the skunk smell from the garden wasn't as strong, and the stars were out, bright and strong. A great longing swept through Ella so suddenly it gripped her like a vice around the heart.

Is Aden with the stars? Her eyes searched the heavens, and she found herself hoping they could speak the answer but knew they couldn't give anything but silence. When she thought the bull would charge, she figured she'd join Aden, wherever he was. *Why wasn't I allowed to join him?* Life could never repay what she had lost. Above her the stars continued to twinkle as her gaze swept across the heavens.

Aden used to watch the stars with her, and now he was gone—yet the stars continued their display. It didn't seem right. Perhaps if the stars could speak to her, but there was nothing. And then—perhaps it was her imagination or was it truly the stars speaking? *Continue on as we continue on until your time is up. Only when your time is completed, will ours ever be.*

Ella looked across the sweep of the sky. *Did Aden send me a message? That's a strange thought. Surely not!* Her people didn't believe in such things. *Instead, this must be* Da Hah *Himself taking time out from all His great works to comfort me and mend my broken heart.*

"Ella, are you okay?" her mom's voice called from the kitchen doorway.

"Yah," she said, "just looking at the stars."

"We really need to get to bed. It's late, and I've already sent the little ones. We'll be all by ourselves for choring tomorrow morning."

"I'm coming," she said. She turned and went inside to find a dressed Dora seated in the living room.

"That lousy skunk," she said, still sputtering.

"You do smell better," Ella said with a laugh.

"Now off to bed, all of you," Mamm ordered. "You need your sleep. The day will be full enough tomorrow."

In her room, Ella lit the kerosene lamp and took her tablet from the drawer. Yes, it was late, but she still felt she must write if only for a few moments.

"Dear journal," she wrote.

It's been a long wild day, to be sure. Eli got injured by the bull but should be okay, Mamm thinks. Right now we're supposed to be in bed and asleep, but I can't stop thinking about Aden. Why did God have to take such a wonderful man? I know I've asked myself that many times, and there still is no answer. I suppose there never will be one—at least this side of eternity.

I thought for a moment tonight that I would get to join him—not in some evil way but in the best way one could cross over. I stood up for Eli in the face of the angry bull. Is that not a good way to go be with the one you love?

It all happened so fast, but I knew what I was doing. Yet I'm still here. I wonder why, and I also wonder what it would be like over there in the place where Aden is. Are there really streets of gold? That seems a little cold to me, in a way, and not at all like what Aden would have wanted.

He liked the stream down by Stoddard Road, the music of the water over the rocks, the glory of the stars at night, and the beauty he said he saw in my eyes. I don't know about that, but I do wonder if those things are over there where he is. I wonder...Does he have a girl there who loves him?

No, I don't suppose they have such things, at least from what I'm told. But I know he does have something so much better. In fact, maybe he's forgotten about me already because of all the wonderful things that are in heaven.

I never thought that I could hurt this way. At first I just thought I hurt because I missed him. Now I know the pain is also because he no longer misses me. The ache is like a great big boulder in my heart, aching for what I've lost and also for what I will never have again—a man who loves me like Aden did.

I'm sure there are boys who will say they do, but I don't want to go to the young people's gathering anymore. I know what will happen. They will say the words, "A beautiful girl like Ella, she shouldn't be without a man." Yet I don't think I'm that beautiful. Aden always said I was, and I believe he meant it. Yet all those who are in love think their loved one is beautiful.

I worry because there will probably be someone who will think they want me now that Aden isn't here. Someone will ask to take me home. I fear it a lot from some boy who maybe already has a girl. It will happen, and terrible feelings will come out of it. Even if I say, "no," which I will, the girl will know.

It's a terrible thing, and I think I'll just stay home for a good long time. For more reasons than my sorrow, it will be for the good of everyone. Oh, dear God, why did You take my Aden away from me?

With tears in her eyes, she closed the tablet, slid it under a dress in her dresser drawer, and climbed into bed to fall into a troubled sleep.

Twenty-four

Ella awoke with the sound of Mamm's tap on the door, dressed quickly, and was downstairs ahead of her sisters.

"I suppose you'll be working inside this morning?" Ella asked. "And Clara too? She's probably still pretty sore from last night."

"That's what I was thinking," Mamm said.

Ella waited until Dora and Clara appeared together at the bottom of the stairs and then said, "Clara's in the kitchen this morning, and Dora's with me out in the barn."

"Thanks," Clara said, looking grateful. "My hands are still hurting."

Ella got her coat and headed outside. In the yard she could already see the light of the gas lantern in the barn shining through cracks around the door. Monroe must already have been up for a while. When she opened the door, the line of cows stood in the stanchions. Monroe, with a milk pail in his hand, glanced at her from between the cows.

"You should have gotten us up," she said.

He laughed, his voice still rough. "I thought with all the ruckus last night, all the girls of the house would be needin' their sleep."

"Yah, yah," Ella said as he laughed again.

Behind them the door opened, and Dora walked in.

"What a stink have we got here," Monroe teased. "Phew, the girl smells. It's enough to chase away the boys from miles around." The boy bent over in his laughter so that he disappeared behind a cow.

"I don't stink," Dora said.

"That's 'cause you can't smell yourself," Monroe said, bending over again.

"It's not true," Dora wailed. "Is it true, Ella? Don't tell me it's true."

Ella smiled and shook her head. "He's just teasing you."

"Well he shouldn't be teasing me. It's much too early in the morning," she said, turning to Monroe. "Just wait till a skunk gets you sometime! Then I'll never let you hear the last of it."

"I don't go throwin' slop on poor little critters," he laughed, pulling his stool up under himself, disappearing behind the cow for good.

"That horrible, horrible boy," Dora muttered, reaching for the washcloth to wipe down the cow's udders.

"There will be better days ahead," Ella said.

Dora only grunted.

With the first round of cows done, they repeated the process to the soft sound of cows munching and milk splashing in the buckets.

"I'll finish the last one," Monroe said.

"Good," Ella said, "and thanks." She left with Dora to change for breakfast. Arriving at the house, they saw that the three younger girls were sitting on the kitchen bench, already awakened and dressed. Ella raced upstairs and changed quickly but wasn't needed for breakfast preparation when she got back downstairs. Monroe splashed loudly outside in the washroom as he cleaned up. Ella took her seat at the table. The absence of her dad and Eli seemed to cut like a knife, as if the whole house was still and they all felt the pain together.

"I'll walk over to Mr. Adams' house right after breakfast," Mamm said as they ate. "You girls can clean up the kitchen, and I'll come back and help if Mrs. Adams can't take me to the hospital."

"There shouldn't be any problem there," Ella said.

"See that Clara gets off to school," Mamm said as she moved toward the bedroom door.

"I'm a big girl now," Clara protested.

"I know you are," Mamm said kindly. "We just have to look out for each other with all the trouble we're having."

Clara nodded, and Mamm went to change. She came back for a final goodbye before she left.

"Are we having morning prayers?" Monroe asked from the living room.

"Not with Daett gone," Mamm said, opening the door to leave.

Ella felt the absence of the morning prayers. Perhaps with so many troubles, they should have more prayers, not less. Even silent prayers—bending her knees in supplications to the Almighty for His mercy—would have been nice. The effort would have seemed a comfort, even without her dad present to lead the family, but tradition must have held sway in Mamm's mind.

There was an aversion to any public approach to God that wasn't led by a proven male presence. *Mamm must think Monroe, at fifteen, is too young to lead the prayer. Eli might have done it even though he isn't baptized, but, of course, he isn't here. Perhaps Eli has been spared because he isn't baptized...And maybe he is being granted time to make his formal peace with God and the church, even though he has never been a wild boy.* Such thoughts were too deep for Ella to ponder.

Ella watched Mamm walk across the yard and glance each way before she crossed the blacktop. Her mother looked stark in her dark blue dress and black shawl as she approached the Adamses' house and knocked on their door. From the motion of her mom's hands and the fact she was invited inside, Ella figured Mrs. Adams would soon be available to take her mom to the hospital.

"It looks like Mamm's going to get her ride," Ella said when she joined her sisters in the kitchen.

"I have to leave for school," Clara said, busy packing her lunch.

"Did you leave the drawing out?" Ella asked.

"You didn't go changin' your mind?" Clara asked, tilting her head.

"Nee, I still want to use it. Mr. Adams brought the quilt back last night," Ella said.

"It's on the pile," Dora said. "It's not even dirty either. I thought there might at least be blood on it, you know, from how Eli looked."

"Don't *say* such an awful thing," Clara said.

"Well, there was blood everywhere. Why wouldn't it be gettin' on the quilt?"

"Because it's Ella's quilt!" Clara said.

"What's that supposed to mean?" Dora asked.

"That quilt is special. I think it helped Eli last night when she gave it to him. I could see it on Eli's face."

"The girl has gone wacky," Dora said, rinsing a dish in the sink, "but who wouldn't be with all that's been goin' on. People dying, bulls goring people, skunks sprayin' me—"

"I'm not wacky," Clara said. "Ella's quilt *is* special."

"Now, now." Ella said as she assumed the mother role with Mamm gone.

"I guess I'm sorry," Dora said. "I really didn't mean it. See? You're still my sweet, sweet sister."

"Yah, yah," Clara said, but Ella saw the smile play on her face as she went out the door, her lunch bucket swinging by her side.

"So what was that all about?" Dora asked with Clara gone. "Are you putting thoughts into the girl's head?"

"Nee, I'm just trying to keep my own mind straight."

"With all that's happening, it would mess up anyone," Dora said, making another trip to the counter with her hands full of dishes.

"So what's on the list for today?" Ella asked as she washed. "Mamm didn't leave any instructions."

"She's got enough on her mind already."

"There's the regular wash tomorrow, but the blankets from last night should be done today. We should probably bake pies, I guess. Though, that could be put off till tomorrow. Bread's low. We should tackle that today, don't you think?"

"The garden could be done," Dora said as if she hadn't heard any of Ella's suggestions. "Mamm mentioned that yesterday. I think we could start on the first planting of onions. They'll get bigger that way. At least

Mamm's a firm believer in the theory. Then the peas could be planted. We could make beds for them, if nothing else."

"I want to work on the quilt, but I guess that can wait."

"That quilt again," Dora said, making a face. "You really think that quilt's special?"

Ella shrugged. "I'm surprised I'm even workin' on it. Maybe that's what makes it special. It seems to heal somethin' inside of me, that and Clara's picture. She really can draw. Maybe that's why she thinks it's special."

Just then the front door burst open behind them, and Monroe's shout startled them. "I've found them," he said, his voice gleeful.

"Found *what*?" Dora asked. "And don't go scaring us like that. Life's short enough the way it is."

"The skunks!" he said, satisfaction in his voice. "They're under the barn—a whole family of 'em. At least I think so from the noise they're makin'."

"You expect me to get close to skunks?" Dora said, glaring at him. "Leave them be is my opinion on the matter."

"I can't," he said. "Something has to be done with them. They have to be gotten off the place. Any suggestions from the female side of the family?"

"What are you plannin' on doin'?" Ella asked. "Not something stupid I hope. We wasted too much time cleanin' up skunk smell last night. I'm not wantin' to go through that again."

"I won't get sprayed," Monroe said confidently. "I'll shoot down the hole and get them all that way."

"You'll do nothing of the sort," Ella said. "There has to be a better way."

"Like leavin' them alone," Dora said. "I learned my lesson last night."

"I guess we could pour slop down the hole," Monroe said, keeping a straight face for a moment before he lost it and burst out in laughter.

"You are a mess of a boy," Dora said before she finally joined in his laughter.

"I have a suggestion," Ella said when Monroe had quieted down.

"What would that be?" he asked. "You gonna sweeten the slop bucket?" His laughter rang through the kitchen.

Ella ignored his remark. "Take a lesson from last night, is what I say."

"Put Dora down the hole?" Monroe said, choking back another fit of laughter. "She could pull them out one by one. I'm sure they're good friends by now."

"If you'll be quiet, I'll tell you," Ella said.

"He's not used to a sensible conversation," Dora said, "the poor little dear."

"So tell me what great wisdom my wise sisters have to share," Monroe said, composing himself somewhat.

"We could put vinegar and baking soda in a bucket of water and pour it down the hole," Ella said. "We cleaned Dora up with those things, and I think that should get 'em out."

Monroe looked skeptical.

"Try it first before you do anything else," Ella said and went to get a bucket of water. Monroe made no move to follow the suggestion.

"It'll work," Dora said, feeling positive about the situation at last.

"That's just because it worked for you," Monroe said. "You're not a skunk, though."

"Thanks," Dora said, rolling her eyes at him. "You can actually say nice things. I didn't know it was in you."

"Sorry," he said. "It just kind of slipped out, and I didn't mean it."

"That's what I thought. If you ever even make eyes at a girl, I'm going to warn her 'bout you."

"Really," he said, snorting, but Ella was sure she caught a worried look in his eye.

"Here's the water. Let me add the stuff, and then we'll see what happens."

"I hope it works," he said. He took the bucket when she was done, and they followed him outside.

"Stay back," he said as he cautiously approached the hole beside the barn. He stood over the opening for a moment, turned the bucket upside down, emptying the contents down the hole, and then backed up to where his sisters stood.

Nothing happened for a long moment. "It's not workin'," Dora said.

"Quiet," Monroe whispered. "I hear somethin'."

With a rustle, little bits of dirt flew into the air, and the striped head of a skunk popped out of the hole. It looked around and seemed ready to return to its refuge when it was apparently pushed from behind. With a grunt, the skunk exited the hole and shook itself as its mate popped up behind. The second one did the same, rubbing its nose on the ground. Behind them three smaller skunks rolled out and proceeded to gallop around the two parents.

The skunk that had come out first gathered itself together, stared at the three humans, and then with great dignity, ambled across the barnyard. Its mate followed behind, and the three youngsters soon tumbled in line.

"Now I've seen everything," Dora said.

"I'll shoot 'em if they come back," Monroe muttered.

"You will do no such thing," Ella said. "Now don't we have work to do?"

They nodded in agreement as the line of skunks disappeared into the fencerow, their tails high in the air.

Twenty-five

"I'll work in the garden," Dora said, standing outside the barn door, "if that's okay with you."

Ella shrugged. "I can't help you with the cultivator just yet. I have to start the bread dough first."

"Monroe can help me," Dora said, quickly opening the barn door.

Ella went inside to start the bread dough. As she measured the flour, she could see through the kitchen window that Monroe was indeed helping Dora. They came out from behind the barn with the large Belgian horse hitched to the cultivator. Dora lined up the horse at one end of the garden for their first pass over the recently disked garden spot. Dirt flew out sideways as they started forward and then reversed themselves and came back the other way. Once the beds were turned up, leveling off the top by hand would be simple, though backbreaking.

When her bread dough was mixed and left to rise for the first time, Ella—mindful of the time lest she forget to go back inside and knead the dough—went outside to help.

With a hoe, she worked on one of the rough dirt hills, smoothing it out and flattening the top. Dora led the horse past while Monroe hung on to the cultivator. He stopped at the end of a row to wipe his forehead even though the weather was barely warm.

"Phew!" he exclaimed. "Hard work, this cultivating is."

"He's just soft from the winter," Dora joked to Ella.

"I'm not," Monroe said. Grabbing the handles, he yelled, "Let's go!"

Ella smiled as they came down a fresh row. It felt good to be outside working in the garden.

When the timer went off in her head, Ella left the hoe lying on top of the bed and sprinted into the house. The cool spring air went all the way through her, invigorating her bones to the marrow. Breathless, she stopped short at the kitchen counter. Another unexpected stab of realization welled up from her heart, *How can I feel so alive when Aden is gone?* Would these sudden reminders of what she'd just lost never cease? She pushed the feeling aside and washed her hands, as if to cleanse them of more than just dirt on her skin.

The dough, deflated under her fingers, was reduced quickly to a quarter of its size. Ella broke off the appropriate lengths, measured them from memory, and placed each piece in a bread pan she quickly buttered. She counted out twelve pans and set them on the table. That would make enough bread for a week and a half. With Eli injured, the bread batch might last more than that. Too much, and they would have stale bread on hand.

Ella left the dough to rise for the final time and rejoined the cultivator crew in the garden. Monroe had apparently just proclaimed his day's work done because Dora stood there with her hands on her hips.

"One more round," Dora said loudly.

"Nope," he said. "I'm done with women's work for the day. I have to take care of things on the farm."

"This *is* the farm," Dora said, glaring at him. "And it's not women's work. I work at hay and plowing! Just remember that."

"I'll see you later," Monroe said, smiling sweetly.

Dora gave in with a huff, and Monroe lifted the cultivator up on its front wheel, yelled to the horse, and was off for the barn. He steered with his body, the lines wrapped around his waist.

Ella worked outside until she figured the bread had risen, and then she stayed indoors to watch the stove while the bread baked. She sent the three young girls out to help Dora and joined them when the bread came out of the oven. Two long even rows of raised beds with droopy planted onions were completed when Mrs. Adams pulled into her driveway across the road.

Mamm and Daett both got out of the car and spoke with Mrs. Adams. Ella noticed Mrs. Adams waving repeatedly as if she was repelling the words her parents spoke. Obviously she was refusing her mom's offer to pay for the trip.

Dora stretched her back and stood up when she noticed Ella's attentive look at what was happening across the road.

"They're back," Ella said, confirming the question in Dora's eyes.

"Daett's with her, which means Eli must be okay," Dora said.

"I hope so," Ella said, motioning for her three younger sisters to come and join them in the yard to wait for the news.

Her dad looked weary as they came across the road. He limped as if his muscles were sore, but his face lit up with a smile as they got within earshot. It was a good thing to see.

"*Da Hah sie lob,*" he said fervently. "Eli will make it. He's got some broken ribs, a ruptured spleen, and a collapsed lung, but Dr. Mast personally stayed till Eli was out of surgery. We'll be bringing him home the day after tomorrow. There's nothing that won't heal up, they said. So it seems *Da Hah*'s will is to give us much grace on this matter."

"Much grace, yah," Mamm said, beaming. "After what Eli's been through, we can be so thankful."

"Has the bull acted up since I've been gone?" Daett asked.

"Monroe's been keepin' an eye on it, and it's running with the cows as usual," Ella said.

"I wish you would get rid of that bull," Mamm said. "I can't stand the thought of keepin' it on the farm."

"It's a good bull, and they're all dangerous—most of them anyway," Daett said.

"But that bull attacked Eli," Mamm said. "It could be one of you next time."

Daett pondered this in silence for a minute and then looked again at the expression on Mamm's face.

Finally, he said, "Yah, I will call right away and have Mr. Wayne come by. His trailer runs through here most days on some errand. If he's in the area, the bull will be out of here by this afternoon. And I'll have a new bull brought in when I get the money from the sale of this one."

"I really do appreciate this," Mamm said, full of relief.

"Do you have lunch ready?" Daett asked in Ella's direction.

"Nee," she answered with a shake of her head, "I guess I forgot. We were so busy in the garden."

"That's okay," her dad said. "I see the garden looks real *gut*. You girls do some *gut* work. I think I'll walk down to the phone now, and perhaps you can have lunch ready when I get back."

"Yah," Mamm said, answering for Ella. When Noah had left, she told the girls, "Wash up, and we'll make lunch quickly."

Ella was the last one in line for the washbasin because she had dashed back to the garden to pick up tools. They were done for the day, and this would save a trip back outside. She dropped the tools off in the basement through the outside steps. She smiled as she remembered Dora's sputtering trek downstairs last night with the flashlight. This would no doubt be a Yoder family story for many a year to come.

Mamm's exclamation reached Ella's ears through the open basement door.

"Who baked the bread? These look wonderful—and twelve loaves at that!"

"Ella did," Dora said. "She's good at such things."

True, she had baked the bread, but Dora could do the job as well as she could. Ella, on the other hand, was not as good with the horse cultivator in the garden as Dora was.

"Dora's better with the cultivator," Ella hollered up the stairs, but no one paid any attention. She decided to repeat the statement when she got upstairs but changed her mind when Dora and her mom were already in a discussion on another subject.

"I think we'll turn the guest bedroom on the first floor into a recovery room," Mamm said. "Eli can't climb the stairs."

"I'd make him," Dora said, teasing.

The meal was prepared well before Daett walked home from the phone shack.

"Mr. Wayne should arrive this afternoon for the bull," he said.

Mamm gave him a grateful smile. "Is Monroe anywhere close to the house?" she asked.

Daett glanced out the front door. "He's unhitching now and will be on his way in."

Minutes later, with everyone seated, lunch was served. After the prayer, Monroe launched immediately into the skunk story, including ousting them from their hole.

"You should have seen the girls' faces when the skunks came tumbling out. I thought they would both run for the house faster than you could say *jack rabbit.*"

"We did not!" Dora retorted. "And it was Ella's idea to add vinegar to the water. That's what girl brains are for, to come up with real solutions that don't have *boom* on the end of them."

Daett laughed heartily. "It was likely just the water that drove them out. They don't like wet beds, but I am glad you didn't let Monroe go shooting them down in that hole."

"They're just girls," Monroe muttered, but he didn't sound too serious. Another story had been added to the family's list to be told at reunions and after Thanksgiving and Christmas dinners. The best thing, though, was her parents' good spirits. It was an amazing thing how laughter could continue in the midst of the sorrow they had experienced already. Like the stars, life just went on with its twinkle.

"We have to wash the blankets this afternoon," Mamm said when lunch was done. "I saw them still hanging on the line."

"I guess we forgot with the garden on our minds."

"That's okay, and I'm glad that's started," Mamm said quickly. "We still have time to wash this afternoon. Dora and I will clean up the kitchen while Ella starts with the blankets."

Ella nodded and left to lug the heavy blankets down to the washing machine in the basement. Later, after they were washed and clean, she would hang them back on the line. Before Ruth came to help her lift the heavy, wet blanket and hang it on the line, the water dripped down the front of Ella's dress, soaking it. They rolled out the wash line together until blankets hung heavy halfway up the side of the barn to where the line was attached.

Ella checked the quilt and decided it really didn't need to be washed, just dusted. If there was time, she might start this afternoon on the center work. Carefully she replaced the quilt in its frame.

With the last of the blankets on the line, Ella checked in with her mom, who was upstairs.

"Is it okay if I work on the quilt until the blankets are dry?"

Mamm thought for a moment and then said, "That might do you a lot of good. Just don't forget about the blankets."

"Thanks," Ella said. She took Clara's drawing down to the basement and carefully traced the outline of the house onto the white quilt block. Just the outline of the drawing—even without the stitches—looked beautiful. It looked as well, if not better, than she had envisioned.

For thread, she chose black, blue, and dark green. She planned to stitch in such a way as to produce a nice shadow effect. Ella completed the first few stitches and then stepped back to examine the results. Her judgment had been correct. The color scheme worked completely.

Ella worked steadily until around three-thirty when, with a bang of the door upstairs, Clara announced her arrival home from school. She soon could be heard bounding down the basement steps.

Clara took one long look and gasped. "It's wonderful, Ella," Clara said.

"I think so too," Ella said. "Would you like to help?"

"I haven't learned those stitches yet. Besides, Mamm wants me back upstairs before too long."

"Well, then, you can do the straight lines on the other side. I'll ask Mamm if you can. It would be a good place to learn."

"Would you really let me?" Clara asked, amazed. "I can really work on your center block?"

Ella nodded, and they went upstairs quickly to confer with their mom.

"I guess what I had planned for her, Ruth can do," Mamm said. "I'll be happy for any quilt lessons you can give her."

They returned to the basement. While Clara threaded her needle, her face aglow, Ella gave instructions. Ella then watched Clara carefully as she started down the penciled line.

"Am I doing okay?" Clara asked, her fingers shaking. "What if I mess up your quilt?"

"Worst case, we can always cut the thread out."

"I don't want to cut it out. It might ruin your quilt."

"You're doing okay," Ella said. "Just relax." She watched for a few more minutes and then went back to her own stitches.

"I think I'm learning," Clara said after a while. "Do you think so? Are the stitches tight enough?"

Ella glanced up, checked, and then nodded.

"Boys are so difficult," Clara abruptly said a few moments later.

Ella pulled the thread through, her eyes intent on the stitch. "They are worth it, though."

"How can you say that," Clara asked, "after you've lost Aden?"

"Because he was still worth it, that's how I know. Whatever you have to go through to find someone like that, it's worth it."

"Won't *Da Hah* just be takin' him away from me, like He did Aden?" Clara paused, her thread held in the air.

"I don't think that's how it works," Ella said. "We're all different, and *Da Hah* doesn't choose the same every time."

"You really think so?"

"I do," Ella said, her needle steady as she carefully pulled it through the cloth.

"Paul makes me feel so *gut*," Clara said. "Not like Ezra, even though Ezra might be a better person."

Ella smiled. "You'll be figuring it out in due time."

"But Paul scares me," Clara said, her voice breathless.

"Paul's a *gut* boy." Ella paused between stitches. "He comes from a nice family, and it's good to be lovin' someone," Ella said, and silence fell between them.

When chore time arrived, they went upstairs to change but were distracted by the angry bellows outside.

"The truck is here to pick up the bull," Mamm said.

Hopefully the departure of the dangerous animal would be complete before she had to see it again. When they stepped outside a few minutes later, Daett had just closed the gate of the trailer, the dark form of the bull inside. He held up his hand to tell them to wait on the porch as the truck drove forward.

"I'm glad it's gone," Clara said, sighing in relief.

"One less trouble around here, that's for sure," Ella said.

Twenty-six

E lla changed the sheets in the downstairs guest bedroom the evening before Eli's planned return home. She fluffed the goose feather pillows and made sure the kerosene lamp on the dresser was filled. From Mamm's description, it sounded as if Eli would need extensive care, perhaps even through the night. In that case, a continuous night-light in his room might be useful.

Last night at prayer, Daett thanked *Da Hah* for His many blessings, in particular that Eli had been spared. This was no doubt the proper thing to say, but wouldn't it have been better if Eli hadn't been injured in the first place? The accident seemed so unnecessary and senseless, and it had spun their world even further out of control. Now it was as if everyone had to spend time catching up.

Does God really have a plan? she had asked herself last night as she prayed, her head on the couch cushion, her knees on the hardwood floor. The answer hadn't come. Acceptance of the Almighty's ways was a firm tenet of her faith, whether one understood or not. Still, there was the hope that perhaps someday it would all make sense.

Her dad's words had caught her attention when he prayed, "Now unto Him that is able to keep us from falling and who will render judgment on that final day, we give thanks, honor, and praise."

Judgment? Is that it? Will the answers come at Judgment Day? Perhaps God allows these things so that He can render judgment to each human heart, give a test so He can see whether we stay faithful, honest, and just through the trials that come our way. It could well be, and I do want to be worthy of that day of judgment, whenever it comes for me.

Later in her room, she took a few moments to make note in her tablet that Eli's homecoming was to happen tomorrow.

Eli is expected home soon, and I hope his recovery will be swift. I can imagine the pain he's in with his broken ribs. Mamm says there's not much that can be done with broken ribs—not like a broken arm or leg where the busted parts are held perfectly still by the cast.

Poor Eli. I suppose he'll learn the lessons God wants him to learn. I can't imagine him becoming bitter about this. His loss is not as great as mine, but I still can take lessons from his good attitude. One must carry on through thick and thin. This is one thing I am thankful for, but I plan not to mention this to them. I suppose Mamm will figure it out anyway. Someone will need to care for Eli on Sundays and perhaps even on youth nights. That someone will be me. I will insist on it. I just don't want to face the world out there yet. It seems so strange and unfriendly without Aden in it.

Ella replaced the tablet and climbed into bed. Sleep came quickly, her weariness deep.

In the morning and after chores and breakfast, Mamm left with Mrs. Adams to go to the hospital. They took the backseat of the van out and spread blankets on the floor in case Eli would need to lie down on the trip home.

"If it's needed," Mamm had said. "It's better to be prepared than to expect Eli to sit up all the way home if he's in pain."

Ella fluffed up the bed one final time and then moved out to the garden to work. She kept watching for the van, and when it pulled into the driveway a little before twelve, Eli was sitting upright on the front bench seat, his face somewhere between a grimace from the pain and happiness to be home again. Ella ran to the van as Eli eased himself to the ground. She would have given him a hug, but he held her back with a raised hand.

"I can barely walk," he whispered.

"You do look *gut,* though," Ella said. "So much better than when I saw you last."

Eli nodded and then grimaced when he stepped forward.

Dora, at work in the basement on the last load of wash, didn't see anyone until she saw them walk past the window. She shrieked and raced up the steps to open the front door.

"So you're not dead," she said, a broad smile on her face.

"Close enough," Eli said as he hobbled painfully inside. "Show me some place I can lay down."

"You're in the guest bedroom," Mamm said. "You won't be climbin' any stairs for a while."

"That's nice," he said, grinning. "It makes me feel special."

"You'd better get well pretty quick," Dora said. "We need you around here so don't go feelin' *too* special."

"I'll be glad enough to get rid of all this," Eli said, lifting his shirt to show them the white strips taped around his torso. He turned around slowly so they could see the supports went all the way around his body.

Ella led the way and held the bedroom door open for him. Eli lowered himself gently onto the bed and sighed.

"My, my," he said, "it is good to be home, and now I want around-the-clock service, all sisters at my beck and call. I want water, candy, and food when I need it and no questions asked. Is everyone understandin' that?"

"You low-down rascal," Dora said, "I do think the hospital has gone and spoiled you already. I think you need to get out and plow the fields. Do you really expect us to obey you hand and foot? I'd say a good day's work in the field would be what you're really needin'."

"How soon the sun hides behind a cloud," he said, grinning. "I thought you felt sorry for me."

"Not *that* sorry," she said. "I now have the wash to finish in the basement, my weak, frail, little brother."

"So I will be dyin' at home in my own bed," he mourned, his body stretched out in hopelessness on the bed.

Ella laughed and left to get him a glass of water. She could hear her mother give him a long lecture on the care of his broken ribs, instructions she apparently had gotten from the hospital. She even went so far as to read them off a paper she had brought home.

"Don't run or climb stairs. Don't cough unless you have to. Have someone help you into and out of bed."

Ella couldn't help but laugh. Eli was not going to like any of this, but at least he was alive. He did look the picture of despair when she walked back in with the glass of water.

"This recovery is goin' to take years," he said, moaning. "Years and years, and I can't even go outside for a good week by Mamm's instructions, mind you. How am I supposed to get better with no sunshine? What is life worth if you have to spend it all inside the house? At least let me go out to the barn when they do chores. I could sit and watch."

"You will do no such thing," Mamm hollered from outside the bedroom. "We've already brought you home sooner than the doctor wanted us to. We don't need you injuring yourself and returning to the hospital because of your foolishness."

Eli groaned at a new thought. "How are we gonna pay for this anyway? The bill has got to be thousands of dollars, and that's just for the hospital bill. Why didn't you just let me die out there? It was my fault I tried to run across the barnyard all to save a little time. I knew the bull was pretty upset that night."

"That's an awful thing to be sayin'," Mamm said. "Life is a great gift, and *Da Hah* takes and *Da Hah* gives it—not us. Don't you ever think something like that again."

Eli glanced at Ella. "I shouldn't have said that. I'm sorry. Aden didn't have any choice in the matter, did he?"

"It's okay," she said, patting his arm. "We're just glad you're back, safe and sound."

He laid back, limp on the bed, and groaned again. "It just hurts all over. Each breath causes pain."

"You'll be better in no time," Mamm said, her voice cheerful now. "I'm out in the kitchen, and Ella and Dora will be around somewhere all day. We'll be checkin' on you. You just holler when you need something."

"It's almost lunchtime," Ella said. "You've got to be hungry, yah?"

"I'd be if I could swallow," he said, holding his ribs. "It was horrible stuff they served in the hospital. Because it hurt so bad to swallow, I only ate a little and didn't care so much. Now here I am with good food and wanting to eat a lot but too hurt to eat."

"Now don't go feelin' sorry for yourself," Mamm said. "Stay in here, and I mean it. No trips to the barn, just the necessities like the bathroom. The walkin' you've already done today has been hard enough."

He grimaced one final time as they all left the room. Ella made and brought an egg salad sandwich—Eli's favorite—from the kitchen. His eyes lit up with delight.

"Oh, you'll be spoilin' me now. Oh, ye ribs, please let me eat," he said, groaning and slowly sitting up in bed.

"Put this over you," Ella said, getting him to lean back and shaking a linen bed sheet out across his lap. "I just cleaned these sheets."

"My mouth waters. My eyes are a achin'," Eli said. With a look of bliss on his face, he bit into the sandwich. A swallow was followed by a muffled howl of pain, but he proceeded to take another bite.

"You don't *have* to eat it."

"Oh, but I do," he said, his voice solemn. "I have to get well. I can't stay in this bed forever."

Ella had turned to go when he asked, "Is Mamm out in the kitchen?"

"Yah, do you need her?"

He shook his head, and Ella moved toward the door.

"Ella, I have to tell you somethin'."

Ella paused and then returned to his bedside when she saw the serious look on his face.

"I met this girl…in the hospital. An *Englisha* girl. She took care of me sometimes. She lives north of here."

"So? They have lots of nurses in hospitals."

"Not like this one. She was just like one of our own people."

"She's an *Englisha*." Ella looked sharply at him.

Eli bit into his sandwich and chewed slowly. "What would you say if she stops by."

"But we can't pay for nurses."

"We don't have to. She'd be stoppin' by to see me. Only don't tell anyone. Mamm will have a fit if she even thinks it's more than a friendly checkup."

"Now wait a minute." Ella put both hands on the bed. "You didn't fall for this girl, did you?"

He grinned weakly and nodded. "I like her…more than I've ever liked any girl."

"She was there to take care of you," Ella said. "She was a nurse. Surely it didn't mean anything."

"Maybe or maybe not," he said.

"Well, if it's true, then I suggest you get over it fast."

He met her eyes, and she knew at once that her words were in vain.

"You'll be seein' when she gets here," he said, "how nice and plain she is."

"So when is she comin'? Will she just walk in here?"

"I told her she could stop by when she wanted to. I told her to tell whoever came to the door that she was one of my nurses from the hospital here to see me. Perfectly normal thing, I would say. Only it's not perfectly normal. I think I'm going to ask to see her once I'm well—in friendship."

Ella regained some of her composure. "Nurses are friendly because they're supposed to be. That's part of taking care of you. That's all."

"Like I said, maybe or maybe not." Eli finished the last bite of his sandwich. "I just wanted at least one person to know about this, and I knew I could trust you."

"Well, all I can say is don't be heartbroken when she doesn't come," Ella said. "Just thank the good Lord you have a decent home to return to, a nice family to take care of you, and a church that watches for your soul."

"I *am* thankful," he said, weariness in his voice and sleepiness in his eyes.

She left him alone. Surely a few days of rest and good food would restore him. What imagination he had and what nerve to invite a nurse home for a visit.

"Is he okay?" Mamm asked.

"I think so," Ella said, trying to smile. "He ate his sandwich, and he's tryin' to sleep now."

Her mom nodded and looked relieved.

Twenty-seven

S upper was over, darkness had fallen, and the gas lantern now hissed above the kitchen table.

"It's time for evening prayers," Daett said, "and we will have them in Eli's bedroom."

Chairs scraped on the hardwood floors as they got up and gathered around Eli's bed. Mamm and Dora brought in chairs so they could kneel.

"Our great God in heaven," Daett prayed, kneeling now, "You who see all things and order the affairs of men, we thank You for Your mercy to us and that Eli has been spared. We ask that You would continue to protect us from evil, from sin, and from the world. Have mercy upon us weak and frail human beings made from the mere dust of the earth. You know that we blow over like the grass in the fields at the faintest brush of Your hand. Remember us, we pray, that we perish not from the face of the earth. Do not forget us in Your great anger. And we give You thanks for the blood of Your Son, Jesus Christ, who washes away our sins. Amen."

Afterward, Eli had tears in his eyes as he whispered, "I'm in pain."

"*Da Hah* will take you through this," Daett said. "He has spared you, and He will allow your body to be healin' again."

"If it be His will," Mamm added with a note of caution, "but we are hoping it is."

Eli nodded and then asked, "Isn't it time for my pill again? Then I'll see if I can sleep for the night."

Dora brought him the bottle of prescription pills that Mamm had bought in town. With the kerosene lamp turned low, they left him alone. Mamm would check on him throughout the night.

Ella went up the stairs quietly and settled slowly on the bed. Eli's information about the nurse troubled her. Eli could not allow himself to get entangled with an *Englisha* girl.

She jumped up at the sound of a buggy pulling into the driveway. What would someone want this late at night? It could mean only one thing—there was trouble somewhere. Ella opened the door into the hallway.

Dora already had her head out of her bedroom door. "Did someone just drive in?"

"Yah. You goin' down?"

"You think it's trouble?"

"I hope not," Ella said. Yet a caller at this hour must surely mean trouble somewhere.

"Maybe someone wants to borrow from Daett," Dora offered.

"This time of the night? I'm goin' down," Ella said, her foot finding the first step in the dark, her bedroom door shut behind her.

"I've heard enough of dark troubles to last me a good long time," Dora said. "Tell me if it's really bad. Otherwise I'm going to sleep." Dora's door clicked shut behind her.

Mamm was at the front door when she got downstairs, the guest bedroom door shut.

"Who is it?" Ella whispered.

"Looks like Uncle Mose's buggy. I can't tell for sure, but Daett's already outside."

Ella stood beside her mom as they opened the front door and listened to the rise and fall of male voices beside the buggy. She couldn't make out what they said, and the tone gave no clue either. There was no laughter or mirth, but that didn't narrow things down much. Mose could simply be interested in Eli's condition. Why hadn't she thought of this before?

"Eli's just home," she whispered. "Mose is askin' about him."

"I thought of that," Mamm said, "but why isn't he comin' inside?"

"Maybe because it's so late."

"Here Daett comes now." Mamm stepped onto the porch as the buggy left.

Daett approached in the darkness, his form barely visible. When he stepped into the faint light from the living room window, Ella saw his face outlined with concern. Surely the news was not good.

"There was an accident just now out on the state road," Daett said, his voice troubled. "Mose's boy and the girl he was with were on their way home from Randolph. A car came across the road from the other way and didn't see their dark buggy, I guess."

"Are they okay?" Mamm asked.

"David is. Mose said he went along to the hospital, but his girl-friend's hurt. He just came from telling her parents. I suppose they'll go down tonight, yet."

"Ach," Mamm said, holding the door open for Noah, "is this never going to stop?"

"It does seem we've had a lot lately," Daett said. "*Da Hah*'s hand is heavy on us, but He knows what He's doin'. Mose said they would let us know of anything new."

"Who's David dating?" Ella asked, unable to remember seeing him with anyone on a regular basis. She knew her cousin fairly well, even though he lived two districts over.

"Menno Beachy's daughter," her mom said, "Melissa. She's nine-teen or so."

"How badly was she hurt?" Ella asked. Surely this would not be an-other parting of a couple like Aden and she had been through. David and Melissa were younger, but the pain would be just as real.

"Mose didn't know," her dad said. "The ambulance took her to Tri-County."

"You mustn't worry," Mamm said, taking Ella's arm. "There's nothing you can do anyway, and we must leave these things in *Da Hah's* hand."

"What if she dies?" Ella whispered.

"Then they will bear the burden as you have borne it," her mom said. "Now, let's see how Eli's doing. Remember, we still have our own to take care of."

Mamm opened the bedroom door, and Ella followed her in. The kerosene lamp threw low shadows on the wall. Eli's face looked almost white, scaring Ella and causing Mamm to run her hand across his forehead.

"He's got a fever," Mamm whispered. "Low grade, I think, but he's got to be watched."

Ella nodded. She had expected something like this since Eli told his tale of the nurse. Her brother had, no doubt, been affected by the fever when he spoke such nonsense.

"I can take a turn now," Ella said.

"Later. I'll watch for a bit. Dora can take her turn first. Tell her to be expectin' it soon."

"Okay," Ella said, giving in and leaving her mom seated by Eli's bedside. Thankfully Eli, at least, seemed peacefully asleep. If he tossed and turned, it could mean even greater danger. She took the stairs slowly, their squeaking loud in the darkness. The world was a dreary and uncertain place. Now, another accident had happened in such a short time. Was this the dreaded series of three? And yet *Da Hah* was in charge, as her dad said. He would do what was best for them in His great wisdom.

Dora came to the door of her room at Ella's first knock as if she had still been awake.

"What was it?" she whispered.

"An accident with David and his girlfriend. They were on the way back from Randolph."

"What were they doing out on a night like this?"

"I don't know. Expect they had business in town."

"It's the third accident now," Dora said, stepping out into the hall and closing the door behind her. "Someone will die this time. It might even be Eli since he's still not over everything, I can tell you that."

"You shouldn't talk like that," Ella said. But then she admitted the truth. "I did think the same thing, though, but we shouldn't plan for the worst."

"I'm tryin' not to, but I just do. It's the way I think, is all."

"Mamm said you are up next to watch Eli. She wanted me to tell you."

"So he is worse?"

Ella nodded in the dimly lit hallway.

"And you want me to…not think the worst?"

"Really, Mamm says it's just a low-grade fever," Ella said, mustering confidence.

"I'll be ready, then," Dora said, her voice resigned. "It'll be a long night, I can tell already."

Ella found her way down the hall, and in the darkness of her room, she reached for a match to light the kerosene lamp. At the last moment, she decided not to write in her journal. It was late enough already. The time it took to write her thoughts would be better spent in sleep.

Sometime later, she faintly heard footsteps in the hallway but didn't wake fully until Dora shook her shoulder.

"It's your turn now," Dora's voice whispered in the darkness. "Wake Mamm in three hours or so. I'll be takin' another turn after that."

With Dora's faint outline in the doorway, Ella got out of bed and found her way downstairs. The stillness of the house was almost complete. Eli's breath in the guest bedroom came even enough, and his face now looked normal from what she could see.

He surprised her when he whispered, "I could use some water."

Ella glanced at the dresser but saw no glass there.

"I'll be right back," she said, finding her way out to the kitchen. The heavy darkness of the night bothered her for the first time as she groped for the water bucket. It would help if at least a few stars were out. On impulse she walked over to the kitchen window and looked out. The skies were blanketed in thick clouds. No rain, but the weather looked like a downpour was possible at any moment.

Ella went back to the bedroom, the cup in her hand, and Eli struggled to prop himself up on two pillows. He finally just sat up completely, reached for the glass, and drank the water in great swallows.

"Best be careful," she whispered.

"I know. That did hurt, but I was thirsty."

"Are you feelin' better now?"

"Yah, I think so," he said, handing her the glass. "Has someone been in here all night?"

"Yah, Mamm and Dora. It's my first turn now."

"I'm not a *bobli,* really."

"You ran a slight fever this evening, and Mamm thought someone should stay with you—in case you got worse."

He lay back in the bed with a sigh.

"You should try to sleep."

"Suppose so," he said but sat up slightly again, resting his head against the headboard.

Ella sat down in the rocking chair in the corner as a wave of sleepiness swept over her. She could see it would be hard to stay awake, and because Eli obviously felt better, the temptation would be even greater. Ready to yield, Eli's voice reached her through the haze.

"So you think an *Englisha* girl is out of the question?"

She awoke with a start. "You mean the nurse?"

"Yah. You didn't take what I said earlier seriously, I could tell."

"There's nothing to take seriously, Eli," she said. "I thought your words were spoken through your fever. It's the only way it made sense to me. You can have nothin' to do with an *Englisha* girl."

"So you wouldn't even consider it? Ever? Even for yourself?" Eli lowered his head back to the pillows.

"Eli," she said, scolding now, "I just lost my beloved Aden, and I don't want anyone else."

"Do you believe that there's only one person in the world for us?" he asked, his face barely visible in the light from the kerosene lamp.

Crazy shadows played on the walls. "Does love really only happen one time?"

"I have no idea what you're talkin' about. Don't you think you should get some sleep? What if Mamm and Daett heard you talk like this? These are awful thoughts to be thinkin', yah?"

"Of a *gut* love?" He laughed softly.

"Of an *Englisha* girl. You know what I mean."

"I think she'd come join us—the Amish—if she loved me." Eli raised his head to look at her. "I really think that."

"This has nothin' to do with love," she said, her voice firm. "We live in different worlds. How can there be love across such a ditch, and a really big ditch? I mean, Eli, for once think about this. You're a boy, and a nice one. I thought girls were the only ones who lost their heads over love."

"I suppose you're right," he said, sighing, "yet it does almost seem possible. You'll see when she comes."

"Eli," she said, "you keep sayin' that. But this *Englisha* girl can't come into our house. You know that. Not in the way you say."

"Don't worry," he said, his voice sad, "I've already told her that. If she comes, she will be careful. She will be comin' as a nurse to see how I'm doing. Mamm won't know any more—that is if you don't tell her, Ella."

She brushed her hand across his forehead, and he smiled faintly.

"Your fever seems to have gone down," she said, taking her seat on the rocker again. Soon his even breathing told her he was asleep. *Surely, he isn't as serious about the* Englisha *girl as he sounds. Should I tell Mamm and Daett about this?*

She rocked slowly and awoke when her mom's hand rested on her shoulder at the first gray hint of dawn.

Twenty-eight

The rainless clouds still had not cleared as Ella headed to the bedroom with Eli's breakfast.

"I want to sit with the rest of the family…at the table," he said, swinging his legs onto the floor.

"Mamm," Ella hollered. This was beyond her jurisdiction. "Eli wants to come to the table."

"Hush," he whispered, trying to stand, but she held her ground. He was stubborn, and so could she be.

"You're not coming out yet," Mamm said from the kitchen. When she arrived, she gently pushed him back onto the bed.

"I think you'd best listen to Mamm," Ella said.

He knew she was referring to more than just breakfast, and he rolled his eyes at her. Then he gave up his protest and accepted the tray of food. What a strange sight he made, her big brother in bed and so helpless.

They were in the middle of breakfast when a buggy turned into the driveway. Daett stood up, his eggs and toast uneaten, and went to greet whoever had arrived. An uneasy silence settled on the rest and stayed until his return. Ella knew by his face that the news wasn't good.

"David's girlfriend passed away last night…on the operating table… at Tri-County."

"The second one. There it is," Dora muttered, her face dark.

Mamm shook her head and made a motion toward the three younger sisters. Dora seemed to comprehend and said no more.

"The funeral's tomorrow," Daett said quietly. "The viewing's tonight at Menno Beachy's place."

Ella felt the wound inside her rip open again. Mamm noticed and gently touched her arm. The tears threatened, but Ella held them back by thinking of the plans that needed to be made.

"I'll stay with Eli tonight," Ella said quietly, hoping the offer would be accepted without much fuss.

"I'll stay with her," Clara said. "I want to stay with Ella if she stays."

"You will go with us," Mamm said.

"Why can't I stay too?" Clara asked.

"Because Ella has her reasons. You don't," Mamm said.

Ella breathed a sigh of relief. It was *gut* that her mom grasped her feelings.

"I don't like funerals," Clara insisted.

"No one does," Daett said, "but it's *Da Hah's* way, and He knows what's best, and so we'd best learn to live with it."

"I'll never learn to live with funerals," Clara said.

"I suppose none of us really do," Mamm agreed. "Now get ready for school because you can't be going late even on a morning like this."

Clara left thirty minutes later, her light raincoat draped over her head. Dora and Ella finished the kitchen. The heavy clouds dropped a light mist of rain, showing no intentions of quitting. They couldn't work in the garden or do the wash. Ella knew there were pies to prepare for the weekend. The food could also be served at the funeral tomorrow. They would need to take something over for the family.

"How about some extra pies?" Ella suggested in mid thought. "If we start now, I can make enough for both us and the funeral tomorrow."

"I can handle that," Dora said. "You can do something else."

"Are you sure?" Ella asked. "You don't need any help?"

"Nee. Dark days like this give me strength."

"You always were a strange one, that's for sure."

"People come in all the colors, I suppose. The world needs someone like me," Dora said, her voice now cheerful.

"Yah," Ella agreed. "Then I'm going to work on my quilt. Is that okay, Mamm?"

"Yah," her mom answered from the living room. "I've got mending to do, but take one of the little girls with you just to keep her busy."

"Must I?" Ella replied. Then it dawned on her that perhaps her mom had only been teasing. She walked to the living room door just to be certain.

"Were you serious?"

"Nee, I just wanted you to feel what it's like to be the Mamm for a while," her mother said.

"I don't want to quilt anyway," Ruth said from the couch. "I want to go to school."

"You will next year," Mamm assured her. "You will quilt sometime too. All my girls will learn because we can't marry you off if you don't know how to quilt."

Ruth burst into laughter at the idea. "Then maybe I won't ever marry."

Ella smiled. *Then that will mean two of us Yoder women will stay single.* She took a kerosene lamp with her from the utility room shelf and headed downstairs. Carefully she lit the flame, set the lamp on the shelf, and continued the tiny stitches.

Perhaps it was the outline of the house, the memories of what they meant, or the news from this morning, but the tears soon came. So many trickled down her cheeks—thick and heavy—she had to stop and find a handkerchief.

Does David feel now the way I had felt? He must even though he is younger and a man. Surely his heart aches the same. Men are not immune from pain, she felt sure. She longed to put her arms around her cousin and tell him everything would be okay, but how was that possible? She didn't even know herself whether such a thing was true.

There were moments with her family when she forgot about the pain and could even laugh. Yet moments like this showed that the wound was still there. Her fingers lifted the needle and then paused as the tears blinded her eyes. She wiped them away and studied the quilt pattern for a long moment.

For reasons she couldn't understand, Clara's image of the house soothed her. Maybe it was because Clara cared so much—enough to draw the picture and insist that she use it.

Ella moved her needle through the quilt and then suddenly stopped to listen. The low murmur of an unfamiliar male voice came from upstairs, apparently in conversation with Mamm. She hadn't heard anyone arrive. With her eyes just dry from tears and likely still red, she didn't want to see anyone, especially unknown males. She continued to stitch.

The door suddenly opened at the top of the stairs, and Mamm's voice called down. "Ella, there's someone here to see you."

She stood in surprise, but before she could move toward the stairs, the male voice said, "I'll just talk with her downstairs."

Ella now recognized the voice. It was Aden's brother Daniel. *But why does he want to speak with me?*

"I can come up," she offered, considering that they might be more comfortable upstairs in her mother's company.

"I'll be comin' down," Daniel said, his voice now muffled since he was already in the stairwell. Behind him Mamm said something Ella couldn't make out.

"Good morning," she said, though Daniel's face was only dimly visible in the soft lamplight. The resemblance to Aden was there, faint but distinct. Yet the realization of it caused an unexpected pang.

"I'm sorry to be disturbing you," Daniel said. "It's just that there's something I need to be talkin' to you about."

"Oh?" was all she could muster. *What can he possibly have to say to me?*

He fumbled for the chair she offered him. "I'm so clumsy."

She smiled and sat down when he did.

He cleared his throat. "Ella, I know it must still be very hard for you, what with Aden not gone that long yet."

"Somehow, it almost seems like years," she said, meeting his eyes. "I know you loved him too."

"I did." He nodded and seemed to relax.

Ella blew her nose, suddenly comfortable in his presence. She had never been around Daniel much, just at his parents' house when she and Aden had been there. He had been kind to her that hazy morning of the funeral. Now that she was fully aware of him, it struck her how different he was from Aden. It comforted her in a strange way. Somehow it would have felt wrong to find someone who was just like Aden but wasn't him at all. She managed another smile in Daniel's direction.

He spoke again. "Did you hear about Aden's horse?"

"No. What happened?"

"The horse got into the feed on Sunday mornin'. It got swelled up pretty bad and didn't survive."

"Oh, no!" she said and then added, "Perhaps it missed Aden." The picture had flashed in her mind of the grand horse she had seen so many times from her vantage point inside Aden's buggy. In a way, it seemed appropriate the horse had joined its master in death.

"It was a grand horse," Daniel said, but Ella sensed he didn't share her idea about missing Aden.

"That it was," she said.

"I hope it's not too early for this," Daniel said, fumbling with his hands. "Mamm wanted me to wait for a while yet, and I suppose that might have been the right thing to do. I didn't tell them I was coming over, but it just seemed to me you should know about what Aden wanted you to have."

Ella couldn't have been more puzzled and searched Daniel's face. "I don't know what you mean," she said.

"Did Aden and you ever talk about the house he was wanting to build for you?"

"Yah," Ella said, "he was going to bring the plans over the Sunday after he passed." At this, she began to tear up again. How could she not. It was her dream house—*their* dream house.

"I'm sorry," Daniel said, getting to his feet. He took her hand and wrapped it in both of his.

She would never have let any other boy do this, but this was Daniel. He loved his brother as she had loved him.

She gripped both of his hands with hers. Daniel said nothing. The moments passed slowly in silence.

"I shouldn't have come," Daniel said. "Mamm was right. I'm sorry, Ella. That's the way I am. I just do things, and they don't always turn out for the best. This all can wait till sometime later." He turned to go.

"Later won't make it any easier," she told him. "I'll listen to what you have to say now."

He turned back and halted a moment and then took his seat again as Ella took hers. A light seemed to go on in Daniel's eyes as he confessed, "Aden was much better at these things than I am."

"You're doing okay, Daniel. Go on."

He relaxed a bit and started afresh. "Okay, then, here goes. As you know, Aden planned to build a house for you. He had the money all saved and the land purchased. If I understood him correctly, he would have started late this spring."

"That sounds about right." Ella nodded.

"Well, the money is still there. There's enough money to build the house even after we pay his hospital bill. The hospital will settle for a smaller amount than normal because we'll pay in cash. Anyway, I know Aden would have wanted you to have the rest of the money."

"Oh, no," Ella replied, recoiling at the thought. "It's not mine. We weren't married."

"But Aden wanted you to have it." Daniel looked at her, his face intense. "He wanted you to have the land, the money, and the plans. And I could build you the house...if you still want it."

"You? For nothing?" She looked carefully at him.

"No," he said. "Even Aden was going to pay me to help. I can do the work for you the same as I would have for him."

Ella's head spun. "Daniel, I don't know. With Aden gone, I don't know if I'd want to live in it without him. Plus, I'm still single. What business does a single woman have with a house?"

"I have the plans," he said, his face hopeful.

Ella felt herself pull back. She didn't want, without Aden, what would have been theirs together.

"I don't want to see them. Really, I don't," she said forcefully.

"I'm sorry," he stood, his face now fallen. "I'm clumsy like that."

"Don't go yet." She stopped him with a raised hand. "Sit down… please. I'm not blaming you at all. Perhaps it's just a bit too soon. But I am glad you told me about it. Even if the house is never built—I mean—you can sell the land, I'm sure. But it would have felt strange to hear about this down the road, as if you knew somethin' and should have told me."

"*Danki,*" he ventured. "I was just tryin' to do what I thought Aden would have wanted."

She met his eyes and knew he told the truth.

"Then should I just wait?" He stood again to go.

"Perhaps. I don't know, though. Really, I don't. Building a house… me?"

"Aden would have wanted it," he said again with conviction as he turned to leave.

Ella watched him until his feet disappeared up the basement steps. He was so unlike Aden, and yet his heart was right.

The whole idea is so unlikely, but perhaps Daniel has a point. Still, the thought of looking at the plans Aden had drawn up is simply too much to even think about. I can't do it.

Her hand reached for the needle again, and her eyes followed the line of the stitches. On and on they went until they formed the outline of a house, her house, her and Clara's house on the quilt. The thoughts just leaped at her. *Can this happen in real life?* The thought took her breath away with its daring audacity. *I don't know if such a thing is even possible! This is definitely a matter that will simply have to wait.*

Twenty-nine

"So what did Daniel want?" Mamm asked when Ella came upstairs.

"He was telling me about Aden's property," Ella said, not wanting to add any details. Her mom seemed satisfied with the meager answer.

"It's chore time," Mamm told her. "Clara's out in the barn tonight, and remember we have to be leaving early."

"Me too? Do I have to go? I thought you said—" Ella asked, leaning on the kitchen chair with both hands.

"I think you'd better come with us," Mamm said. "I know it will be hard, but if you start avoiding the hard things in life now, life will only get harder."

"Perhaps for just this one time?" Ella asked, searching her mamm's face.

"Please?"

Mamm considered it a minute but then said, "Ella, I'm thinking of you, but I'm also thinking of the grieving family. Your presence there might be a big help to David and the others. If they can see that you have been able to survive, it might give them hope."

"I hadn't thought about that," Ella said.

"I can do three cows tonight," Clara shouted from the living room.

Ella smiled at her sister's newfound confidence, and the two went upstairs to change. Dora passed them on the way down, already changed into her chore clothing.

"What was Daniel here for?" she asked. "He waved to Eli in the guest room but was obviously more interested in you."

"He was telling me about Aden's property," Ella repeated her answer.

"Sounds fishy to me," Dora said.

"He was just bein' Daniel," Ella said.

Dora shrugged, apparently satisfied.

When they had changed and were on their way to the barn, Ella asked Clara how school was going.

"Okay. We're practicing the last day of school program."

"How's Paul?" she asked with a tilted smile.

Clara colored a little, "Teacher gave us—Amanda, Paul, and me—a poem-reading part in the program."

"A nice poem?"

"Yah, Paul stands between the two of us, and we quote it in turns. Katie set it up that way."

As they approached the barn, Ella relished in the familiar smell of the farm. It was so wonderful to return to what was safe, especially after Daniel's visit. *Could I actually dare have my own home without a husband? The idea itself seems impossible, let alone getting the approval from either set of parents!*

Clara finished the first cow in record time, Ella noted with satisfaction. Her milk strokes were still unsteady, but the improvement had come quickly. When Clara finished the second cow before either Dora or she was done with their third, Ella allowed her to start another one. At the end, Ella switched with her and finished.

After choring was finished, supper was served. With their plans for the evening, the meal was rushed and with few words.

"Who'll stay with Eli tonight?" Mamm asked. "Ella's coming with us, after all."

"I will," Monroe spoke up.

"You?" Mamm sounded surprised. "I thought Dora might want to."

Dora shrugged. "Let him. I don't care."

"I'll still hitch up your horse," Monroe said.

"Let's get these dishes off the table, then," Mamm said. "We have to get on the road soon."

"Yah, I'll go get the horses right away," Daett said with a nod. Together he and Monroe got up and left for the barn to ready the two buggies.

"Eli, don't you leave your bed—even with Monroe here." Mamm left her last instruction for Eli, the girls already on the way out the door.

Ella expected Monroe to release their horse when Dora and she had climbed in, but he waited while their mom climbed in the second buggy. This took extra time, Ella knew, and she appreciated the effort. With Eli being so stubborn over this *Englisha* girl, it was good to see maturity in one of her brothers.

When their dad had passed them, Monroe released the bridle, and they were off. Ella gave him a wave of thanks as they went by. The road was fairly open until they got within a mile from the Beachy home. Then the long line of buggies began. At times they came to a complete halt, only to move slowly forward and stop again. Eventually they reached the turnoff and were directed into a field behind the barn to unhitch.

Ella pulled up beside her dad. They both got out of the buggies and began to unhitch the horses.

Dora glanced around quickly. "Looks like some of the others are just tying their horse to the back of the buggies," she told Ella. "Apparently the barn is already full."

Ella looked around and agreed with her. Several horses were already securely fastened to the buggy boxes. She did the same as her dad headed for the barn. He was braver than she was to face the packed barn of horses, but then he was a man.

The two walked across the pasture as fresh waves of pain rushed over Ella at the sight of the yard full of people. Dora noticed her sister's discomfort, reached for her hand, and held it for a moment. Ella wished a thousand times she hadn't come, but that wasn't possible either. Attendance was expected. She only hoped that Mamm was right and that her presence there would give hope to those who felt the loss most.

In the yard the long line of people inched slowly forward. Ella thought it seemed like hours before they reached the living room. Inside the house, the line went into the bedroom and out again. Ella stepped back so she could be the last of her family in line. The furious ache in her chest didn't go away, but she felt safer at the end, as if the position gave her some protection for what lay ahead.

When she reached the casket, Ella forced herself to look. Not to look would seem disrespectful. Inside, her whole body screamed in rebellion. It was too soon for her to have to behold another face in death. The obligation seemed more than should be expected of anyone.

Ella whispered a prayer for strength and stepped forward.

Melissa's face looked peaceful enough. Her head covering had been carefully placed, and she wore her black dress. Ella forgot her hesitation during this moment of grief. Here before her lay a young girl, one whose hopes had been high, her love alive, and all this was taken from the world. The face wasn't Aden, but the result was no different. In death, they were the same. Ella's hands gripped the sides of the box for support, and she let her head fall forward as the sorrow came over her in great waves. Mamm stepped out of the line and came back to stand with her arms around Ella. Tightly she held her daughter until they were able to move forward together and shake hands with the family.

Eventually they stepped up to where the still-recovering David was seated. He stood awkwardly when she approached, and she gripped his hand with both of hers. She wanted to give him a hug and would have if this hadn't been a public place, but even in the presence of death, tradition held firm.

The silence of the room had already been heavy. If possible, it now became greater as the people noticed Ella and David softly weeping in sympathy. Mamm had her arm around Ella, and David's daett soon came and stood with him. Time seemed to stand still. Finally she found the strength to move on.

Mamm led Ella to a bench, and Ella lowered herself down, her knees ready to buckle. Yet for some reason unknown to her, Ella felt strangely comforted, like the great gash in her heart had a few stitches placed across the wound. The thought repelled her, as if it violated Aden's memory, but still Ella knew it was true. In her shared sorrow with another, she had felt a glimmer of wholeness. How that could be, or even should be, she couldn't explain. Perhaps her coming *had* been a good idea. Good for both David and for her too.

The benches behind them filled up, and soon the pressure to make place for others became apparent. Mamm went over, spoke briefly to David's mom, and then moved toward the front door. Ella stood to follow, and Dora did the same. Daett and the girls soon joined them in the yard.

The girls hitched their horse to the buggy while their dad was still in the barn, grappling with how to get his horse out. They waited patiently for him, and not until he had left, did they join the line of buggies driving out of the field. Ella held the reins tightly as they bumped out onto the road.

"So this was the second death," Dora declared. "Part of the series everyone is expectin'."

"I don't think you should bring things like that up," Ella said. "It's not right…in some way."

"What if there is something to it?"

"Then we can't do anything about it."

"One of the girls talked to me just before we left. She thought Eli might have really been the second one, but that he might have been spared."

"I'm really not interested, Dora. I've had 'bout all the pain I can take, and if Eli was spared, then so much the better."

"I still think we should be prepared for the next one."

"We all should be prepared, Dora. Each and every day, we should be. Isn't that what the preachers say?"

"This is different. It's like you have a real warning, something to see with your own eyes. It could even be *me* because it seems to follow the family—Eli, now Melissa, although probably not you. That wouldn't make any sense at all."

"Would you just stop thinking about this? It bothers me," Ella said. Darkness had fallen, and Ella turned on the switch for the buggy's low-beam lights. Her heart thudded when the lights didn't come on.

"The battery must be dead," Dora whispered in horror. "Why isn't it charged up?"

"Probably because Eli usually does it, and Eli's laid up."

"It's a *sign*," Dora whispered. "A *terrible* sign it is. This time it really could be me! Please, God, help me be ready if it's me You're calling."

Ella laughed in spite of her best intentions. "You're just scaring yourself, Dora. Now get the flashlight from under the seat. I know Eli keeps one there."

Dora reached back, banged her hand around for a long moment but came up empty-handed.

"There's nothing there, and it's going to happen. I can *feel* it. Eli always keeps a flashlight around. Oh, Ella, this is how Melissa went! I know you'll live through the accident, but it will be me who dies this time."

"Oh, stop it, Dora! Now you're scaring *me*," Ella said. It was enough to deal with a buggy without lights, let alone a panicked sister.

"Mamm and Daett are ahead of us. Let's catch up," Dora's voice was urgent. "This is just awful."

Ella slapped the lines briskly and urged the horse on. The horse responded, but even around the next bend in the road, she couldn't see the lights of her parents' buggy.

"It's our fate," Dora moaned, "and here comes a car from behind. Oh, Ella, pull over quickly."

Ella responded with a tug on the lines, pulling the buggy to the right. She stopped when the ditch embankment was too steep. Ruts came up on the gravel, and they bounced furiously inside the buggy.

"You'll break a wheel, and then we're gone for sure!" Dora grabbed the left line and jerked back. The horse turned sharply as the car passed only inches from them.

"You're the one who'll get us killed! Now get control of yourself."

"I'm sorry," Dora said, settling into the seat. "Here comes another one."

Lights flashed and bounced over the hill as Ella pulled into the ditch as far as she could safely go. The ruts were almost as bad, but Dora stayed silent this time.

"I don't think I've prayed so hard in a long time." Dora let her breath out slowly and quietly said, "I don't want to die. Please, God!"

"I don't suppose Melissa wanted to die either, but she did," Ella said, surprised to find bitterness rising up in her heart. It wrapped its fingers around her heart, freezing her body like ice. *Not again. Why must these waves of anger and hurt return again and again? Didn't I feel better just minutes ago while sharing David's grief?*

"Daett would say it was *Da Hah*'s will. He called her," Dora said.

"But *why*?" Ella fairly screamed, the coldness in her voice filling the still night air. The horse jumped, ran hard for a few strides, and then slowed again.

Dora's eyes became wide when she heard her sister's outburst. Still Ella went on. "Tell me *why*! Why didn't Melissa and David deserve the right to love, the right to marry, the right to have children, the right to leave someone behind them, and the right to grow old together like others? Does *Da Ha* have something against certain people? Does He just pick this one and that one, saying to one, 'You die' and to the other, 'You live'? Why do you and I have the right to go on with life? Why, Dora? *Why*?"

Dora reached with both hands for the lines. "Do you want me to drive, Ella, because I can?"

"Why should you? I can drive just fine."

"I think I should," Dora said, not taking her hands off the reins.

"Oh, Dora, I'm not trying to kill you," Ella said, guessing Dora's thoughts, her voice now void of emotion.

"I'm not so sure," Dora said, pulling on the lines. "You're way too upset to even think of driving. We should all have known that. You're grieving yet. Why, Ella, you're not even fit to be out of the house."

"I'm *fine.*" Ella pushed Dora's hands away and slapped the reins. She pulled toward the ditch as another set of lights approached. This time there was room enough and fewer ruts to contend with, but Dora froze beside her until the car passed.

"You didn't take the battery out," Dora asked, her voice trembling, "or hide the flashlight?"

"What are you talking about? The battery's just dead."

"You're hurting pretty bad, and we should have known that."

"I wouldn't do such a thing, Dora," Ella said as she carefully pulled up to a stop sign and then turned left.

Dora seemed lost in thought. "I'm not so sure I believe you," she finally ventured. "I just thought of something else."

"Yah, and?" Ella waited. Another set of lights appeared and passed safely before Dora answered.

"Clara told us how you went and jumped in front of that bull. She said it was the bravest thing she had ever seen. But I just thought of something. You were hoping the bull would kill you, weren't you? You wanted to die."

"Well…" Ella paused, searching for the right answer, but she knew from the sound of Dora's sharp breath, her sister wouldn't believe a denial. She said the words anyway, "Not like you're saying it. It was that I wanted to protect Eli. Yah, and in doing so, if I had died…it did seem to be a good thing at the time."

"So you *did* take the battery out?"

"Nee, I didn't do that. And I wouldn't try to kill myself—or you."

"I suppose if someone had been through what you have—had loved as deeply as you did—this would be understandable, yah?"

"I didn't do it," Ella said, her voice firm. "It's against the will of *Da*

Hah. He doesn't welcome into heaven those who take their own life. Remember, I do want to be with Aden again."

"You know, I'm going to ask Eli."

"That's fine." Ella smiled in the darkness. "I don't know what he'll say, but I didn't take the battery out."

When they arrived home, Dora helped unhitch and then made a beeline for the guest bedroom. Ella saw her in conversation with Eli when she came inside.

"Well?" she asked when Dora came out of the bedroom.

"Eli said he took it out to charge it before he was injured." Dora smiled weakly. "But you sure had me worried." She awkwardly reached out to hug her sister.

"I'm glad you cared," Ella said as they clung to each other.

Thirty

The house was silent. Eli lay asleep in the guest bedroom. Ella thought of work that could be done, but with the rest of the family at the funeral, the idea of working didn't seem to fit the day. It was as if this day was like an additional Sabbath—sacred to those who had to bury their loved one.

Ella checked on Eli again and then went downstairs to work on the wedding quilt.

With a cloudless sky outside, she didn't need a lamp to work on the stitching. As the needle moved smoothly in her hand, thoughts of Daniel's visit came to her, faint but persistent. In many ways, she couldn't believe he had been here—right here by the quilt.

A house for me without Aden—it was an impossible notion. Yet Clara's drawing of the house lay before her, almost speaking to her. Thoughts she hadn't expected began to rise up; thoughts of hope, of a future, and of a way to go on with life. The half-penciled house now seemed as if brought to life by Daniel's words.

Her thoughts were interrupted by a distinct knock upstairs on the front door. Someone had arrived, perhaps a tourist or someone who thought they had a shop in the house. Even though no sign was in the yard, people stopped in every once in a while.

Ella quickly went upstairs, her feet noiseless on the basement stairs. She glanced in Eli's room before she answered the door. Eli was still asleep. She then peeked through the front window to see who was at the door. A woman Ella didn't recognize stood at the door, and then she knew. For a quick moment, she almost decided to pretend no one was at home. But in good conscience, she couldn't do that. It would somehow be wrong.

Ella opened the door, and the woman smiled and asked, "Is this the Yoder residence where Eli Yoder lives?"

Ella nodded. She had guessed right. Eli's *Englisha* nurse had come.

"I'm Pam Northrup. I was Eli's nurse at the hospital, and I told him I'd be by to see how he's doing." Ella had to admit Eli was right. She did have a distinct plain appearance, though clearly not Amish.

"Yah," Ella managed, "this is where he lives."

"How's he doing?"

"About the same," Ella said, considering how she might deny the woman entrance and tell her she was not welcome. Instead she opened the door and forced a smile. "He was asleep when I last looked in."

"I'll just peek in on him," Pam said quite confidently as if she visited Amish patients all the time.

Eli must have heard them approach because when they entered, he was propped up on his pillows, smiling his boyish grin from ear to ear.

"Hi," he said, extending one hand awkwardly while using the other to smooth down his tousled hair.

"Hi to you," Pam said, taking his offered hand and then his wrist as she calculated his pulse. When she finished, she asked, "How are you feeling?"

"I ran a fever the first night home. Nothin' serious, I'm thinkin'. Mamm took good care of me."

"Are you taking the antibiotics the doctor gave you?"

Eli nodded.

"You should be okay, then, but I bet those ribs still hurt."

"Of course," Eli said with a grin.

"Is this your sister?"

"Yes. I'm sorry, I should have introduced you," he said. "The rest of the family is at a funeral."

As Pam turned to shake hands with Ella, Eli made a quick face and motion, which Ella easily interpreted as Eli wanting her to leave them alone.

Anger rose in her at his success in arranging this visit without their mom's presence. Mamm would know what to do, but she wasn't here. In her place, Ella decided she would deal with Eli later. There was no sense in a scene now, and she didn't like scenes anyway.

"I'll leave you," she said, managing another smile as she backed out of the bedroom but leaving the door cracked open. That was one compromise she wouldn't make. The soft murmur of their voices rose and fell, and she paced the kitchen floor for thirty minutes before Eli called for her.

"Pam's ready to leave," he said with a weak smile.

"You behave now," Pam said to Eli, "and take care of yourself."

Ella led the way to the front door and held it open for her.

"You have a good day," the girl said and turned to wave at the bottom of the porch steps.

"You too," Ella offered. She waited until Pam got in her car, waved again, and backed out of the driveway. She was a nice girl—but *Englisha.*

Ella marched straight to Eli's bedroom. At the moment she didn't care if he was sick or not. "How dare you!" she demanded. "What would have happened if Mamm had been at home?"

"Thankfully she wasn't," he said, wearing his boyish grin, "but it would have looked like a nurse on a visit."

"Have you totally lost your mind? She's an *Englisha* girl, Eli. Can't you see that?"

"Doesn't she look kind of plain?" he countered.

"Maybe a little, but it makes no difference. She's not one of us. She never will be. They live in their own world. They can't just come to ours like that, and they never do. You know that, and you're certainly not

going to hers. You're too decent for that, Eli. You've never been wild.
You're a *gut* boy. You've all kinds of chances with our own girls. I could
name three nice Amish girls right now who would love some attention
from you. With those kinds of doors open, what's wrong with you?"

Eli stared at her, his smile frozen in place under the attack. "Relax.
She won't be stoppin' in again. I told her today not to come again."

"But you will go to her, won't you? Eli, don't you know you can't see
her again. Not just here, but anywhere. If this comes out, even a whisper of it, it would take you years to live it down. And the other girls
would quickly forget you and fly into the arms of the other boys."

"Ella, don't you believe in love," Eli asked, "and that it comes just
once in a lifetime?"

"Where on earth did you hear something like that?" she demanded.
"Have you been reading love stories or something? Those *Englisha*
books from the library? Where, Eli?"

Eli grinned knowingly. "Not from books, Ella…from watching
you and Aden."

His words froze her.

"Aden and me?"

"Yah, you had that kind of love. It just happened that you were both
Amish. How can I know it won't be the same for me?"

"That's different, and you know it," Ella said, gasping.

"I love the girl," he said. "So, yah, I might see her after I'm well
again."

"Love," she said slowly in search of words. "How can you tell so
quickly? It doesn't come all at once, at least ours didn't." Her face softened. "I guess I don't know how you feel, or how she feels. But she's
Englisha, Eli. You must be careful. Can you be thinking of marrying
her? What will this mean? Will she come your way? Rarely does anyone come to our faith from the outside. Think about that, yah? And I
just can't see you goin' her way. Would you?"

He shook his head.

Ella was surprised how easily her anger had been tempered by Eli
pointing to her and Aden as examples of being in love. "You must

be wise, Eli," she said. "Really wise even if you think this is love. The kind Aden and I had, I just can't imagine this can happen with an *Englisha* girl. But don't tell anyone of this, not till you're certain. It will be an awful thing to break Mamm and Daett's heart with such news. It could almost tear them apart. I guess only you can know whether that's worth it. Can you really be loving someone and losin' what you now love so much? That's a hard question, I know. But I'm afraid neither of us may be wise enough to find the answer. At least not me. So what will you do now, Eli?"

"She left me her phone number, and I can call from the pay phone—once I'm well."

"Then I suppose you must do what you think is right, but there will be much sorrow, Eli, when Mamm and Daett find this out."

"You won't tell them?"

"No, but you will have to eventually if anything comes of this."

"I will tell them when I'm certain." He settled back down on the bed, his face weary.

"You'd best sleep now. Do you want somethin' to eat first?"

"Later," he said.

Ella left him to work on her quilt again.

A little after noon, she made him a sandwich. He looked pale and offered no further comments about the girl's visit. With a shudder she thought of what would happen if Eli did indeed love this girl, Pam. There would be many tears and great sorrow in the Yoder house. It would be even worse than the bull attack. A fear would grip them. It would be more than what they felt when they thought Eli had been fatally injured.

Life is a burden too difficult for a human to carry, she thought. *Only God can help. I doubt silence about the girl's visit is the correct choice, but I gave him my word. Perhaps Daett can persuade Eli better than I was able to. I will say nothing.*

She wondered if she should try harder to persuade Eli to reconsider, but she knew it would be best to allow him to find his own way. If pressure were brought to bear too soon, it might push him further away. Eli was like that—stubborn. Fervently she prayed, hoping she had made the right decision.

After the others came home from the funeral and chores and supper were completed, Ella went upstairs and got her tablet out. She wrote to calm her mind.

> I write this down carefully, but I must write it. If I don't tell someone, it feels as if I will explode. My brother Eli has gotten the most foolish thing in his mind. He thinks he loves an Englisha girl.
>
> I'm afraid that in the terror of the moment, I was way too hard on him—especially after he said such nice things about Aden and me. I had no idea he felt we were such an inspiration. The knowledge breaks my heart all over again, if that were possible.
>
> I pray that God will help us all. There was another funeral today, and I know there is fear around that this is not the end. All of this make no sense to me, but then neither did Aden's death. Perhaps God has a reason for it all. I hope so. It sure costs a lot on our end. I suppose He somehow takes that all into account. But then perhaps I am just trying to make sense again.
>
> Please help us, dear God. We really need it.

Thirty-one

Eli's body became stronger each day, but as the weeks wore on, he still required attention. Ella's willingness to care for him provided the excuse she needed to avoid the youth gatherings.

In church on Sundays, Ella easily avoided any eye contact with boys. A proper period of mourning would be respected but might end sooner than she wanted it to. Avoiding contact was the best insurance against any young man misunderstanding.

One morning as Eli made his way gingerly to the breakfast table, he said, "I'm attending the school picnic."

"You're not ready yet," Mamm said.

"I'll sit in a chair in the yard, but I'm goin'," he said. "I've recovered enough for that."

"But why?" Mamm asked. "It's just another day, and you've been there before."

"I'm tired of the house," he declared, "and I'm goin' if I have to crawl down the hill to get there."

There was no persuading him otherwise. Ella saw the stubborn look on his face, but she was suspicious of his motives. That evening during kitchen duty, she confronted him.

"You're up to somethin', Eli. I know it."

"I just want to attend the school picnic." he said. "I don't need any other motive."

Ella considered this, but as she sliced the celery for the evening soup, she figured it out. Glancing at the clock, she decided she had time and went directly to the bedroom.

"I know what you're up to," she declared. "It's your first chance to be usin' the pay phone. You plan to call that girl."

"Shhh." he whispered, his face giving him away.

"Why are you doin' this to us, Eli? I thought you might give up the idea."

"I can't." He hung his head. "I can't get Pam out of my mind. It's love—I know it. It's the kind you and Aden had."

The look on his face touched her, and she softened.

"Please! Don't tell Mamm and Daett," he pleaded.

"I'll not betray my convictions," Ella declared.

"I'm not askin' that," he said, and then with a grin, he added, "I'm not askin' you to date an *Englisha* man."

"Don't be jokin' about this, Eli. It's serious."

"Yah." He sobered up. "It is serious. I don't want to miss my chance at love, a love that will last a lifetime."

"I don't think you'll find it with an *Englisha* woman." Ella sighed and then felt the bitterness rise again. "I found love, and then *Da Hah* took it away."

"I'm sorry," he said and reached out to touch her hand. "I wish there was somethin' I could do."

"There is nothing." She turned her head away. "I can't go around blaming *Da Hah* for it. I know that. I just never thought it would be this hard."

"I'll never understand how you do that…or show such kindness to me—most sisters wouldn't understand their brothers like this, especially if they sneak around and see *Englisha* girls."

"You're wrong about that, Eli. I don't understand you," she said. "I don't think I ever will."

"But you are patient," he said, his voice low. "Ella, do you really think I'm wrong to love someone like Pam?"

She wavered as she faced that question and the pleading look in Eli's eyes. Ella felt the worlds collide inside of her. She had no answer, and its absence frightened her.

"What's wrong with me?" she asked, her face a contortion of conflicts. "I suddenly don't know."

"Dear God," he whispered. "You really don't know. Then I'm right!"

Ella caught herself, but the damage had been done. "Of course it's wrong. It can't be right."

"There was a part of me that hoped you'd know for sure," Eli said, "but you don't, and now I know I have to call her. I have to find out for myself. Ella, I don't want to lose what I have. I love our family. I was never plannin' to leave the Amish. And I hope it never happens. It's like you said—I'm not wild as some are. I'm easy. And yet I find a happiness in Pam's eyes that's unlike any I've experienced with our own girls. I can't turn back now, Ella. Not till I know for sure. Can you be understandin' that?"

"No, I don't think I can," Ella said, "but I guess you'll have to find your own way through this. I just hope you don't do the wrong thing."

"Thanks." Eli squeezed her hand.

"My supper," Ella gasped and raced for the kitchen.

When Mamm and Dora came in from the barn, she was late with the mashed potatoes. Her mom looked at her strangely. "Is something wrong? You're never late like this."

"I was talking to Eli," she said, managing a smile, "and time got away from me."

Mamm went toward the bedroom and quietly asked Eli something Ella couldn't hear. Apparently the answer was satisfactory because nothing more was said about the uncharacteristically late supper.

They had just had prayer when a buggy pulled in and tied up at the hitching post by the barn.

"He must plan to stay," Noah said dryly. "I wonder who it is."

"Not more bad news surely," Mamm said, getting to her feet.

"It's the third death. I know it is," Dora spoke up, her voice mournful. "At least this awful dreading will be over, then."

"Would you quit this moanin' and carryin' on?" Mamm said as she headed for the front door.

They all heard the front door open and then shut as if whoever it was wished to speak outside on the porch. Long minutes went by, no one speaking, just waiting.

"No one has died," Clara said. "If it was that, Mamm would already be back in by now."

"You can never be certain," Dora said. "She might be in tears, depending on who it is. It would take time to recover."

"No one has died," Noah said firmly. "*Da Hah* is a merciful God, and He does not give us more than we can be handlin'."

The sound of the basement door swinging open beneath them reached the kitchen table. Dora looked at Ella with the strangest expression on her face but said nothing. Moments passed with the sound of faint noises in the basement. First they listened to the murmur of voices, and then they heard their mom's footsteps on the stairs. She opened the door and joined them at the table again, all without a word. Her face bore no hint of expression.

"Well…who was it?" Daett asked. "And why did you take him to the basement?"

"Shhh, not so loud," Mamm said. "I'll talk to you after we finish supper."

"So no one has died," Dora asked as if she were disappointed. "This thing just goes on and on."

"I told you to stop that," Mamm told her.

Dora apparently hadn't run out of ideas. "It's Deacon Shetler come callin'. Monroe must have done somethin', and he's waitin' in the basement for him. Eli couldn't have done anything because he's laid up, and it's not Saturday night so it must be something awful to be in this big of hurry."

From how white Monroe's face turned, Ella considered Dora's guess might have hit the bull's-eye.

"So what did you do?" Ella asked.

"I didn't do anything," he said.

Ella thought his face was still white, but a weariness came over her at the thought that another of her brothers was up to no *gut*. "Can't boys ever behave themselves?" she asked.

Monroe's mouth was open, but Mamm spoke first, "It's not the deacon."

There was silence for a few minutes, and then Dora asked the obvious, "So what was Monroe so scared about?"

"He did look kind of startled," Noah agreed. "Perhaps he'd better tell us. Why were you afraid of a visit from the deacon?"

Monroe shook his head but offered nothing.

"You'd best tell us," Ella told him in her lecture tone.

"I think you should tell us," Daett said.

"Here?" Monroe croaked.

Daett nodded. "We should always be sure our sins come out. It might be time to practice now. It might keep you from committing these wrongs in the future."

Horrible confessions flashed in Ella's mind—visits by girlfriend nurses, secret phone calls to *Englisha* girls, and scandal and disgrace. All would be horrible things to spill into her three little sisters' ears. "Don't be sayin' it here," she blurted out.

"You know what this is about?" Daett asked, his spoon now set on the table, concern on his face.

"Oh, no," Ella gasped, "of course not."

"She doesn't," Monroe spoke up in her defense. "It just happened a few days ago while Ella was at home. I'm sure no one else heard about it. Deacon would be first to know, and he'd come to me—not spread it around. That's why I thought he was here."

"So why don't you tell us," Mamm said, "this thing you did, which the deacon but not your parents knows about."

Monroe took a deep breath. "It's really nothin' much. We took off from town the other day when Daett sent me in for a part at the hardware. Roman, the deacon's son, was there ahead of me in his buggy when we left town. Well, on that straight stretch of road when no car was coming, I tried to pass him. I don't how it happened, but I got into his wheel spokes. When I turned too sharply, I caught just the edge of my wheel. It knocked out three of Roman's spokes and marked the rest up a bit."

"Do you know how dangerous that was?" Mamm said. "You could both have been hurt badly."

"Not to mention damage to the buggies," Daett added, "and the horses. What if traffic had been heavy? Two Amish boys racing down the state road would have caused quite a scandal!"

"I thought of all that…afterward," Monroe said, hanging his head. "Roman said he would try to fix the buggy down at the blacksmith shop with his own money, and I'd pay half too. We thought we could straighten things out that way."

"Things will be straightened out when you boys stop actin' like that," Daett said. "We'll talk about this later, and I think you should pay all of the damages."

"Yah, Daett." Monroe nodded. His relief at apparently getting off easy showed on his face.

"Now who's downstairs in the basement?" Daett asked.

Mamm got up from her chair. "I think you and I are needin' a talk—in the bedroom."

Daett glanced up at Mamm, stood, and followed her without a word.

Thirty-two

"What was that all about?" Dora asked when their parents had disappeared in the direction of the bedroom.

"I'm sure glad it wasn't about my sins," Monroe said with a sigh of relief.

Ella felt a great fear creep over her. She put a hand to her head as the plates on the table went around and around in little circles in front of her eyes.

"Are you okay?" Dora's voice reached her faintly through the fog.

Ella had no idea what she said, if anything.

"She's knows who's down there," Dora whispered to Monroe. "Who in the world could it be?"

"I don't know," Ella croaked in protest and then cleared her voice. "I really don't."

"Then why are you acting so strangely?" Dora asked.

Ella didn't answer. Out of the corner of her eyes, she noticed Dora and Monroe look at each other.

"What are Mamm and Daett doin'?" Clara asked, entering the exchange.

"They're talking about something," Ella said. If the topic was what she suspected, then Clara would be the last person who needed to know. Her world had already been upset enough by recent events.

Mamm appeared in the kitchen doorway. "Ella," she said, "come in for a minute."

Ella felt the fear return as she slowly rose and walked toward the bedroom. She felt Dora and Monroe watching her all the way to the doorway.

Ella didn't dare ask her mother what she feared. She just meekly followed. There seemed nothing else to do. Her mom held the bedroom door open and shut it behind her. Even then her parents still spoke in whispers.

"It's Wayne Miller," her mom said, "young Bishop Miller, and he's come to ask for your hand in marriage."

Ella gasped and then shook her head silently. She knew who Bishop Miller was, and it was out of the question. But Daett slowly raised his hand to stop her protestation. "I can understand how you must feel, but you must not be hasty. I know little time has passed since Aden's death, yet you must consider what a privilege this is. Never has this been offered to any of our women before. He's just a young man who's never dated much. He's a good farmer and a brilliant thinker. Many say he knows half the Anabaptist stories in the *Martyrs Mirror* by memory, never married, and yet ordained a full minister at age twenty-five. Such opportunities don't just happen to anyone, Ella. Wayne Miller is quite an exceptional man."

"I can't," Ella choked.

"But think," her dad said, his eyes pleading with her, "what an honor this is. Word has it that he has never seriously considered any of our girls to be the right one for him. He is a man uncommon amongst our people. For the girl who is asked to be his wife, I can't imagine any greater hopes one could have."

"But I loved Aden," she said, trying again, "and I don't want to be marryin' anyone."

"I understand that," her mom spoke up. "It's a little early for you, and we know that. It's why we're tryin' to help out. Ach, why didn't the man know to wait a while yet if he's supposed to be so smart?"

"Sometimes men are *clumsy* in the ways of the heart," Daett mumbled.

"You can say that again," her mom said and then lowered her voice. "It's just that you shouldn't be hasty, Ella. Tell him you need some time to think about this—maybe six months. He'll understand that. He's a *gut* man. You don't want to make a quick decision right now, especially while you're still grieving like you are. Don't go making a choice you might be regrettin' years later. Really, Ella, you have to think about this. You can't run away from men forever."

When Ella remained silent, her mother began again.

"Some girls could possibly just shut themselves away like you have the last few weeks and never move on with their lives. We understand how you feel, Ella, but you can't shut out life forever. *Da Hah* took Aden away from you for reasons we don't understand, but we must accept His will. You can't stay single, Ella. You simply can't."

No, they don't understand. Not really. Ella's heart was numb with how alone this conversation made her feel. *I'm all alone against the world— even my own family does not stand with me.*

Her mother spoke again, "You'll never get a better offer than Bishop Miller. You really won't, Ella. Your daett and I are here to tell you what must be very hard for you to hear."

Ella swallowed hard. Her worst nightmare had not just come as a dream but was playing out right before her eyes. *What am I to do? Give in to my parents...and Bishop Miller? Forget Aden forever?* She knew she couldn't blame her parents for being concerned about her welfare. She couldn't stay shut up forever, and she couldn't keep saying no forever. Her honor, her faith, and her love for her parents demanded it. Every exit where she cast her eyes for escape was shut off. Only her will and determination stood in the way, but would it be enough?

"I will speak with him then," she relented, her voice a bare whisper.

"I'm so sorry for you." Her mom wrapped her in her arms. When she let go, Ella saw tears in her eyes. "I wouldn't have chosen this path for you in a thousand years, I wouldn't have. Yet *Da Hah* has seen fit to have you walk it. Why? I don't know. It must be because you are so loved. You are a wonderful girl, Ella. You'll be a great woman of our people. I know Aden was the best for you. Bishop Miller is perhaps *Da Hah's* answer to your loneliness."

"I'm not promisin' to marry him," Ella whispered.

"No," her mom replied as she shook her head, "just tell him you need time. Just time, and *Da Hah* will do the rest."

Ella found the doorknob of the bedroom, the steel cold to the touch. With great effort, she forced her feet to move toward the front door. She still had enough presence of mind to avoid the kitchen—and Dora and Monroe's questioning eyes. Better to go around to the outside basement door.

Each step felt like a descent into destruction. The familiar concrete took on sinister forms, and the hardness under her shoes sent shocks upward through her entire body. She pulled her head covering forward and tightened the strings before she opened the basement door.

Her eyes searched for a form in the flickering display of light and shadows from the kerosene lamp. Bishop Wayne Miller had already risen from the chair beside her quilt. He stood, motioned with his hand toward a chair beside him, and nodded in greeting.

"*Gut* evening," he said. "*Da Hah* has given us beautiful weather. I hope I haven't disturbed your supper."

Ella shook her head while her feet somehow found the energy to move forward. She wondered where the bishop had found the other chair. For some reason she couldn't remember it having been there the last time she quilted. But then, perhaps Clara had brought the chair down. She sat down only inches from the bishop's knees and noticed that her hands were trembling.

He cleared his throat and began speaking. "I wish to express my deepest sympathies for your loss...first of all. I didn't come to the funeral because I expected the gathering to be quite large, and Aden wasn't from my district. Yet I knew of Aden. He was a man of firm faith, a man who loved his heritage and would have been an asset to any of our districts. I regret I never got to know him better."

Ella kept her eyes on the floor. She had seen what she wanted to see for the moment. The bishop had come in his Sunday best, which meant he took this seriously. His voice was gentle enough, soft almost, and not unpleasant.

He seems sincere, and he certainly is handsome. She could tell that even in the low light of the kerosene lamp. *His young face, weathered by outdoor work, is framed by his lengthy, well-kept beard. He does not have a pound of fat on his tall frame. I understand why people are in awe of the man. His presence quite fills this room.* These thoughts all seemed like terrible things to think and made her feel awful disloyal to Aden. Yet the thoughts came unbidden.

"I suppose you're wonderin' why I've come so soon after the tragedy. And I know it is soon. I told your mamm so. Yet I have searched my heart, and I could not wait. *Da Hah* moves in mysterious ways, Ella, in ways we cannot understand sometimes. I do not wish you to think of me as untoward or out of order. With this thought in mind, I won't pressure you or rush you, but I do want to make my interest known, yah, my interest in your future attention. It is my hope that, perhaps with time, you might become my wife. I know this must come as a great shock since you hardly know me. I can understand that, and I can have patience. It's just that I wanted to approach you before it's too late. I never could forgive myself, Ella, if I failed to speak with you and some other man expressed his interest first. I hope you understand that. I say that not to disrespect you or your love for Aden—I know it must have been great—yet *Da Hah* is the one who works the hearts. He can turn them in any direction He wishes."

Ella could barely listen. She wanted nothing more than to be upstairs sitting at the table with Dora, Monroe, and Clara. Still, the bishop went on.

"Even after great tragedy, He can heal hearts and turn them where He wishes. I want to tell you, Ella, *Da Hah* has already turned my heart toward you. I have never thought of another woman like I have thought of you these last weeks. A great love has been forming in my heart for you, a love like I've never had for a girl before. I tell you that not to hurt you or to take away from how Aden loved you. I would never do that. I hope you understand my heart. The same God who created Aden's love for you has created my love for you. And, in time, perhaps you too can learn to love me. I am willing to wait, Ella, as long as you wish if you will just consider my words seriously."

Ella searched for words that wouldn't come. Finally, she raised her eyes to his, noticing for the first time that they were blue…and full of kindness. Yet behind them was power, strong church power of the kind that caused her to tremble on her chair.

"I'm sorry if I have frightened you," he said when she didn't speak. "I didn't mean to. This has all been so sudden, perhaps."

"Yah, it has," Ella said, her voice shaking. "I loved Aden greatly, and I really don't feel right talking about this so soon. I buried him not that long ago."

He smiled gently. "You have a tender heart, and so loyal. This only increases my love for you, Ella. I have no way to tell you how much your answers please me. Any woman who didn't feel what you feel and answered as you answered, after such a loss, would not be worthy of my love. Yet *Da Hah* has time, which He uses to heal so many things. I believe with all my heart yours will be healed. When it is, I wish you to know of my love. Can you understand that?"

Ella wasn't certain she understood, but she nodded.

"Then perhaps we can speak of this again when some time has passed and when you've healed some more and have considered my proposal. Perhaps six months? I know that seems like a long time, but it will pass quickly. At the end of that time, would you consider then whether your heart is prepared to love again? I would consider it an honor if at that time you would speak with me. I will come to you, and we will speak again."

Ella's mind raced, but there seemed no other possible answer, and so she nodded again. Perhaps, she decided, between now and then she would find the strength to say no. Now, the strength simply wasn't there.

"It is agreed, then," he said as if he closed a church matter properly decided in his favor. "I will come again at that time." Then he got up, touched her arm lightly, and walked out. The basement door closed behind him, and the lights of his buggy soon went past the window. Ella sat frozen, unable to move, until her mom's footsteps could be heard coming down the wooden basement stairs.

Thirty-three

Mamm approached Ella and laid her hand gently on her shoulder. "Are you okay?"

"I don't rightly know," Ella said

"You didn't send him away for *gut,* did you?"

"Nee, he suggested waiting six months, and I agreed."

"Then he's a wise man, yah?"

"I don't want to marry him," Ella said, her voice firm now.

"You don't have to. But it's wise to wait until later when you can think more clearly."

"But you and Daett want me to marry him."

"Yah, we do, and I don't think you could go wrong with Wayne. But that will be for you to decide all in its good time, of course. I'm just glad you didn't send him away for *gut.* The decision doesn't have to be made tonight. It can be made in six months. By then things might look different. Really, Ella, outside of Aden, I don't think a better match for you could ever be found. Bishop would make a *gut* husband, as *gut* as you can do now."

"I'm not going to marry," Ella said.

"Now, now, don't think about it, at least not tonight or even in the days ahead. Let's go on with your life. *Da Hah* will move in your heart as He sees fit." Her mom took her hand and helped her stand.

"Is the kitchen work done yet?" Ella asked.

"Dora and Clara are about done, and I can help them. You best go up to your room for the night. It's been a hard evening for you. Just remember that *Da Hah* has His own plans for your life, and all we can do is submit to them."

"Do they know who was here?"

"Yah, we told them, and they understand."

"I feel ashamed," Ella said, a deep blush spreading over her face. "It's as if this is all my fault."

"It's the way of men and women." Her mom grasped her arm. "It's *Da Hah*'s doin', so there's nothing to be ashamed of. Even in your pain, you must not forget that. This is a great honor, the young Bishop Miller himself—here so soon—to seek your hand in marriage. You must not let your eyes be blinded, Ella. Many, so many of our girls, they would consider this a *gut, gut* thing."

"Then I'm not one of them."

"Ach, that's why you need time—time to be healin', to think, and to see the ways of *Da Hah*. Come now, a good night's sleep will do you wonders. Get some sleep. Our day's work is full tomorrow, as always."

Ella followed her mom upstairs. Dora, soapsuds on her elbows, caught her eye from the kitchen sink. She smiled a weak, sympathetic smile, and Ella squeezed back the tears.

Daett stood when she came into the living room. He came over to take both her hands in his. "This is hard on you," he said in earnest. "My heart is hurting for you tonight. I wish you could have been spared, but so soon it has come. No matter how much we wish it otherwise, it simply was not to be. Perhaps we can help you bear this burden in some way. This sorrow of yours, I wish we could…"

Ella could only nod.

"You did decide to wait for some time?" Daett asked.

Ella whispered, "Yah." It would have broken his heart if she hadn't. But in another six months, his heart will be broken anyway. The impossibility of the situation was so complete, so undoable whichever way she turned.

"It has been too much already," Mamm said from behind them. "She should rest for the night."

"You shouldn't have been asked to bear so much," Daett conceded, "but you have also been offered a great honor. That is how *Da Hah* works. He gives and He takes away. We will pray for your strength to return."

Ella gathered herself together and found the knob to the upstairs door even though her eyes were blinded by tears. In the comfort of her own room, she lay on the bed and sobbed till exhaustion came.

Dora woke her when she tiptoed in the room. With darkness outside the window, Ella knew she had been asleep for some time.

"I just thought I should be checkin' on you," Dora whispered. "You're still dressed. Here, I'll help you get in bed."

"I'm not a *bobli* anymore," Ella said, but Dora wouldn't take no for an answer. Dora wouldn't consider leaving until Ella was undressed and tucked under the covers.

Seated on the bed, Dora held her hand until Ella laughed. "Now you make me feel like a real *bobli*."

"You are one—right now at least. And I'm going to take *gut* care of you, poor little girl. What a rough time you've been havin'."

"Don't make me cry all over again." Ella propped herself up on the pillow.

"He really asked to marry you?" Dora's eyes were wide in the starlight.

"Not in that many words. He would have if I'd acted open, so he just wants time. He wants me to wait for a spell."

"Then he came just in case someone else comes with that same interest?"

"Somethin' like that."

"Bishop Wayne actually said that?"

"Yah."

"My, you have a chance to be a bishop's wife, and not just any bishop—Bishop Wayne Miller. My sister will walk with the great man of the church. Can you imagine that, Ella? Your children will be the mighty people in the land. No one will be able to punish you for anything you do."

"You have fallen sick," Ella said. "My own sister is betraying me in my own bedroom. I'm not going to marry him."

Dora laughed, "Sorry, I guess I got a little carried away. But you will forgive me, I know you will."

"Yah, I already did," Ella said, knowing her words had fallen on deaf ears. Dora's mouth was wide open, a look of pure delight on her face.

"Oh, *lieber Gott im himmel.* Is this not something? I know it's hard for you to see, especially right now, but believe me! Mamm and Daett are right. This could not be a better turn of things. It was terrible that Aden passed away, but this is a sign *Da Hah* has not forgotten you. Oh, Ella, just wait, and you will see it. I know you will. Before many days have passed away, you will surely see it."

"So where's your usual gloom and doom?" Ella asked. "No troubles ahead, have we? No clouds with thunder and lightning? Can't you understand this? I'm not going to marry anyone."

"Oh, Ella," Dora said, moving closer and grabbing her arm. "There's not a cloud in this sky. But you are so wonderful and so loyal, and that makes this so much the better. If you could see what we see, but you can't right now, and that's okay. Time will bring this all out for the best."

"What if it doesn't? What if I refuse in, say, the six months the bishop has set?"

Dora shuddered. "I guess Mamm and Daett wouldn't understand, and I don't know that I will."

"Don't you think we ought to sleep?" Ella was weary of the conversation. She felt shaken but not enough to change her mind. A solid night's sleep might help restore her resolve. Apparently she would need all she could get in the days ahead.

"I suppose so," Dora said, getting up to go and shutting the door gently behind her.

Ella laid back and tried to nod off again, but sleep had fled. Her future stared her in the face. Her parents wouldn't force her into any marriage, but they would be troubled, and concerned if she refused the bishop. They would be heartbroken if she rejected what they considered such a blessing from *Da Hah*.

In desperation, she lit the kerosene lamp, put on her heavy housecoat, and found her way downstairs. Even with the usual squeaks on the steps, no one seemed roused from their slumber. She carefully opened the basement stair door and made her way downstairs as the quilt drew her. Whether it was the memory of Aden or its connection to him, she didn't know. The need to quilt, to run the needle through the cloth, to make beauty out of the mundane gripped her. Perhaps comfort and sleep could be found in action.

With the lamp lit and set close by and her hands busy, she let her thoughts run over her possible future. *Should I allow myself to become the wife of Bishop Miller?* Her stomach churned at the thought. She told herself to remember what had been said all night about the need to wait, but would that really make it any better?

My decision will not be any different in six months than it is now. Aden's love was real, and I won't settle for anything less than that. There was but one Aden, and one love we shared. That life could produce another such love seems unlikely—it certainly didn't come with the Bishop's visit.

Her body weary, her mind distraught, the thought that came to her didn't register at first. But then Ella paused in amazement, dropping her needle and slowly running her fingers over the quilted outline. "That would make sense," she whispered. *So is this my answer? Do I really dare...have my own house? I wouldn't hurt Mamm and Daett, then, at least not as much. And they wouldn't feel as responsible if I was out of the house.*

Her mind ran back and forth over the idea until she was satisfied. The last reason, which made the whole thing fall in place, was Eli. In a wild flight of fancy, she imagined the romance between Eli and the *Englisha* girl discovered and Eli forced away. He certainly couldn't stay at home for very long, and she could give him shelter with her own house.

But is Daniel really serious about the house? The question raced through her mind. *Yes, he is surely serious.* Now that the solution was so obvious, she was gripped by the fear that it might be taken away from her like Aden had been.

"Dear *Gott*," she prayed, "have mercy on me. Let Daniel mean what he said. Surely You wouldn't break my heart all over again. Please remember me."

Feeling comforted and having hope that sleep would now come, she took the lamp and went upstairs. Apparently her mom had heard something because she came out of the bedroom.

"I'm going back to bed," Ella whispered. "I couldn't sleep."

"What were you doing?"

"Quilting just a little bit."

Mamm nodded. "Good night, then, and sleep good."

Ella managed a smile and shut the stair door behind her. In bed, excitement ran through her and prevented her sought-after sleep. *There is so much to be done! I have to speak with Daniel as soon as possible. Is there time yet? Six months seems like enough, but is it? Winter is just ahead, and the house will have to be completed before the Bishop calls again.*

Downstairs the clock struck one o'clock, and then Ella remembered nothing else until Dora knocked loudly on the door.

Thirty-four

Whether it was because she just felt better or because she had found a way out of her bishop dilemma, Ella wasn't certain. Whatever it was, Ella surprised herself on Friday night.

"I'm going along," she announced.

"You're comin' to the youth gathering at widow Miller's?" Dora asked in surprise.

"Yah," Ella said without any hesitation. "Eli still needs looking after, but Mamm can handle him."

Dora looked at her strangely but decided to leave well enough alone.

Ella helped with the chores, milking extra fast. They were done early. Supper was eaten quickly, and Ella sat in the cramped middle of the buggy seat with Monroe at the reins. Once Eli was well again, they would go back to their routine of taking two buggies. For now, the ride had to be what it was. Amish frugality demanded the choice. Two buggies for three people would be extravagant.

Ella hadn't yet mentioned her house plans to anyone. She had high hopes Daniel would be at the gathering tonight. Such an event usually brought out a fair-sized crowd. The garden planting for the widow Esther Miller should be attended by the youth from several districts.

Her eight children could have put her garden in, but the fun was greater this way. The work would give the youth a reason to socialize and a break from volleyball games.

Monroe pulled into the driveway, and Ella noticed several boys were already out with hoes, hard at work. From the looks of things, they planned to form the beds by hand. Three girls with plants in their hands waited for the completion of the first row. Esther was in the garden, her hands waving around wildly, giving instructions on where she wanted things planted.

Behind them a line of buggies dotted the road. Ella jumped down, shook the wrinkles out of her dress, and took a deep breath. This was her first youth gathering since the funeral. From the beat of her heart, she knew this wouldn't be the easiest thing to do. Yet her heart felt comfort and purpose in the evening. It would not be wasted. She was here to talk with Daniel. *Is this how time goes on and how life begins again after having been torn apart? Does it start with an unexpected reason and a sudden purpose such as this?*

Ella removed the hoes from the back of the buggy as Dora stepped down. Monroe barely gave Dora time to clear the wheel before he pulled forward with a jerk. Dora stuck her tongue out at the back of the buggy, which brought an unexpected but welcome laugh from Ella.

"I'll train mine better than that," she sputtered.

"Your brother?" Ella asked.

"My *husband*," Dora proclaimed. "I'll be trainin' him better than that."

"You'd best be askin' questions before you marry, then. Questions like does he act so now? How does he treat his sisters now? That's the place to start, they say."

Dora made another face, and Ella handed her one of the hoes. The other two she carried with her. Monroe would come for his if he chose a task that required its use.

"You can't trust boys," Dora whispered as they approached the girls in the garden. "They all fake it while they woo you, and then it's back to their usual selves after the wedding and vows, of course, vows from which there is no escaping for us."

"You do see the dark side of life," Ella said, surprised at how lighthearted she felt.

"So what have you two got up your dress sleeves?" Linda Mast asked, onion plants in her hands.

"Just brothers," Ella said, "that and Dora's future husband."

"Didn't know she had one," Linda said with a laugh. "Did something happen in secret perhaps? Did you get the bishop up in the middle of the night?"

Even Dora had to grin, as laughter rippled across the garden.

"It wasn't me," one of the boys hollered. "I'm still single, and I for sure was sound asleep that evenin'…whenever it was!"

There was more laughter, and then Dora shot back, "Maybe if you'd be nice to your sister, then she wouldn't have to worry about her future husband either."

"Ohhh—" the boy groaned and clutched his chest. "*Sie shoot'th mich im herzen*. It bleedeth on the ground."

"Let that be a *gut* lesson," Dora told him, her voice light, as laughter rose and fell all around.

The mood darkened later when more youth had gathered.

"Anybody thought about the next death—the one after Melissa Beachy?" one of the boys asked.

"I don't believe in such things," a girl said, and there was a murmur of agreement.

"I don't know about that," the boy retorted. "It scares me."

Ella could feel fear run through the gathered youth, and her own heart ached for them and for herself. They were not timid people and likely to tremble without a reason. Death, even if it came unexpectedly, had an order to it. They could handle that, but to have it stalk them, with the certainty of a calculated killer, unnerved them.

So far death's choices had been young people. From what Ella could gather in the murmur of voices, they expected this pattern to continue. On the basis of this logic, some young person was meant to die soon.

Tonight could be the last night, perhaps, for the one beside you, perhaps the very face you glanced toward, the one whose voice you listened to. Ella felt the chill in her own heart and expected the others felt the same.

The voices rose and fell, and the mood changed again. It was hard to stay focused on death in the midst of such vibrant life. Males and females, none of them married and yet bursting with energy, encouraged each other. The excitement of life accented the night air and the hearty work their hands engaged in.

Ella pushed her dark thoughts away and looked around for Daniel. She still had not seen him all night. Perhaps he hadn't come. The possibility was easy to imagine, but this would only delay her. She would speak with Daniel whenever next she had the opportunity.

"Did you hear the news?" one of her cousins whispered in her ear.

Ella smiled, drawn out of her mood with the usual buzz of gossip. Wedding gossip, she expected. The time spent in speculation and guesswork around a dating couple who both passed the twenty-one-year-old mark could be immense.

"Yost and Linda are gettin' published on Sunday, I think," Mary Ellen said. "My brother saw them at the bishop's house last night right after dark. They were sneakin' in, I suppose."

"That's one nice thing about livin' round the bishop's house like you do," Ella said, laughing. "You get to see stuff like that."

"Not always," her cousin was quick to say. "They get smarter all the time. Last year Amos and Mary actually came in the middle of the day a half an hour apart. They quite pulled the wool over everyone's eyes."

"I guess Yost and Linda should have tried that."

"I know." Her cousin joined in the laughter. "Everyone knows, I guess, what you're up to after dark, especially if you're young and at the bishop's house."

"Yah," Ella allowed as her spirits sank, "though I'd have given a lot for the chance to go anytime of the day with Aden."

Her cousin glanced at her quickly. "Ach, I'm so sorry. I shouldn't have brought up the subject. It hasn't been that long at all."

Ella wanted to tell her cousin that it had been long enough for a serious proposal of marriage from a very insistent suitor, but she bit her tongue. Not only would this have been improper but disrespectful to Bishop Miller.

Her cousin grabbed her arm. "Ach, Ella. I'm just terrible. I'm worse than that. I'm a beast, a cow from the barn. Please forgive me and my klutzy, clumsy tongue."

Ella shook her head and whispered, "Nee, it wasn't you. I was just thinkin' of somethin' else."

"Of course, it was me," her cousin said, insisting. "You are, as always, too kind."

"It's really okay," Ella said, smiling weakly. "This will happen for a while yet, I suppose."

"I would imagine."

"It's also my first youth gathering."

"Then I'm really sorry," her cousin said, on the verge of tears herself. "What must it be like, I can't image. Losing Harold? Ach, we've dated for three years already. Why, it would be like half my heart was gone."

"Something like that," Ella agreed, "but like they told me, life goes on, and *Da Hah* does give grace."

"You always were the brave one."

Behind them, Esther came out into the yard and waved her hand. "I have the food ready. Well, almost," she proclaimed as high as her voice would go. Ella smiled at the joy it contained. It did make you feel good when you made other people happy.

"I have rolls and apple juice. Just the ice cream is yet to be made. If two of you boys will go to the basement and bring up the ice, we can start makin' it now."

The volunteers ran for the basement. Homemade ice cream was loved by all. Moments later, an ice block was brought up, still covered with sawdust. The block was broken up in a burlap bag and dumped around the freezers. A line of boys soon stood behind each ice cream freezer, taking turns at the handles. Most settled down to a steady pace after the first few energetic hand spins. Salt was applied as needed till the ice cream thickened, and the paddles froze in place.

"We're done plantin'," Monroe, who happened to be the one in line at the moment, hollered. "And the first freezer is finished."

A cry of, "We're done too," came immediately from the other line.

An old table was carried out from the shed while plates and spoons were brought out from the house. A line formed quickly. Ella finally spotted Daniel as she took a small dip of strawberry ice cream, an even smaller piece of a roll, and a glass of apple cider. Her appetite, even after the garden work, wasn't that great, and it left her completely now that she had seen Daniel.

She tried not to be conspicuous as she worked her way over to where Daniel stood. He still had not gone through the line, but it might be better to let him know she wanted to talk.

"Good evening," he said with a smile.

"Good evening," she replied.

The boy beside Daniel moved away, apparently drawn by his hunger to the table, or perhaps as Ella suspected, he knew she wanted a private conversation. Ella was self-conscious and sure she had the look of someone who wanted privacy. She suddenly shuddered to think of what Daniel or anyone else would say if they knew of her real reason. Daniel must never know—or anyone else for that matter.

"I see you have your plate already," he smiled.

"Yah. I've been looking for you all evening," she said, trying to keep the tremble out of her voice. What she wanted wasn't wrong, she tried to assure herself, but the tremble remained.

Thirty-five

"Oh," Daniel said, lifting his eyebrows, "you wish to talk with me?"

Ella nodded. "What you came for the other day—about the house—I'm ready to accept. That is if you still can do it."

"So you have made up your mind? I'm glad to hear that. I feared I might have offended you."

"Have you spoken with your parents? Do they approve of this gift from that money Aden left behind?"

"No." He shook his head. "I haven't talked to them, but they won't object. I'm sure about that, but I will speak with them. I should also explain this to your parents, don't you think?"

"Yah," Ella nodded, liking the idea, "you'd better because I don't know if I can say it so they'll understand. And I need to show you the house anyway—the one on the quilt. That's the one that has to be built. The one Clara drew."

"So you won't use the plans Aden drew up? That was what he planned for."

Ella whispered softly, "Please, don't even—perhaps ever—show them to me. It hurts too much. I don't think I could stand it, and it's much better this way. If we use what Clara drew, it will be my house.

I don't think I could live in what would have been *our* house. I hope you understand."

"I think I do. How about tomorrow night, then?" Daniel asked. "Is that too soon?"

"You can speak with your parents that quickly?"

He nodded. "Tonight perhaps. If not then, I'll speak to them in the morning at breakfast time. This is kind of sudden, I know, but we really need to get started before my other construction works starts. It'll be ready to begin soon, since I'm startin' with a fresh crew. I'm tryin' to go on where Aden left off, not that I really can because Aden was much better than me."

"You'll do fine," Ella said. She wished he wouldn't be so insecure. "After supper tomorrow, then," she said and moved away. Already some of the girls had noticed the lengthy conversation. Slowly Ella lowered herself down on the grass beside her cousin, who glanced up, obviously curious.

"Talkin' about Aden's things," Ella said to satisfy her. What else could she possibly say?

How did one say that a house was being built by people who were supposed to have been your in-laws but now wouldn't be? If she added the bishop's proposal, which she had no intention of doing, eyebrows would really be raised. It all left her with a strange feeling of excitement.

Ella picked up her spoon and scooped the last of the melted ice cream from the bowl. In her mouth, the sweet coolness was delightful. Ella felt a twinge of guilt at the pleasure and at her excitement. So quickly she had moved on.

Above her the sky had darkened, and the first stars twinkled with vigor. Ella focused on a bright one just above the horizon. The answer to her guilt came suddenly and with great clarity, as if from the heavens themselves. She drew her breath in sharply and was startled, surprised, and filled with joy. Her bowl dropped from her hand as she thought that somehow surely Aden had seen this evening and had smiled. He had. With an absolute certainty, he had.

At the dropping of her bowl, her cousin put an arm around Ella and said, "I'm so sorry. Perhaps you've ventured out again too soon."

Several of the other girls also gathered closer.

"It's her first youth gathering since…" The cousin needed to say no more as murmurs of sympathy were offered.

Ella managed a quick smile of sorts. "Sorry," she whispered, wishing she could share that she was feeling a sense of joy, not sorrow, at the hope of Aden's approval of her plans.

No one said anything, but Ella could feel the heavy mood. She had only succeeded in reminding them that death could find any of them tonight, tomorrow, or the next day.

"I'm so sorry," she whispered.

"It'll be okay," her cousin said softly, giving her another hug. Ella smiled her thanks and got to her feet. Several of the boys had already gone to the barn to get their horses. They silently drove their buggies out and collected the girls. It was almost as if they willed death to stay away and held it back by their own careful action.

Monroe brought his buggy up, and Ella climbed in after Dora. As they rode in silence, Dora finally burst out, "This has got to stop! This thing hangs over all of us."

"It's just superstition," Monroe said, slapping the reins sharply. "We shouldn't let it bother us."

"For once I hope you're right," Dora said, "but I've got to say this scares me."

They rattled onward into the night, silence again settling over them. Monroe drove recklessly, considering the circumstances, Ella thought but didn't mention it.

Dora sighed in relief when they pulled into the driveway. Monroe glanced at her but didn't say anything. Ella jumped down first and started to unhitch her side. Dora held the horse's bridle until Monroe had the other side done. Ella watched until Monroe and the horse vanished into the darkness toward the barn. Dora was already at the front door but waited for her to catch up. Together they walked inside. Mamm and

Daett were still up, the gas lantern hissing quietly in the living room, the house silent with no sign of Clara or the younger girls.

"So you made it through your first youth gathering, Ella. I'm so glad you went," Mamm said, getting up. "Was it too bad?"

"So-so." Ella tried to smile. What she wanted to say couldn't be uttered.

"She had a hard evening," Dora spoke up, "as all of us did. I tell you, this death thing hangs over our heads, and I'm tired of it. I so wish it would just be over and soon."

Mamm shook her head. "You must not speak so, Dora. Death is in the hands of *Da Hah,* and we must abide by His will when it comes."

"He gives much grace," Daett said from the hickory rocker. "I don't want to hear anymore complaining about what happens in our lives. We must submit as obedient children." He rocked slowly to the squeak of the wooden rocker as silence settled on the house again.

"Daniel's comin' over tomorrow night," Ella said, daring to speak up. There had been enough talk of death tonight. "I spoke with him tonight, and he wants to explain some things about Aden's plans before he died. He said he'd come after supper if that's okay."

"It must be important?" Mamm said, a puzzled look on her face.

"It is," Ella said. "He wants to speak with all of us, and it's kind of important to me."

"Speak to the whole family?" Dora asked. "What kind of trouble could that mean?"

"There is no trouble," Ella said.

"We'll see, then," Mamm said, dismissing them upstairs with a wave of her hand. "It can't be too serious, not with Daniel involved. Now go and get your sleep, and…tell Eli goodnight. He's upset he couldn't go with you tonight."

Dora and Ella put their heads in the bedroom together, smiling fake smiles, and hollering "Hi." Eli glared at them, and they laughed.

"Whoa, whoa," he said as they turned to go. "I have to have some news at least. You can't just go and leave me without anything."

"You tell him," Dora said, turning on her heels. "I can only think dark thoughts anyway."

"Don't mind her," Eli said. "So how was the evening?"

"Okay, I guess, for my first time out," Ella said. "We did the garden work, and then the boys made ice cream. I got a little teary-eyed at the end, but I'm not going to tell you why. It concerned Aden."

"I understand," Eli said, nodding. "You loved the boy."

"Yah," Ella said, "but there's more. Daniel is coming tomorrow night for a family meeting. He has something to say about the plans Aden had. It might involve you, Eli."

"Mysterious," Eli said. "I would be glad to be involved in anything to do with you and Aden. You are the best sister around."

"I'm not," Ella said but appreciated the compliment. How could such a stubborn boy who flirted with the dangers of the *Englisha* world be so sweet? It was one of life's mysteries. "But thanks anyway."

"Goodnight," Eli said and settled down on his pillow. "I think I can sleep now, but may the day come quickly when I can get out of this bed."

"It will come." Ella shut the door behind her and took the steps slowly, each squeak a comfort to her heart. At least there were some things in life that didn't change. In her room she prepared for bed but knew she couldn't sleep yet. With the kerosene lamp turned up high, she grabbed her tablet out of the drawer and wrote furiously.

It's late spring now. In some ways it seems Aden's been gone for years now, and my worst fears have come to pass. Even Dora, with her wild imagination, couldn't have seen this one coming. Mamm and Daett say this is all a sign of Da Hah's doings, but I tremble with disagreement. I simply cannot believe what has happened.

Bishop Wayne Miller has showed up and almost outright requested my hand in marriage. He had more manners than to ask point-blank. I think my resistance to his talk slowed him down a bit because if I hadn't showed my rejection of his obviously upcoming question, I have no doubt he would have asked me right then and there to be his promised.

The thought sends chills up and down my spine. No man other than Aden has ever had my love nor ever could. I cannot give my heart to another even if I wanted to. It seems the most serious breach of loyalty my heart could ever make. To allow another to touch it, place his arms around me, or draw me into his embrace is just not possible.

My heart cries tonight again with a great longing for Aden and an even greater longing to have been his wife. If I could have been his wife for even a night or a week! To have him taken from me before we could ever be truly one seems the cruelest thing of all. It seems to me that if we had been together, I could bear this so much better.

I suppose Mamm and Daett have little sympathy for my sentiments. Love comes again, they say. The heart heals and, besides, they say marriage is more than just emotions. It's about living together, trusting each other, being loyal to one another, and bearing children. They have a point that the Bishop would supply these as well as any man could—except Aden, and Aden is gone.

The way Mamm and Daett act does have an effect on me. Still, I will not give the bishop any favorable answer either now or in the future. If I ever allow another man into my heart, it won't be like this. I'm really afraid of what Mamm and Daett will say when they find out I must turn the bishop down, not to mention what the bishop will say.

Surely, he won't harm them. They aren't in his church district and don't disobey the Ordnung anyway. Yet one never knows. The bishop looks to me like someone who's used to getting his way, especially with girls. I doubt he has ever had one reject his advances. He's got an awful lot of power from what I could tell. I wonder what he will do when it is challenged, as I surely will.

That's why the answer is so clearly in Daniel's solution with the house. It will solve so many problems. And if Eli persists in this foolish pursuit of the Englisha girl, I could even give him temporary shelter. That would get me in trouble, but better me than Mamm and Daett. I have less to lose, and this might even cool the bishop's desire for me.

Wouldn't that be a good test for him? Does he love me—Ella Yoder who sheltered her brother who ran around with the Englisha girl? Yah, if Daniel doesn't let me down, we will build the house. I will help build it myself, if necessary, so urgent is the matter. Six months will come around much sooner than one imagines.

Then the sweetest thing happened tonight. Now it seems like it was likely all in my head, but it did so comfort me. Tonight at the youth gathering, I was all torn up after speaking with Daniel and the decision to meet here tomorrow night. I've never done things sort of behind Mamm and Daett's back.

Anyway, I looked at the stars like I used to do with Aden. A really bright one had just come out and twinkled away. And then it happened. It seemed like Aden smiled one of his smiles at me just like he used to—only this time it came out of the sky, from faraway. Yet it felt exactly the same, as if he sat right beside me like always before, perhaps even a little warmer, if that is possible. I couldn't do anything but cry for a while.

Ella closed the tablet, placed it carefully on her dresser, and, once in bed, fell instantly asleep.

Thirty-six

The quilt should be finished today. Ella awoke with the determination that it must be so. Somehow she needed to find the time to finish the quilt, but she wasn't certain how to do that. She dressed in the darkness and was already on the stairs when Dora's alarm clock went off.

"*Gut* morning," she said to her mom in the kitchen. "I'm heading for the barn."

"Monroe isn't even up yet," Mamm said in surprise. "What's the hurry?"

"The quilt," Ella admitted sheepishly. "But it doesn't have to be done if we don't have time." And yet she hoped her mother would understand somehow.

"I don't think we have too much on the list for today," Mamm said.

"Thank you," Ella whispered and left.

In the barn she opened the gate to let in the first round of cows. They mooed wearily, as if they didn't wish to be up yet, and ambled slowly in. She had them locked in the stanchions when Monroe and Dora, all sleepy eyed, showed up. Daett walked in a minute later, a big grin on his face.

"My, my, someone's up early this mornin'."

A flush of emotion ran through Ella. The day was starting out good.

"She can milk my cows," Dora grumbled. "I feel like I've been beaten on the head all night long, as if maybe I'm the next one to leave this world."

"Get off that horse," Monroe said. "I'm *gut* and tired of hearin' you drive it."

"That's in *Da Hah's* hands," Daett said, "and we'd best be leaving it there. So let's not hear any more about it. I'll do the silage, Monroe, and help on the next round of cows."

"Let's hear no more about it. You hear that, Dora?" Monroe said when Daett was out of earshot.

Dora didn't say anything. She grabbed a milk bucket and began her work, making the milk ping loudly against the bucket's metal sides.

"Just leave her alone," Ella said in Monroe's direction. "She's had a hard night."

"Yah, leave her alone," Dora grumbled as if she wasn't there.

Ella laughed as she got her own milk bucket but got no response from Dora. Her spurt of energy and good feelings continued.

"What's the hurry?" Dora grumbled when Ella quickly finished her first cow.

"I want to finish my quilt today."

"You would think of that—and first thing in the mornin'," Monroe spoke up from a few cows down.

"Just mind your own beeswax," Dora retorted.

Monroe made a sputtering sound and then was silent. Ella figured his compliance had more to do with disinterest in the subject than consideration for Dora.

Daett came in to help on the last round of cows, and they finished in record time. Dora and Ella left for the house while Monroe stayed behind to finish the final chores. The stars had already begun to dim from the rising light of the sun in front of them. It filled the sky with a reddish hue as they made their way up the walks.

"What does Daniel want tonight?" Dora asked, her curiosity still aroused.

"He wants to talk about Aden's things. You can hear it from him when he comes," Ella said. She didn't want to say more. Daniel could explain this all better than she could. It would be better coming from him. That would look better than if her family got the idea she had cooked up the plan.

"You and Daniel are up to somethin'." Dora eyed her sharply in the early morning light.

"You'll find out tonight." Ella stuck with her plans. Dora's curiosity would just have to wait.

"I think I figured it out," Dora declared. "You're planning to steal him from Arlene."

"Dora!" Ella exclaimed.

"It has something to do with Bishop Miller," Dora continued, apparently rattled by the outburst. "This is a way to get around what Mamm and Daett want you to do. What's puzzling is you've never been stubborn before, but you seemed to have changed lately."

"You're not even close," Ella said with an edge in her voice.

"So you're takin' the next brother," Dora continued in the same tone. "They used to do that in the Old Testament. Yah, when an oldest brother died, the sister took the next one. Arlene will be heartbroken."

"You have lost your mind," Ella said, suddenly more amused than angry.

"No, I don't think I have," Dora grumbled, following her into the washroom. Ella let Dora take the first turn at the basin and then started as Dora wiped herself with the towel.

"Should we throw the water out?" Ella asked when she was done.

"No," Dora said, her voice dark. "The boys never do it for us. Anyway, we aren't dirty like they are."

"That is a point." Ella laughed. She couldn't believe how happy she continued to be and smiled at what Dora would surely say about the "dark clouds following soon enough."

Clara and Mamm had breakfast set out, and so Dora and Ella sat down to wait for the menfolk. Mamm stepped over to the stair door and hollered up, "Time to get up, girls."

Soft footsteps soon were heard coming down the stairs, and Ella smiled as the younger girls appeared one after the other. They seated themselves on the back bench well before the bangs and splashes in the washroom began.

"How can two men be so noisy?" Dora commented. "Seems like they could keep the noise down."

"They're men," Mamm said. "Just be thankful they are. *Da Hah* has been good to us."

"A man is a bad thing," Dora said, her face resting on her hands.

"Don't be listenin' to her," Ella told Clara, who was smiling.

"She won't anyway," Dora retorted.

Monroe entered the room loudly and sat down, and Daett came in right behind him. Eli, awakened by all the noise, hollered from the bedroom, "I'm hungry."

"I'll bring you a plate later," Mamm called back. "We have to have prayer first. Pray in there, will you?"

Eli mumbled something they couldn't hear. After prayer, Mamm loaded a plate of food and disappeared in the direction of the bedroom only to return shortly, saying, "He's looking much better this morning."

"*Da Hah sie lob,*" Daett proclaimed, eggs and bacon piled high on his plate. "Soon the boy will be on his feet again, and I sure can use him in the fields."

"Do you want one of the girls to help?" Mamm asked. "I can spare one of them today."

"Might have to," Daett said with a nod, "now that I think of it. Monroe and I have our hands full with the back field. We're disking and planting the corn. The front, behind the barn, still has a day or so of plowing to be done. It sure looks like rain, maybe tomorrow already. The sky was mighty red this mornin'."

"Ella can help," Mamm volunteered. "She knows the most about plowing and handling the Belgians."

"Are you up to plowin', Ella? All day? Cause I sure could use you," Daett said.

"You'll make a farmer's wife out of the girl yet," Dora muttered.

Ella swallowed hard, her plans to work on the quilt in jeopardy.

"Yah, I can," she said quietly, "if the horses don't get away from me."

"They won't." Her father seemed satisfied. "Monroe will get them harnessed up right after we finish with breakfast, and you can use the single bottom plow. The double is too much."

"Oh, I guess I can plow," Dora said, "since Ella wants to finish her quilt."

"It's okay," Ella said. "I'll do it."

Daett's face lit into a wide smile. "I'm pleased to see that your heart is healin' like that, Ella. *Da Hah,* He is always faithful, but I suppose the quilt can wait. It's not going to run away."

"Yah," Ella simply said.

"If we are all done, then, can we have prayer?" Daett asked as he got up. "The day is getting away from me."

They all followed him into the living room. Monroe made quick gulps of his last spoonfuls of oatmeal and took up the end of the line.

With a soft rustle, they knelt as their father began to pray, "Our merciful and great heavenly Father, Your grace is new every morning. Grant us strength for this day, wisdom for our tasks, and courage to face our duties. We thank You again that Eli was spared and ask that Your healing would continue in his body all according to Your most gracious will and desire. In the name of the Father, the Son, and the Holy Spirit."

With a shuffle of feet, they rose, and Dora made a beeline for the kitchen.

"My, she's in a rush," Mamm said. "Ella, you won't do any kitchen work this morning because you're helpin' outside. I suppose Monroe can use your help with the Belgians since Eli isn't around."

Ella nodded and followed Monroe out the door. She didn't have any problems with horses, even huge ones. They seemed a delight to her. In the barn she dished out the grain while Monroe gave each horse a quick brush down. She waited while Monroe threw the harnesses on and then tightened the straps. Monroe led the two horses out of the stall, gave one to Ella, and followed her with the other. Outside, the Belgians blinked their eyes sleepily. Two killdeer were disturbed behind the barn, took flight, and shrieked their disapproval. The horses by force of habit easily got in line in front of the plow, its single blade pulled out of the ground.

With the tugs fastened, Ella shook the reins and yelled loudly, "Get-up!"

The horses obediently lurched forward and headed for the field. With her foot, Ella disengaged the plow blade, and the sharp point plunged into the black soil. Out of the corner of her eye, Ella saw the look of approval on Monroe's face. Apparently he was still surprised that a girl could do a man's work so well.

At the end of the long field, she repeated the motion in reverse and brought the blade up for the turn. Carefully she watched the horses for any signs of exhaustion. They seemed to be fine, but she gave them a short rest when the end of the second row was reached. Her father was a firm believer that horses were meant for work and not abuse.

The hours rolled by. The horses kept to a straight line, and the black dirt curled under her feet with the engaging and disengaging of the plow blades. Ella felt an occasional pang of regret that her quilt wasn't completed, but the glory of the spring day surrounded her and worked its way deep into her consciousness.

The two killdeer were back, flying off every time she came close to the barn. Both would flutter their wings and drag them on the ground in desperation in front of the team.

Ella wondered if the killdeer already had laid its eggs. It seemed early in the year to already have a nest built, but she wasn't certain. When she allowed the team its next rest, she walked to the barn for a drink of water. Along the way, she looked for any signs of the nest. This produced great distress in the two birds. They landed only a few feet from her and appeared to be desperately protective of something, but she saw no sign of any eggs in the shallow gravel bed.

At lunchtime, she waited until Monroe came in from the back field to help unhitch. They led the horses to the barn and fed and watered them. Inside the house, Mamm had sandwiches ready.

"Makin' good time," Daett commented, his eyes warm. "Couldn't have done the morning's plowing better myself."

Ella nodded her appreciation for the praise. Another day would come for quilt work, and the plowing did need to be done today.

After lunch, Monroe helped get the horses out again, and the afternoon dragged on. The sun grew warm on Ella's back and shone brightly in her eyes when she went the other direction. Ella thought of a trip to the house to get her bonnet but decided against it. The pleasant feel of the sun on her face more than made up for any discomfort.

She thought of Daniel, of tonight, and of how strange her life was turning out. Who would have thought she would be capable of what she planned to do. Not that long ago, she was to be the future wife of Aden, comfortable, secure, and undisturbed. Sure, one always looked for the unexpected but not like this. People got sick, and babies were born—sometimes with trouble but mostly without.

Ella reached another turn and guided the horses back the other way. Before her the fields spread out for what seemed like miles, the valley dipping and rising gently. Her dad's farm stopped two fencerows down, and the rest belonged to other Amish neighbors. So solid, the earth was. You plowed, disked, and planted it, yet it always, somehow, stayed the same.

Why couldn't people—or life—be like that?

As the minutes slipped by, she continued in her thoughts, almost missing disengaging the plow for the next turn. The horses stopped suddenly, their noses tight up against the fence. The two looked back at her as if they questioned her sanity.

"Sorry," she said out loud. Now the struggle would be to make the turn. Disengaging the plow from the ground was the first thing. She finally managed by applying the full pressure of both her feet to the lever.

Slowly the horses backed up in response to her tugs on the reins, but she barely avoided a serious tangle of harnesses. Once she was turned around and the plow was back in the ground, Ella sighed with relief. Monroe would have laughed if he had seen her. Now, no one needed to know her misstep.

Monroe came to help her unhitch when she pulled up to the barn when the sun was low in the sky.

"Looks nice for a girl," he said. "Maybe Daett should ask you to help more often."

Ella ignored the remark. Brothers could be such an ornery lot.

Thirty-seven

Daniel arrived after supper, his buggy rattling loudly into the driveway. Ella was in the kitchen helping Dora and Mamm wash and dry the pile of supper dishes.

"You'd better go let him in," Mamm said. "He's tying up at the hitching post."

Ella dried her hands and went to the front door just as Daniel was ready to knock.

"Good evening." She welcomed him with a smile. "I'm glad you could make it," she said, motioning him into the living room.

"Good evening." Daett greeted Daniel from his rocker. "Nice day today. Ella helped us with the plowing. She's a good worker." Then, without mincing words, Daett continued, "Ella says you have something to tell us tonight."

"Yah, I do," Daniel said nervously, taking his seat and glancing up as another buggy pulled into the driveway.

Daett got up, took a look out the window, and then called toward the kitchen, "Lizzie, it's Mary Stutzman. You'd best go see what she's wantin'."

Mamm rushed into the living room, her apron still on, nodding to Daniel as she went by. Ella glanced into the yard and hoped the conversation between her mom and Mary would be brief, and from what she could see, that seemed to be the case. Both women acted in a hurry. Thankfully, Daniel took time to get up and put his head through the bedroom doorway and greet Eli.

Eli mumbled something that Ella couldn't hear, and then Daniel shut the door behind them. Their voices rose and fell inside. Daniel soon came back into the living room and took his seat again.

"Construction work comin' along?" Daett asked cheerfully, and Ella relaxed a little. "I know it must be hard for you...startin' back up again like that."

"Yah, it is," Daniel agreed, "but I have some good boys to help me. Menno's two and the Troyers' boy. We're starting some jobs soon."

"I'm glad to hear that," Daett said as Mamm came back inside. Ella had seen the buggy leave, and concern now gripped her at the look on her mother's face. *Surely,* she thought, *this evening won't be spoiled by some more bad news.*

They all waited silently as Mamm stood still by the door.

"Is somethin' wrong?" Daett finally asked.

"Lois Stutzman passed away this afternoon," Mamm said.

"Preacher Stutzman's wife?" Daniel asked in surprise. "He's in our district."

Mamm nodded. "Ivan's wife. It happened sometime after the child was born around two o'clock. The midwife thought everything had gone well. Then the bleedin' started, and she couldn't get it stopped. Ivan drove for the clinic with the spring wagon, but they didn't make it in time."

"Why didn't they ask the neighbors to drive?" Daniel asked. "They live close to at least one of the *Englisha.*"

"Ivan did. But no one was at home because it was the middle of the day. The poor man. Mary said he drove his horse like the wind."

"*Da Hah's* will be done," Daett said, his voice filled with sorrow. "Our people have been much troubled lately. Now a preacher's wife has been called home."

"The poor man," Mamm repeated, taking a seat on the couch. "I just saw her not that long ago. One never knows when the last sight of a loved one will come. Lois is gone, and yet Eli was left us. *Da Hah* does work in mysterious ways."

"They are all things for our own *gut,*" Noah said softly. "*Da Hah* knows what is best."

"And three girls are now left behind," Mamm said. "I suppose his sister can step in for a while. I think he has an older one who's still at home."

"Susanna." Daniel supplied the name. "Though his parents are up in age already, Susanna spends a lot of her time takin' care of them."

"I'm sure they'll work it out somehow," Daett assured them. "Now we must not keep Daniel any longer than we have to…even with this news."

"The viewing is tomorrow night," Mamm said.

"Another funeral," Daniel said, his face drawn. "It wasn't that long ago since Aden's funeral. The living and dying keeps going on."

"*Da Hah* has His time for everything," Daett said.

Silence settled around them, and Ella stared off into space. *What else could happen?* Out in the kitchen Dora must have bumped the stacked dishes because one rattled to the wood floor. Daniel jumped and then smiled nervously.

"What I came for, yah—" he began, taking a deep breath. "Well, first of all, when Aden passed away, he left a large sum of money. Most of it he planned to use for his house. Well, his and Ella's."

Daett and Mamm nodded, and Ella felt like she couldn't breathe. Her parents' faces were impossible to read.

"Only now that he's gone and the money and land are still here, I want to speak about what is to be done with the money."

"But weren't there hospital bills?" Daett asked, clearing his throat.

"They are all paid off," Daniel said, "and I believe I know what Aden would have wanted the rest of the money used for."

"You have spoken with your mamm and daett," Noah asked, "about this matter?"

Daniel nodded. "I have. We spoke last night and before that, as well. Mom wanted to wait at first, but now they have agreed."

"And Ella?" Daett asked.

"I have spoken to her."

"Does she agree with this plan, which you think Aden would have wanted? I don't want my daughter to have money that is not hers to receive."

"It's not money," Daniel said. "She would receive very little—if any—of the money. What we believe—my parents and I—is that Aden would still have wanted the house built for Ella. It should be hers—that and the land."

"A house?" Mamm asked. "But Ella's not married. A girl cannot be livin' alone like that."

"But I'll be twenty-one," Ella protested. "I can rent part of it out, if it comes to that, or have someone live with me."

"I see you have thought much of this already," Daett said. His words came slowly. "Yet you have not spoken to us about it."

"It has not been that long since Daniel mentioned it," Ella said, her heart sinking.

"It is what we as a family want," Daniel said, choosing his words carefully. "Mamm and Daett and I. It is also what Aden would have wanted. I hope you do not hold this against Ella because this might be *Da Hah*'s gift to her to help her move on with life."

Ella could see her father almost bite his lip, as if words pushed to come out. No doubt he wished to tell Daniel his daughter was recently spoken for and that no more care was needed. Yet he said nothing, and his face did seem to soften after a moment.

"There has been much suffering lately," he finally said. "We must not be adding more to it. Do you want this, Ella? Does your heart really desire it?"

"Yah," she said as guilt gripped her heart. It felt like betrayal since her father had no way of knowing what she really wanted the house for. She managed a weak smile.

"What do you think, Lizzie?" Daett asked.

She turned to Daniel and asked, "Will this house be paid for? All of it?"

"It will," Daniel said. "There's enough money and, perhaps, a little left over."

"It couldn't be much," Daett protested.

"No," Daniel said, smiling, "not much."

"Then this can be done," Daett decided suddenly. "We must not stand in the way. Don't you think so, Lizzie?"

"I hate to see my daughter…all grown up and gone," she replied, sighing.

"It is the way of *Da Hah*," Daett said, turning to Daniel. "So when can this house be built?"

Daniel leaned forward. "Because of our other work, this should be done soon."

"Then life must move on, and Ella's must too." Noah nodded his approval and seemed to relax back into his chair.

Ella felt a great joy rise up inside of her. The wonder of this turn of events thrilled her. Then just as quickly, her spirits fell again as she remembered why she might need the house and that Aden would never share it with her. To drive her dark thoughts away, she turned to Daniel.

"I must show you the drawing," she said. She went upstairs to get Clara's house picture and returned to the living room. She held it up on her lap and showed it to Daniel.

"Is this what you want?" He took the drawing from her, his eyes fixed on it.

"Yah," she nodded, "I want the house as Clara drew it."

"It's *gut*," he agreed, "and it's easy to build, I must say. It's a real *nice* Amish house."

"That's what I thought!" Ella said, laughing for the first time.

"It is *gut*," Noah said over their shoulders.

Ella noticed her mother didn't come close and that she had wiped a tear from her cheek.

"I'm sorry," Mamm whispered. "Just too much goin' on, I guess. So many new things, and now you're leavin'."

"I'll still be your daughter," Ella said, putting her arm around her mom.

"Well, I really should be goin' now," Daniel said, getting up. "I will take this with me, then. Is that okay, Ella?"

Ella nodded, and he left silently out the front door. Moments later they heard his buggy rattle out the driveway.

"I heard all that," Dora said, sticking her head through the doorway.

"We weren't hiding anything," Mamm said. "You could have come out if you wanted to."

The stair door opened behind them, and Clara came in.

"What did he want?" she asked.

"Ella's buildin' a house," Dora said, "and Preacher Stutzman's wife died in childbirth this very afternoon. When it rains, it pours, if you ask me. Now at least the cloud no longer hangs over our heads. That will make this the third death."

"You sound so…cheerful," Daett said. "It's not just numbers, Dora. One of our men has lost his beloved wife, and we should all weep with him."

"Yah, Daett," Dora said, her voice contrite, "I guess I got carried away."

"Are you done with the kitchen?" Ella asked.

Dora nodded. "There wasn't that much left to do anyway."

"Will someone pay some attention to me?" Eli hollered from the bedroom. "All you do all night is talk and talk, and no one comes to take care of me. And what did Daniel want anyway?"

Mamm went into the bedroom while Ella and Dora left for upstairs. Dusk had already fallen, and the evening was getting on. At the top of the stairs, Dora stopped in Ella's room and shut the door behind her. Ella couldn't find a match, and she groped around for a moment before her fingers found one. It struck on the first try, and the flame quickly transferred to the wick. With the glass chimney back on, the lamp filled the room with a soft glow as Dora sat down on the bed.

"I'm not leavin' until I get the whole story," she declared. "Mamm may not know everything, but I'm going to find out. I'm getting to the bottom of this little well of water."

"What you know already is enough," Ella said firmly.

"It's not. Something is up. I can smell it in the air, even with my own nose off the ground. You're hiding something."

"What if I'm not," Ella asked, "and you're just worryin' about nothing?"

"You're leaving. I'll be the oldest sister at home. I deserve to know what goes on."

"Well…" Ella wavered, drawn in by Dora's logic. With Dora's eyes on her, she gave in. "Okay, then, but you'd best not tell Mamm and Daett, at least not until it's time. In fact, best not till you ask me if you can talk. I don't trust your thinkin' on the matter."

"That's fair. Tell me."

Ella glanced around and then lowered the shade for what reason she wasn't certain, but it seemed the right thing to do. Her voice low, she began. She told Dora about Eli, about the bishop, and about what the house really was for. "Now you'd better tell no one," she concluded.

"So what if Daett could save Eli from this *Englisha* girl?" Dora asked.

"So much the better, but Eli's bullheaded," Ella said. "He will come to see his own mistake. I cannot but think this will turn out okay."

"You're a good sister," Dora said. She stood to go and walked over to pull up the blind. "That was no use," she said with a smile. "Goodnight, now." She gave Ella a big hug.

When the door shut, Ella blew out the light. In the solid darkness of the night, she slipped under the covers.

Thirty-eight

Ella rode to the viewing with Dora in the single buggy. In front of them, their mamm and daett were in the surrey with Clara and the younger girls. Monroe had stayed home with Eli, who hobbled outside for the first time that day. The mischief those two might get into at home together gave Ella a shudder. Dora and Mamm had baked cinnamon rolls, and the three plates of them were stored in the cupboard for Saturday and Sunday. Ella could well imagine an entire plate of rolls gone by the time they returned even though Eli and Monroe already had hefty servings for supper. But the evening's occasion was sacred, and so perhaps this would carry over to Monroe and Eli's attitude about things.

Ahead of them a sea of buggies were parked behind Preacher Stutzman's barn. Ella waited for the familiar stab of pain and for the memories from the recent past to tumble back into her heart. She was surprised when the feelings didn't come. Perhaps she was healing.

"Glad it wasn't one of the young people to finish out the third one," Dora said as they pulled up to park behind their mom and dad's buggy.

"It was someone's wife and someone's mamm," Ella reminded her, thinking of the three small Stutzman girls left behind. She had vague memories of them, lost in the sea of faces from many families. They would be here tonight, pain and bewilderment in their hearts—a feeling Ella knew only too well.

"Still I'm glad it wasn't. It wouldn't have been fair at all since we already lost two of our own."

"You'd best leave those decisions to *Da Hah*," Ella said, getting down to unhitch.

"Suppose so," Dora said, her voice muffled from the other side of the buggy.

Ella led her horse toward the barn, with Dora behind her. She wondered how she would get inside without one of her brother's present to accompany her. The crush of horses was a challenge to navigate and not one she relished. *Daett will help me, no doubt, if I want to wait while he takes his horse inside first. No, that would draw too many curious glances—a girl standing and waiting alone with her horse. One of the boys is sure to offer help—but exactly which boy matters.* It might be perfectly harmless, but after the bishop's visit the other evening, Ella's nerves had not returned to normal.

Just then her dad motioned with his hand. "I can take both horses in, yah," he whispered with a smile. "It's a little rough inside for my daughter."

Ella gave him the reins just as a boy she didn't know came out of the barn. He saw her dad leading two horses and took one from him. She would have offered him a grateful smile if he had glanced in her direction. Seconds later, she caught herself. Smiles to boys, whether stranger or not, might be very unwise at the moment.

With Dora in the lead, they followed their mom past the long line of men and boys. They were just a sea of black pants and shoes to Ella because she kept her head down. What if Bishop Miller was in the line somewhere, his gaze following her? She almost stumbled but caught herself just in time.

Ella took deep breaths. Her face under her bonnet must be brighter than a beet. Hopefully the line of men would just see her as another girl passing by, a little clumsy but still a decent girl. In a moment the house would be reached, and the bonnet removed. Then they would know that she was Ella Yoder.

Thankfully the line of women just outside the door of the washroom was long enough to get rid of the red face. Ella removed her bonnet and shawl as she stepped into the utility room, keeping her face toward the house just in case. She left her wraps on the pile and got in the line moving slowly toward the bedroom where the body was. Two small girls were seated on the bench in the kitchen just outside the bedroom door. They must be Preacher Stutzman's girls since he sat with them, his arms around the shoulder of the oldest. The youngest, her head in his lap, was asleep.

Ella's eyes fixed on the oldest girl, her face so forlorn and tear stained. Her sister and her dad were exhausted. Preacher Stutzman's beard was unkempt, his hair was uncombed, and his eyes were red and swollen. Ella searched the face of the man. He wasn't the dreaded Preacher Stutzman—the terror of a hundred fierce sermons and the harsh voice at Aden's funeral—but a dad and husband, broken in his sorrow.

She gasped. This was different than her loss, but the hearts involved had equally been rent in two. Heads turned toward her, drawn by her display of emotion, but their questions turned to understanding when they saw who she was. She could almost hear their thoughts, their sympathy.

Ella wanted to take the little girls in her arms, comfort them, and tell them that everything would be okay, but, of course, she couldn't. It wouldn't be proper, and they didn't know her. No doubt they had aunts on both sides of the family who had done that very thing with about as much success as she would have. A heart so broken could not be hurried or made better quickly.

The line moved forward, and Ella followed. Inside the casket, she saw the face of Lois, pale, drawn, and at peace. Ella thought Lois looked much older than she must be as a mother of only three young girls. But at least she had a husband and children before she was called away. Aden and she had been denied that.

Yet, *Da Hah* knew what He was up to, and she must trust Him.

He certainly had helped out in her situation. There was no question there. Who would have thought that Aden would leave enough money behind to build a house, a house she now desperately needed. Aden's mom and dad could have said no. And Daniel could have refused too. Even her own parents could have resisted. All in all, there was little doubt *Da Hah's* hand had been in this.

As the line moved out to the kitchen, Ella considered that truly the One in the heavens gives and takes away all for His own reasons. She took a seat on the bench beside her cousin who had helped out at the youth garden project. Across from them, Arlene, Daniel's girlfriend, sat. Ella nodded and smiled when Arlene turned around to glance at her.

In the stillness of the room, her cousin leaned toward Ella and whispered, "Did you hear the news about the angels?"

"No," Ella said.

"Arlene just told me a real tender story. I guess now they can tell it around. They didn't want to before this, lest they cause more fear than there already was. Arlene's brothers, Norman and Mervin, saw three angels in the sky just after Aden's funeral. They were flyin' low, one after the other. One left toward heaven, but two of them stayed. I suppose they were waitin' for the souls of the departed. Doesn't that make you feel good?"

"Oh," Ella said, not surprised. The story didn't sound any stranger than the smile she had felt come from the sky the other night. That would stay a secret, though. Angels—now that was something everyone could understand.

Arlene must have heard their conversation because she turned around. "It's true," she whispered. "We were keepin' it a secret, though Daniel was told. He thought it best if we kept the story quiet. A lot of our people were mighty scared already, but this ought to build their trust in *Da Hah's* doin's, don't you think?"

Ella nodded and said with what bravery she could muster, "I guess so, though the pain is still there. But it's good to know that your loved ones are in the arms of angels."

"I can understand a little," Arlene smiled in sympathy. "I can't quite imagine losin' my Daniel, though. But they say there is grace for every trial. *Da Hah* helps even when He takes away."

"Poor little girls." Ella motioned with her head toward where Preacher Stutzman sat. The youngest daughter had now awakened and leaned against him. Her face was wrinkled from her dad's pant leg, bewilderment in her eyes.

"Ach, one could cry all night," Arlene said with a catch in her voice.

"Yah, one could," Ella's cousin echoed. "The angels do leave much sorrow behind."

"*Da Hah* will comfort them, yah," Arlene said. "He'll send them another mamm maybe. They are so sweet and so lost by themselves."

Ella felt too choked up to say anything, but the two seemed to understand her silence. In front of her, Dora and Mamm got up and moved toward the front door because of the swell of people behind them. When Ella stood up, her cousin stood too and followed her to the door.

Outside, the line of men and boys was less, but Ella still kept her eyes on the ground. She was still fearful about seeing Bishop Miller around somewhere. She had forgotten about him once she was inside the house and now was thankful that he didn't live in their district. That would have been simply awful.

She would have had to listen to and look at him while he preached on Sundays. If she didn't, people would notice. One could only keep one's gaze lowered to the floor for so long, especially when a minister spoke. People would soon put two and two together or think her strange, which might even be worse.

At the barn, her dad brought her horse out first. Dora climbed into the buggy after they got the horse hitched and tried the lights first thing. Her sigh of relief when the lights flashed on made Ella laugh. "Surely, you don't think I'd have driven this thing twice without a battery."

"Yah," Dora said, "but not on purpose, of course."

"I didn't check tonight," Ella admitted, "but I did put one in after last time."

"See what I mean?" Dora settled back on the seat. "At least we have one now. That's good enough for me. You scared me so bad last time that I just about couldn't sleep all night."

"That was a bad one," Ella agreed. "We can be thankful nothing serious happened."

When they crossed the little creek bottom, fog hung thick along the roadside. The buggy lights did little to penetrate the dark gloom. Dora's voice trembled, "I'm glad the three deaths are over with. Nothing will happen to us now."

"Did you hear the angel story?" Ella asked.

"Yah. Do you think it's true?"

"Of course. Aden's in heaven. I know that."

"I hope he thinks about us poor creatures still left on this earth," Dora muttered, putting her head outside of the buggy into the thick fog.

"He does," Ella said, a gentle smile on her face, although Dora couldn't have seen it in the darkness.

They soon broke out of the fog, and Dora settled back into the buggy seat. She stayed there and breathed deeply until they arrived home.

"I'll take the horse to the barn," Dora offered when she had the tugs off and the buggy shaft safely on the ground.

"Thanks," Ella said, grateful for the offer. She pushed the buggy out of the way while Dora disappeared through the barn door with the horse. Briskly she walked toward the house. Once inside, she stopped in the bedroom to check on Eli. He looked like he was asleep. Certain that this was a trick, she went back to the cupboard to check on the cinnamon rolls. All three plates were still there untouched.

Monroe's light was out when she got upstairs. She lit her kerosene lamp, wrote a few lines in her tablet about the day's events, and then blew out the light.

Thirty-nine

The evening before the school picnic, Eli hobbled out to the barn for chores to prove he was up to it. "At least it gets me out of the house," he muttered darkly, "but my ribs are too sore for milking yet. I squeezed them half to death trying."

Ella thought he looked healthy today among the other young boys his age, almost as if he had never been injured. When he moved, though, he had a careful way in which he turned his arms. He was in deep conversation with a friend at present but would leave soon to make his phone call to that *Englisha* girl. Hopefully the girl had come to her senses by now, if Eli hadn't.

A softball game was organized and in full swing. Ella decided not to play for various reasons. For one, she had Eli on her mind. Not that she could do much about that, but it did feel inappropriate to play with such potentially life-changing things underfoot. Secondly, there were plenty of people to play, so she wasn't missed.

The crack of the bat came clearly, loud enough so that several heads turned. Ella couldn't make out for sure who had been up at the plate, but the boy tore around the bases while a wild dash was made to gather the ball from the outfield.

The throw reached third base too late, and the boy made his race for home plate in plenty of time. He bent forward, gasped for air, and flopped out on the grass behind home plate. Ella had figured out by then who he was. He was one of the young Mast boys who dated her cousin.

Ella glanced around and caught her cousin's eye. She had watched the race too and broke into a broad smile. A sharp pain ran through Ella. *How is it to have the one you love, alive and well and out on the ball field? Aden would have been there. He never passed up a chance to play softball, and he was good at the game. I'll never have that again. Youth has failed me and torn love from my heart like it was a thornbush in the pasture to be uprooted and cast away forever. Now there is only the young bishop who wants my attention, and that I have to get away from.*

After lunch and the program, Ella had obtained permission from her mom to drive over and see how the progress on the house was going.

"The footers are poured," Daniel had whispered to her after the youth singing on Sunday night. Whatever that meant, she planned to find out.

The itch was strong to be involved as much as possible. Daniel wouldn't object, she assumed. If he did, he could say so. Today, she couldn't stay long at the site, but if things worked out with her mom, she would return other days with time for actual work.

Her eye caught sight of two boys making their way down the hill from the schoolhouse. One of them was Eli, and the other one was their cousin. Below the hill, the pay phone stood. Surely, Eli hadn't taken his cousin into his confidence. She could imagine he needed cover for the stroll, but things would not go well with him if the cousin passed on any information.

They soon moved out of sight, and so she could do nothing but worry, distracted with her concern. Clara came up and touched her arm from behind, and Ella jumped.

"Sorry," Clara whispered. "Do you think I'll do okay with the program?"

Ella gathered her thoughts together and gave Clara a quick smile. "Ach, yah. You know the lines well. I've heard you say them at home many times."

"But I have to be standin' beside Paul." Clara glanced up at Ella. "What if I turn red?"

"No one knows the difference," Ella assured her. "They'll just think you're nervous about readin' the poem, which is perfectly normal. You don't have to be ashamed of it, anyway, even if people find out you like him."

Clara smiled and seemed to relax. "I'll be glad when it's over, though. He makes me nervous and shaky."

"You'll be a big girl before too long, all grown up and running with the young folks." Ella gave her a hug. "And Paul can take you home, then."

"I don't want to think about that. I try not to think about him at all—especially today when I don't want to turn red."

"You'll do okay." Ella squeezed her arm. "It's almost lunchtime."

"I'm hungry now." Clara glanced at the table set up with casseroles, meats, pies, and cinnamon rolls.

"Here comes the bishop," Ella whispered. "I expect it's time for prayer."

Bishop Hostetler walked to the front of the schoolhouse, cleared his throat, and began, "It's time to eat, everyone. Would someone run outside and let the children in the ball field know, and then we can get to all this food. I'm sure none of us are any hungrier than the children are."

There were vigorous nods from several little boys, and two of the older men went outside. They waved their arms toward the ball field and shouted, "Lunchtime, children!" Young children came at a run from all directions, followed by the more dignified older ones.

Inside the schoolhouse, the bishop said, "We have all gathered now. Let's us go to *Da Hah* in prayer."

He had a clear voice that carried well, trembling only slightly for an older man. His long beard was a solid grey already, and his step was still steady. His gaze was that of a man used to the exercise of power. Ella had known him all her life.

When he was done with the prayer, a line immediately formed. Ella waited until her cousin and Dora came forward and then joined them. She noticed Eli and his cousin coming back up the hill at a slow walk. He didn't look sheepish, but she doubted if that meant much. When Eli did what he thought was right, he didn't look sheepish, regardless of what others thought. He had a strength that could well turn into a weakness, as far as Amish ways were concerned.

With her plate full, Ella found a seat beside her cousin.

"I see you found some of my mamm's chicken casserole," her cousin said with a glance at her plate.

"Looks *gut*," Ella told her with a smile. "I didn't know it came from your mamm."

"Mamm tried it for the first time. The recipe came from her sister in Holmes County. That's kind of dangerous, I thought, to use a recipe for the first time here, even if your sister says it's good. I told her she ought to practice on us first, but that's how mamm is. She likes to try new things right away."

Ella lifted a spoonful of casserole to her mouth and carefully savored the bite. "I don't think you're mamm could go wrong," she said. "She's known for her tasty cooking. Tastes really delicious."

"Still makes me nervous," her cousin muttered. "The way mamm does her things."

Ella glanced nervously in Eli's direction as the conversation rose and fell around them. Eli was in the middle of a real big laugh about something with boys gathered around him. Certainly the joke wouldn't be about any *Englisha* girl. Likely as not, it was a cover for his actions. Eli usually stayed pretty calm in public.

Ella finished her lunch and then helped clean up the tables. Containers of leftover casseroles and pies were taken back out to the buggies, and the place was swept up quickly. They were barely done when the senior teacher walked up to the front of the schoolhouse.

"And now for our school program," he announced. "If all of you will please find seats, we can begin."

Ella quickly found a front-row seat and sat down. Halfway through the program, Clara's part came up. She stood there bravely beside Paul, her chin firm, though Ella thought her fingers trembled a little. Her voice was strong and steady as she went through her part of the poem without a hint of any blushes. Paul was a nice young man, and it was easy to see why Clara would be charmed by his attentions.

Ella didn't dare show her pleasure until Clara had taken her seat. When Clara glanced back, she gave her a big smile. The red then spread slightly up Clara's neck, but disappeared a few minutes later. *Clara will soon be all grown up, married, and gone before I can blink an eye. Me? I will be nothing but an old maid, stuck safely in my house.* The dark thoughts had come quickly, and Ella caught herself before her glumness showed on her face. *Life has to be taken one step at a time, and today has sufficient trouble of its own. I know what needs to be done today, and the rest will work itself out in its own good time. Life will be less attractive than when Aden was here, but still I must step onward.*

With the program over, she got the horse ready with Monroe's help. No one gave her strange looks when she drove away. Already other buggies were hitched up to leave. Her heart hurt as she drove down the gravel road and past the creek and Aden's old home place, but already the pain was a little less.

She followed Daniel's directions and found the site on the corner of Chapman and Young. The land rose gently in the west, a great mound of dirt off to the left. With the horse tied to a fencerow, she approached the activity at the house site. Daniel waved and came to meet her.

"Well, I've come," she told him with a smile, a little breathless from the walk in from the road.

"We're layin' block today and for the rest of the week, really," he told her. "Come on up close, and you can watch."

"Can't help much with that," she said, "but I want to come back later and actually help out. We had our school picnic today, and I have to get home for chores before too long."

"I heard," he said, grinning. "Ours will be next week."

He led her closer to where blocks were brought in by hand and placed on boards. Several men moved about, trowels in their hands, spreading mortar and setting the blocks in place one by one.

"How many men have you got," she asked, "working for you full-time? Surely, not all of these. That would be a lot of men to keep busy!"

"No," he said and shook his head, "these are masons. Only four of us make up the usual crew. Presently we are just helping them because we don't know much about layin' block."

Ella watched with fascination.

"I can help carry several of those things in," Ella said, pointing to the block pile. "They don't look too heavy."

"You sure?" Daniel tilted his head sideways. "They're heavier than they look."

"Ach, yah," she said. "I'd like to help, and this, at least, would be a start."

Daniel waved his hand toward the wall he was on.

"Okay, strong woman, I'll take some over here."

Ella grabbed the block with both hands. The rough edges bit into her fingers, and she found the block heavier than she expected, but she managed—to the encouraging smiles of the boys around her.

"She can do it, yah," one of them with a big smile on his face said after her third trip.

Ella felt joy rise in her heart. The work of the house building would do her a lot of good. Surely *Da Hah* was in this. His ways were mysterious, but she would just continue to follow where He led.

"Got to go," she told Daniel a few minutes later. "Chore time for me."

"We'll be here most every day unless it rains," he said.

"I'll come when I can," she said and smiled with happiness in her heart.

"You sure you want to?" he asked, his brow creased. "We can manage."

"I want to," she assured him.

He got down off the wooden plank and walked her to the road. She untied her horse and got in while he held the horse's bridle. With a quick wave, she went past him and turned left, down Chapman road toward the south.

At home, after chores, she caught Eli alone. "I want the whole story," she whispered. "And I mean the whole story."

"I called her," he admitted sheepishly, "but don't be tellin' Mamm and Daett because I suspect I'll see her once, and then it'll be over with."

"You'd best not see her at all," Ella said, but that stubborn look crossed his face, so she dropped the subject.

Later in her room, Dora stepped in. Ella told her and wrote the event in her tablet but hoped with all her heart the matter would go no further. Eli could make an awful mess out of his life if he wasn't careful about this.

With a prayer on her lips, she gazed at the stars for a long time, and then blew out the light.

Forty

E lla sat at the kitchen table, staring off into space. There was work to do and plenty of it. *I really should get up and get started, but I wonder what Daniel is doing at my house right now. Is he setting walls yet, or, perhaps, he's ready to work on the subfloor. Daniel said yesterday that the first load of wood from the lumberyard in Randolph is going to arrive today. How wonderful it would be to watch them unload it and marvel at that pile of lumber that will become my house! But today is a day to be home, and that is that.*

"Why don't you take all week off and spend it with your house building," Dora said, popping her head into the kitchen. "I can see your mind isn't here, and I'm willing to take the extra load. If you ask nicely, I'm sure Eli and Monroe will also agree to help wherever they can."

"Oh, would you?" Ella said, leaping to her feet. "I would so love that, but I don't want to put an extra burden on everyone."

"If you help chore in the mornings and evenings, that will be enough until the house is done," Mamm called from the living room. "I can understand that your heart would be with the house building."

"Oh, Mamm," Ella said, rushing to the kitchen doorway, "you are being way too nice."

"It's the way it should be," Mamm said as a matter of fact.

"And I'm getting better at milking," Eli said from the couch. "First one cow at a time, and now I'm almost back with my full load. I might even venture out to the fields today."

"So that's decided," Mamm said. "Now let's all get busy with our work."

"Then I'll go work on my quilt," Ella said, "and thank you all so much. One more day with the quilt, and then I'm off to Chapman Road to watch the house."

"That's a good girl," Dora said, slapping her on the back. "Now get busy."

Ella laughed, running down the stairs.

"You're going to trip and kill yourself," Dora hollered after her.

"I was being careful," Ella said. "Now *you* get back to work."

With a smile Ella pulled a chair up to the quilt. Dora was often the one in a dark mood, but deep down she was the sweetest thing. How wonderful it was that things were slowly returning to normal. Even Eli might soon be well, and she would have her house completed soon.

Ella stitched rapidly, taking only a short break for lunch. An hour before chore time, she finished and stood to stretch her weary back. With a sigh she climbed up the stairs.

"Eli's already left for the barn," Dora said, busy at the stove.

"But it's early," Ella said, glancing at the clock.

"He won't start before it's time," Dora said. "He just needed to get out of the house."

"Then I'm going to make sure he doesn't," Ella said, walking toward the front door. "And thank you so much for taking on my extra work."

"Don't worry about it," Dora said, frowning. "You'd do the same thing for me and then some."

After chores the next morning, Ella hitched the horse to the buggy and drove out of the lane at a fast clip. The sun hadn't been up long, and perhaps Daniel wouldn't be on the job site yet. She wanted to be there early just in case.

While driving down the hill and past the schoolhouse, she waved to the teacher walking into the schoolyard. At the bridge, Ella never slowed. She took the winding roads at a fast trot. Finally arriving at the site, she tied up along the fencerow and walked up the hill. Already men were pulling boards off the pile of lumber and busily cutting with saws.

"So the strong woman is back," Daniel said, laughing heartily.

"I'm here to help," she said. "How fast things have changed since I was here last."

"That's because we're such good workers," Daniel said.

"You're also full of yourself right now," she said, "but tell me what to do."

He pointed toward the floorboards. "How about putting nails in those?"

"If you show me a few times," she said, taking a deep breath.

"Well," he said, picking a nail out of his pouch, "this is how you hold it."

"I already know that," she said.

"But there's more to it than that," he said. "You place four nails in between these marks and pound them in."

"I can also do that," she said, picking up more nails.

"Practice there first," he said, pointing toward a piece of wood.

Grimly Ella bent over and started pounding away.

"Again, just for practice," Daniel said.

Slowly Ella repeated the maneuver, and Daniel waved his arm toward his men.

"We're ready to go, so bring another board in," Daniel said. "That was really good work, Ella."

"You're just saying so."

"No, I'm not," he said, moving the next piece of board in place and nailing one section while Ella pounded her nail in as quickly as she could.

"Almost as good as a boy," Daniel said, laughing. "By the time we're done, you can join the crew."

"Don't tease me. This is hard enough," Ella said as they brought in the next board.

"You're a better worker than my sisters," Daniel said. "I'm not teasing."

"Well, it's wonderful to help," she said, bending over to hammer as another board came into place.

The hours went by quickly, and they ate lunch sitting against a lumber pile, shielded in part from the bright sunlight. By early afternoon the last of the floorboards had been nailed into place.

"We're ready for plywood next," Daniel said, pointing toward the pile of flat lumber.

"And what am I to do?" Ella asked.

"Just wait while we carry the pieces in, and then you can help hammer."

Wearily Ella stepped back and watched as they glued the edges of the upright boards and allowed the pieces of plywood to fall into place with a sharp bang. Then they pounded the tongue and groove edges together with sledgehammers.

"There's the work that needs to be done," Daniel said, shouting above the noise and pointing out the lines on the plywood. "We need nails all the way across about eight inches apart."

Ella glanced at the piece of plywood and then across the still unfinished subfloor.

"That's an awful lot of hammering," she said.

Daniel laughed. "We will help, so don't worry."

Ella pounded away and was joined by all the men at the end of each row.

"We have to keep up before the glue dries," Daniel said. "It's not that we think you're slow."

"Stop worrying about me," she said.

"Tired and snappy already," he said with a grin.

"I guess," she said. Daniel was being wonderful, building her house. It was going to be wonderful even though it didn't look much like a house yet.

"We're making *gut* progress," Daniel said when she stopped to catch her breath.

"Yah, and it seems like the house is getting smaller instead of bigger."

"That's the nature of things with homes," Daniel said, pausing to look around. "They always look smaller when only the foundation or sub-floors are in. Once the walls are up, the true size becomes apparent."

The rest of the crew nodded, and Ella paused to look back across the plywood they had put down.

"It still looks small," she said, and they laughed.

By late afternoon they were three quarters of the way across, and Ella stood to leave. Daniel waved as she climbed down the ladder and turned to walk back to where her horse was tied along the fencerow. The horse still had a few nibbles of hay left from what she had given it at lunchtime and was trying to dig them out of the grass. She backed the horse around and climbed into the buggy. The horse started with a jerk, heading home with eager steps.

By midmorning the next day, the floor plywood was down, and Daniel marked off the boards for the wall construction, laying them in place along the outer edges. Ella watched them place a few studs between the marks and then grabbed a handful of her own. When they came to the end of the wall, she turned to look behind her. Daniel had been correct. Already the stretch of laid-out wall made the house look larger.

"Nail in a stud where each set of marks is," Daniel said, bending over to trace the marks with his finger. "You use two nails for each stud, and these double marks are for windows and doors. The boys and I will finish those. All you have to do is leave a stud out wherever there is a zero inside the set of marks."

Ella glanced up and down the lines. "It looks easy enough," she said, her hammer ready.

"Oh," Daniel said, raising his hand. "I just thought of something. Do you want to know how things are laid out on the inside—since you've not seen my plans yet?"

"Of course," Ella said. "And you'd better show me where the front door, living room, and kitchen are. I need to see how they flow together."

"Then let them work on the wall," Daniel said, waving his hand. "Come over here and show me what you want."

Ella followed him to where he had the plans open on a piece of plywood, watching as he traced the blueprint lines with his pencil.

Do I dare make suggestions? Things look fairly decent already, but this is my house, after all. She cleared her throat and, glancing at Daniel's face, said, "I'd like the kitchen moved to this wall so that it looks out toward the back."

Daniel shrugged. "Hey, it's your house. We can still change most anything right now. And what you just moved requires only the change of one wall, which isn't really too bad."

"I think that's all I want changed," Ella said.

"Just speak up about any changes that you want," Daniel said. "As long as we catch things in time, I don't mind. Maybe you should look things over a little more."

Ella studied the print for a few minutes and shook her head, "I think the kitchen is really my only concern. And the rest doesn't really matter as long as it flows together."

"And you think it flows well?" he asked.

"Yes, I think it does," she said with appreciation.

They then joined the others who were constructing the wall. The gas-powered saw roared all day long as one person cut the boards to correct lengths, and the others put things together.

"You can work on the headers," Daniel said, hollering above the noise.

"What are headers?" she asked.

"The headers are made out of this pile of boards, and they need plywood nailed between them."

Ella nodded as he set two of the boards out on the plywood floor.

"You have to be careful," Daniel said. "Each edge of the board has to be lined up fairly close otherwise you get a crooked header."

"What happens then?" she asked.

"It can allow the wall to settle later."

Ella gasped. "I don't want my house falling down on my head. Maybe you'd better do this part of the job."

"No," he said, laughing, "it's not hard at all so don't worry. Simply take this square and hold it against the board on each end, and you should be okay."

"Okay," Ella said, kneeling on the plywood floor. She started the nail on the first board, pushing the square tight against the two stacked boards. Holding them together with her knee, she pounded away. With the two nails in, she sighted down the edge and then tried to adjust them. They still didn't look right, and so she pounded some more.

"You don't have to be that careful," Daniel said, standing at her shoulder. "Just as long as it's close, it's good enough."

"Then why did you tell me earlier to be so careful?"

"Maybe I made it sound too serious," he said, kneeling beside her and sighting the two boards with his eye.

"Is it good enough?" she asked.

"It's very good," he said, "so stop worrying."

"Okay," she said as he moved away.

Daniel was a *gut* boy, and he was trying hard to help her. Aden would be glad if he were here and could see them. A cloud passed over the sun, and Ella wiped her eyes. Aden wasn't here, but she was moving on with life now, and Aden would also like that.

Ella laid the square on the floor again. Taking a careful look, she started the nail. On the other end, she repeated the maneuver, lifting the header to sight down the edge when she was done. It would have to be good enough even though the edges weren't exactly perfect. This wasn't quilting, it was house building. Finishing the header, she added it to the pile.

Chore time came quickly, and Ella climbed down the ladder to leave.

"See you tomorrow," Daniel hollered after her, and the others waved.

She stopped a distance from the house to look back at the work they had done. One of the long walls and the end was up, held in place on the inside with two by fours nailed to the floor. It didn't look like much, but this would be her house, and she would soon live here.

Ella smiled, and giving her horse a gentle rub on the neck, she turned it around on the road to drive home.

The week went by quickly, and the plywood second floor was down by Saturday. Ella helped hand up materials to the upper level on Monday morning, pushing up boards with one of the men until her arms ached.

"Ella," Daniel yelled down from the second floor, "that's enough of that. Come up and help with the walls again."

"I'm fine," she said. "I can help down here."

"I said come up," he said, glaring down through the open stairwell.

"A little bossy, are we?" she said, teasing.

"Just come up," he said, not moving away until she climbed the ladder.

"Satisfied?" she said, standing on the second floor, strapping on her nail apron.

"Yah," he said, turning toward the wall he had marked off. "That's much better."

"You still don't have to be so bossy," she said to his retreating back.

"I just don't want you to get hurt," he muttered.

Ella smiled as she began to work on the headers again. It was *gut* to feel looked after, but Daniel didn't really need to worry. She knew how to work hard and was used to it.

Forty-one

The load of trusses came the next week, and Ella watched as the men set each one by hand. At the end of the day, they stood like spiny skeletons, outlined against the evening sky, their centers having been guided in place by the string along the top. Daniel began working on the roof plywood that afternoon and completed it two days later, rolling out the black tar paper before Ella left for her chores. She walked up the field behind the house, where the ground rose to the highest level, and looked back on the house. The outline of the house was now in place. All the windows were in, and the roof was a black shiny surface, waiting for the shingles to be added tomorrow. The sight took her breath away.

Clara's house was a reality, or almost one. And how strange *Da Hah*'s ways were. Even before Aden passed away, Clara had been given the inspiration for the way the house would look. If there ever were doubts in the future, here was the proof that when things had made no sense during her darkest hours, *Da Hah* had been with her.

That night after chores, Ella walked out behind the barn and looked again for the killdeer nest. Both parents raised a terrible racket, flying almost to her feet and then taking off in their fluttery attempts at flight. Carefully she searched the ground and found the four chicks, just hatched, their fluffy heads and bodies flat against the gravel nest.

"Hello," she whispered, bending low over the nest. They didn't move, their feathers almost a perfect blend with the surrounding soil.

Ella watched the little birds for a few moments while the fuss from the parents grew to a furious pitch.

"Don't worry," she whispered, but they only dashed to her feet to make their objections all the more obvious. Apparently they were convinced she meant them only evil. Slowly she backed away and made note of where the nest was. It lay out of the main path they used for field work but might still be in danger from some of Eli or Monroe's ventures with the teams.

Glancing west, Ella saw great stacks of dark storm clouds working their way across the mountains. Lightning bolts lit up the sky, and the whole system headed their way. Ella shivered, going inside to help with supper.

"It looks like quite a storm's coming up," Mamm said.

"Yes, it does," Ella said, glancing out of the kitchen window.

"Is your house in danger?" Mamm asked.

"Not with the way Daniel builds," she said with a smile. "We might lose some tar paper, though. They didn't have time today to get all the shingles on."

"That's good to hear," Mamm said, bustling around the kitchen with Ella joining in to help. By the time the men rushed in from the barn, followed closely by the sharp lash of the storm, supper was on the table.

"Perhaps we'd better head for the basement," Daett said, approaching the table.

"Not tonight," Mamm said. "I don't think there are any twisters. It's mostly lightning strikes, and those will reach us in the basement as well as up here. We have to trust in *Da Hah*'s protection."

"He has been good to us," Daett said, sitting down with a sigh. "And may He watch over us tonight as we sure do need the rain."

With the rest of the family at the table, Daett bowed his head in prayer, and then the meal began.

"I found a killdeer nest," Ella said, turning to Eli and Monroe, "and

I want the two of you to be careful when you take the team out to the fields. The nest is to the left of the lane, close to the fencerow."

"My, my," Eli said, "the woman builds a house, and now she wants to run the place."

"That's what I say," Monroe said. "I'm surprised she can still sit with us at the table."

"Boys, boys," Daett said, laughing as the rain lashed the kitchen window, "we can all be thankful that *Da Hah* has allowed Ella to move on with her life. I know it's not exactly what we expected, but it is His will."

"Thank you," Ella whispered as tears formed at the edges of her eyes.

"She's going to have me crying soon," Eli said, faking a sharp sniffle. Ella glared at him, and he burst out laughing.

By bedtime the storm had quieted down, and Ella climbed the stairs, entered her bedroom, and sat on the bed. She sat in the darkness for long moments, finally getting up to light the kerosene lamp on the dresser and pulling it closer to her.

"Dear Journal," she wrote.

> Work on the house is now progressing quite well, though I never would have thought such a thing was possible. I, little Ella Yoder, am building a house for myself. Yet Da Hah has seen fit to allow it as He has seen fit to allow my Aden to be taken.
>
> Daniel is confident he can be done in another month or two. He has quite a lot of work lined up for himself after that, and I have my twenty-first birthday coming up. It will all come together so well. I find myself comforted even when my heart bleeds again for Aden, as

it does often—especially on nights like this when a storm has just blown through. Somehow it reminds me of my loss, and what will never be again.

Weary, Ella closed the notebook, climbed into bed, and drifted off to sleep easily.

In the morning, her mom softly called to her from the bottom of the stairwell. Ella dressed slowly, rubbing her arms and legs. She was only used to using muscles that farmwork required. If things continued on like this, a month might be a long time to keep up the heavy work schedule she was on. Yet, it was also a great joy even with the pain.

"Good morning," Mamm said when Ella walked into the kitchen. "Happy this morning?"

"Tired and happy," Ella said with a smile. "I guess I'm out in the barn for chores this morning."

"That would be the best if you're up to it. You've been working hard."

"Oh, yah," Ella said, grabbing her coat as Dora and Monroe came down the stairs. She waited a few minutes and walked outside with them. The cool morning air filled her lungs, and she took deep breaths, waving her arms around in the air.

"Stop that," Dora said. "You're making me tired."

"It feels so good to be alive," Ella said, suddenly stopping to listen. The first streaks of dawn painted the eastern sky in front of them as they turned to look down the road and toward the sound of rapid horse hooves.

"It's Daniel's buggy coming," Monroe said, squinting into the semi-darkness. "I wonder what he wants this early? Probably something to do with Ella's house. I sure hope that thing gets done soon, and every-one stops pestering us."

"The house," Ella said, not moving. "Did something happen to the house?"

"It probably burned to the ground in the lightning storm last night," Dora said.

"Dora," Ella said, hardly able to breathe, "don't say things like that."

"I'll go out and see what he wants," Monroe said, his voice full of concern.

"No," Ella said, holding up her hand. "I'll go talk to him myself. I might as well face this."

The two looked at her, shook their heads, and walked on toward the barn. Daniel was still seated in the buggy when she reached him, holding the reins limply in his hands. He looked as though he hadn't slept. His hair was disheveled, his clothing was soot-stained, and his eyes were red. He hung out of his buggy and coughed, apparently too exhausted to climb down.

Ella's heart pounded furiously. "What's wrong?" she whispered. "Did the house burn down?"

"No," he said, mustering a smile. "I'm sorry for scaring you like this, but lightning struck a tree behind our corncrib, and we didn't see it till it was almost too late. I was up most of the night with Daett moving what corn was left inside the barn."

"Did the corncrib burn up?"

"Partly. But we put the fire out with two water hoses from the barn."

"Then the house is okay?"

He nodded. "I came to tell you that I won't be working there today. The boys will, but I have to get some sleep."

"Then I won't either," she said, "but that's okay. I'm so sorry about the corncrib."

He smiled weakly. "That's much better than if the house had burned."

"Yah," she said, "so will this slow down the work?"

"Oh," he said, "I might as well tell you since I'm here. Dad talked with the bishop last night and gave him the whole story about the house we're building."

"Oh!" Ella gasped, her hand flying to her mouth. "And what did he say?"

A broad smile spread across Daniel's face. "He wants to have a work frolic on Saturday and, perhaps, one after that. Just think—we could be done with this very quickly, which is one of the reasons I don't feel too bad about taking off today."

"But what about Preacher Stutzman? Doesn't he have objections?"

"The bishop said he's a broken man since his wife passed. Stutzman still sorrows, the bishop said, and won't stand in the way of the community helping with the house."

"This is such wonderful news and after such a scare," Ella said. "I can hardly believe it."

"Well, believe it," Daniel said, slapping the reins. "I have to get home, so have a good day."

"Thank you," Ella whispered as his buggy wheels rattled out the driveway.

"So the house didn't burn down," Dora said when Ella walked into the barn. "I'm glad, Ella."

Forty-two

On Saturday morning, Ella stood on the hill behind the house and watched as the buggies pulled in for the work-frolic. They had to be coming from five and six districts away, the men spilling out into the yard and shouting to each other as they made plans for the day. A wagon pulled in, and planks were unloaded that quickly became scaffolding around three sides of the house. Men began to nail the wooden corner beads on, followed by the vinyl siding pieces. At this speed they would be done on the front before lunchtime.

Daniel was somewhere in the group, but it was impossible to find him in the sea of hats and bonnets.

"Ella," her daett shouted from the edge of the crowd, "come down here. They need you."

"What can I do with so many people around?" Ella asked, walking up to where he waited.

"The women want you in the house while they paint," he said with laughter. "I think it makes them feel better."

"Then I'll help with the painting."

"Just come," he said, leading the way through the crowd and holding the front door for her. "Go in there and tell them they're doing great work."

Ella squeezed past two women who were coming out with empty water buckets in their hands. One of them stopped and took Ella by the arm.

"Ella," Lester Raber's wife, Kristine, said. "You're the very person we're looking for. Where do we find the well? The women need water for their washrags."

"The well's behind the house," Ella said, motioning through the walls with her hand.

"Thanks," Kristine said. "We can't find anything around here with all the people running around. But it's going to be a wonderful day, and everyone should get lots of work done."

"I know…and thank you," Ella said as the women rushed outside to the well with their rags.

As she walked into the room that was to be her living room, Ella paused to watch the men nail the sheets of paneling to the walls. They had the ceilings already done, and through the open doorways, other men were visible busily hammering away.

"We need you, Ella," Mamm said, pulling her against the wall as a long line of men went by carrying paneling into the rooms.

"What are we going to do with all this mess going on?" Ella asked. "I wasn't expecting it to be quite this busy. It's certainly not like working with Daniel and his men."

"Don't worry," Mamm said, smiling broadly. "They're all doing as well as Daniel, and there are more of them. We need to start painting this room as soon as they're done in here. That's what the women are waiting for."

"Then I'll help," Ella said. "It might help to calm my nerves."

Mamm laughed. "I'm afraid your nerves won't calm down all day, but I don't want you working. What you need to do is walk around and assure everyone that they're doing what you want."

"That's what Daett said, and I guess I can do that," Ella said, taking a deep breath.

"The room is all yours. We're moving on to the next room," one of the men shouted so loudly that Ella rubbed her ears.

As the men left the room, women carrying paint rollers and pans scurried about. Some laid drop cloths on the floor while others started trimming the room's edges with brushes. Four women who had extensions for their paint rollers started on the ceiling. Ella watched, smiling and nodding whenever one of them glanced in her direction.

"It looks beautiful," she said as they started on the walls.

"We need you over here," Mose Stutzman's wife, Martha, said, looking in from the other room. "We're ready to start painting in the next room."

Ella followed her to the kitchen area, the walls still bare of any cabinets.

"Do we paint everything in here?" Martha asked.

"Well," Ella said, "cabinets still need to be installed—"

"Is the kitchen ready for me?" a male voice hollered from the door opening.

Ella turned to see the face of the local cabinetmaker, Eldon Raber, smiling in on the sea of faces.

"No," she said, returning his smile. "We're trying to figure out what needs to be painted."

"Hah," Eldon said with a wave of his hand, "with so many hardworking women around, just paint the whole thing. That way I don't have to worry about anything, and I can hang my cabinets where I want to."

"Well," Ella said, "there's your answer. Paint the whole thing."

"Do you want to see the cabinets?" Eldon asked as the women laid out the drop cloths and started painting.

"I'd love to," Ella said, following him through the crowded rooms to the outside.

"There," he said, pulling back the blankets on his spring wagon. "That's only the first load, but you can see what they look like."

"They're lovely," she said, rubbing her hand gently over the smooth finish, "but you didn't have to make them out of cherry."

"That was Aden's choice," he said. "He had already talked to me about making them before he passed on."

"Oh," Ella said, "I didn't know."

"I'm sorry," Eldon said. "I guess I should have mentioned it before, but it didn't seem appropriate until Daniel asked me to make the cabinets a few weeks ago."

"I can never thank you enough," Ella said, wiping her eyes. "Everyone is being way too nice today."

"We only want to help," he said. "We all loved Aden. He was a *gut* man."

"Yah," she said, "he was."

"I shouldn't keep you," he said. "The women need you inside, and I have more cabinets coming."

Ella nodded, turning to go inside. Pressing through the crowd, her mamm waved at her to come toward the back of the house.

"The main bedroom is ready to paint," she said. "The women want to know whether the light blue is what you want."

"That's what I told Daniel to get, but let me check," she said, following her mother into the bedroom.

"We're sorry to bother you," Kristine Raber said, "but we wanted to be sure."

"It's perfect," Ella said, holding the paint lid up to the light streaming in from the open window.

"I think it dries a little darker yet," Bertha said.

"But that's what you would want," Mamm said, and Ella nodded.

"And all the bedrooms down here get the same blue," Ella said.

"I think there should be enough paint," Bertha said. "I saw a dozen gallons outside."

"I would think there's enough because Daniel's good at figuring such things," Ella said before her mamm pulled her aside.

"I hope you haven't told Daniel to get more than two colors for the house," Mamm whispered in her ear.

"We're doing a darker blue on the whole upstairs," Ella whispered back. "Surely that's not too fancy. Daniel didn't think so."

"I guess not," Mamm conceded, "but it's pushing things. And I don't know if you should depend so much on Daniel's opinion. You should have asked someone older."

"I think it'll be okay," Ella said. "Really, Mamm, it will be."

"Okay," Mamm said, seeming to relax. "And I am glad for the *gut* sense that you do have."

"Thanks, Mamm," Ella said, squeezing her arm.

Soon after eleven, Ella joined the women outside. Someone had brought in the church wagon, and they set up the long tables in tight rows on the grass. Bertha Raber set the younger boys to work rolling out the tablecloths. They lost control of the first one in a gust of wind, which lifted up the back end and tossed it over their heads as they reached desperately skyward, trying to grab on. The cloth came flapping down across the whole line of tables, slid off onto the grass, and rolled farther down the hill.

"That's it," Bertha said. "We're doing the tables without tablecloths today. I can't afford to have the white cloths all grass strained."

"They might stay down once there is food on," Esther Yoder suggested.

"We can't take that chance in this wind," Bertha said. "The first thing we know, the whole thing—food and all—will be up in the air and down the hill."

"Well, we can't let that happen," Esther said, "so I'm agreed. We'll just have to scrub the benches clean afterward."

"We'll tell the men to eat carefully," Rosemary Miller said. "Maybe they can keep from spilling their plates."

Laughter rose from the women within earshot, and Ella joined in.

"Let's get busy, then," Bertha said. "I think most of the food is still in the buggies."

Ella helped them move the food to the tables. They took the hot dishes to the two woodstoves someone had brought in and set out in the open away from any buildings. They were belching smoke out of the backs, the fires tended diligently by several young girls.

"Have you got it good and hot?" Ella asked young Irene Raber, her face red from the heat.

"As hot as I can get it in this wind," Irene said, stuffing more wood into the firebox.

"It shouldn't take long, then, to warm up the dishes," Ella said, unwrapping the casserole she carried from the thick quilt. Gingerly she opened one corner of the foil-wrapped top as several women behind her did the same. Ella opened the oven door and slid her casserole in, stepping aside as the other women followed suit. Ten minutes later Ella opened the door to check, peaking into the open corner.

"It's boiling," she said, pulling her casserole out to wrap in the quilt again.

Walking over to the tables, she set it down and headed out to the buggies again. By noon they were almost ready, and a portable dinner bell was rung loudly. The men lined up at the washbasins, scrubbing their hands and splashing water on their faces. They dried their hands on towels draped over chairs.

Several of the young boys started splashing water and snapping their towels at each other.

"Young Henry, here, thinks he can hold a sheet of plywood overhead with his hands and start the nail with his toes," Emery Mast said with a great laugh.

"Well I can," Henry said, waving his hand towel around. "I had to do that this winter when we worked out in the barn. I don't know why you don't believe me."

"That's because I want to see tall tales before I believe them," Emery said. "You could have showed us in the house."

Henry shook his head. "There were too many women around for such a thing."

"Hah," Emery said. "Did you forget to clean between your toes last morning?"

"Wait till we tell Emma Rose about this," Mose Yoder said.

Henry's face turned bright red. "It's not a fitting posture for a young man to stand with his foot stuck up in the air around women, but I can do it. And all of you had better mind your own business with Emma Rose."

"I was thinking of asking her home myself," Emery teased. "And I think this dirty toe business is the exact opening I need."

"You'd better not," Henry said, snapping the towel in his direction.

"Hey, I need that towel," Bishop Miller said, reaching for it, his face dripping with water. "I hope none of you young boys plan to act up at Ella's house building."

"No," Emery said, "we're good as gold. We were just teasing Henry a bit."

"That's *gut*," the bishop said thoughtfully, wiping his face and long beard. "I'd say we all go get a bite to eat."

"I could use that," Henry said. "I'm starved from all this nailing with my toes."

They all laughed and followed the bishop over to the table.

The bishop stood at the end of table. He looked out at the people before drawing in a deep breath and speaking out.

"We are all gathered here to build Ella Yoder's house today," he said, his voice carrying out to the hot stoves where the young girls turned to listen. "Let us give thanks today to God who has blessed us with so many things. He has kept us safe and given us the blessings of our families, of our faith, of our communities, and now this food, which has been prepared for us. Let us pray."

He bowed his head, and they all followed.

Ella stood at the edge of the crowd as they filled their plates and sat down to eat. These were her people and her life, and today they had gathered to help her. She pushed the stray strands of her hair under her *kapp* and turned into the wind to dry her eyes.

By evening the house wasn't finished, and Daniel found Ella standing outside in the yard.

"Don't worry," he said. "We'll all be back next Saturday for another frolic."

"I'm not worried," Ella said with a smile. "It's just such a *gut* feeling to have the support of the people—our people."

"Yah," Daniel said, "it is *gut*. It is the way of our people...and the way of *Da Hah*."

The following week Daniel and his crew started another job, but on Saturday they showed up with the smaller crowd who would help put the finishing touches on the house.

By the time the sun was setting, the last of the trim had been placed, the hardwood was given a final coat of varnish, and the knobs were placed on the doors.

After the last buggy left, Clara came sneaking up the hill, struggling with a plastic wrapped bundle.

"What are you doing?" Ella asked.

"I was waiting until everyone was gone," Clara said. "I hid the quilt in your buggy this morning."

"Ah, so we can see how it looks in the house," Ella said, breaking into a weary smile. "I think that's a great idea."

Together they walked into the house, pulled off the wrapping, and carefully unfolded the layers. Ella spread the quilt out on the countertop, and, taking Clara by the arm, stepped back a ways.

"It's so beautiful," Ella said, pulling Clara into a tight hug. "And it was your idea to begin with."

"I was glad to help," Clara said, "and, yes, it is beautiful."

After both girls wiped away tears, Clara said, "We'd better go now. Daett wants help with the chores, I'm sure."

As they turned to leave, Ella looked back for a final glance at the quilt, still draped over the counter. Then she took Clara by the arm, and together they walked a distance up the hill for one more look before returning home.

"It *is* your house," Ella whispered, "just as you drew it. Truly *Da Hah* has given, and *Da Hah* has taken."

"Yah," Clara said, "and with a lot of pain, but now it's done."

"You're sounding like Dora," Ella said as they laughed together.

Behind them the last rays of the sunset broke through the low clouds, painting the house a brilliant red. They stood unmoving until the color faded away. Slowly Ella started the walk down the hill with Clara following. The horse shook its head as Ella turned the buggy around on the road and threw Clara the reins. She climbed up and grasped the lines, hanging on tight as the horse dashed eagerly down the road toward Seager Hill.

Discussion Questions

1. How well did Ella do struggling with the question of why God allows sudden tragedy in our lives?

2. Was Ella justified in wanting God to show some expression of His sorrow in the storm which came after the services at the gravesite?

3. How well did Daniel do in his attempts to comfort Ella?

4. Would you have shared Ella's feelings when she faced the bull over Eli's fallen body?

5. Are the justifications Eli gives Ella for the risks he's taking with the English nurse, Pam, his real reasons?

6. Was the young Bishop Miller's visit to Ella appropriate so soon after Aden's passing?

7. What are Daniel's motives in offering to help Ella build her home?

8. How will the death of Preacher Stutzman's wife affect him in the future?

9. Is Eli planning a serious relationship in his continued contact with the English nurse, Pam?

10. Will Ella's house give her enough courage to say no when the young Bishop comes calling in six months?

About Jerry Eicher...

As a boy, **Jerry Eicher** spent eight years in Honduras, where his grandfather helped found an Amish community outreach. As an adult, Jerry taught for two terms in parochial Amish and Mennonite schools in Ohio and Illinois. He has been involved in church renewal for 14 years and has preached in churches and conducted weekend meetings of in-depth Bible teaching. Jerry lives with his wife, Tina, and their four children in Virginia.

Coming April 2011

Book two in Jerry Eicher's Little Valley series, *Ella's Wish*

Ella Yoder has moved into her dream house. In the stillness of the great house, Ella ponders her options. How is she to survive on her own? How will she ever forget Aden? What is to become of her?

Two would-be suitors soon make their intentions known, but Ella is unsure of her own feelings. As she agrees to take care of Preacher Stutzman's three motherless girls, Ella's heart is touched by their love for her. Could their affection be the answer to Ella's quest? Can God speak through the love of a child?

Readers of Amish fiction will fall in love themselves with Ella Yoder and be hoping she finds the love and happiness she seeks.

The Adams County Trilogy
by Jerry Eicher

Rebecca's Promise

Rebecca Keim has just declared her love to John Miller and agreed to become his wife. But she's haunted by her schoolgirl memories of a long ago love—and a promise made and a ring given. Is that memory just a fantasy come back to destroy the beautiful present...or was it real?

When Rebecca's mother sends her back to the old home community in Milroy to be with her aunt during and after her childbirth, Rebecca determines to find answers that will resolve her conflicted feelings. Faith, love, and tradition all play a part in Rebecca's divine destiny.

Rebecca's Return

Rebecca Keim returns to Wheat Ridge full of resolve to make her relationship with John Miller work. But in her absence, John has become suspicious of the woman he loves. Before their conflict can be resolved, John is badly injured and Rebecca is sent back to Milroy to aid her seriously ill Aunt Leona.

In Milroy, Rebecca once again visits the old covered bridge over the Flatrock River, the source of her past memories and of her promise made so long ago.

Where will Rebecca find happiness? In Wheat Ridge with John, the man she has agreed to marry, or should she stake her future on the memory that persists...and the ring she has never forgotten? Does God have a perfect will for Rebecca—and if so how can she know that will?

Rebecca's Choice

Popular Amish fiction author Jerry Eicher finishes the Adam's County Trilogy with an intriguing story of a young couple's love, a community of faith, and devotion to truth.

Rebecca Keim is now engaged to John Miller, and they are looking forward to life together. When Rebecca goes to Milroy to attend her beloved teacher's funeral, John receives a mysterious letter accusing Rebecca of scheming to marry him for money. Determined to forsake his past jealousies and suspicions, John tries hard to push the accusations from his mind.

Upon Rebecca's return, disturbing news quickly follows. She is named as the sole heir to her teacher's three farms. But there's a condition—she must marry an Amish man. When John confronts Rebecca, she claims to know nothing. Soon Rachel Byler, the vengeful but rightful heir to the property, arrives and reveals secrets from the past. Now the whole community is reeling!